Black, White, Other

BLACK, WHITE, OTHER

Joan Steinau Lester

ZONDERVAN®

We want to hear from you. Please send your comments about this book to us in care of zreview@zondervan.com. Thank you.

ZONDERVAN

Black, White, Other

This title is also available as a Zondervan ebook.
Visit www.zondervan.com/ebooks.

This title is also available in a Zondervan audio edition.
Visit www.zondervan.fm.

Requests for information should be addressed to:

Zondervan, *Grand Rapids, Michigan 49530*

Library of Congress Cataloging-in-Publication Data

Lester, Joan Steinau, 1940-
Black, white, other / Joan Steinau Lester.
p. cm.
Summary: Twenty miles from Oakland, California, where fires have led to racial tension, multi-racial fifteen-year-old Nina faces the bigotry of long-time friends, her parents' divorce, and her brother's misbehavior, while learning of her great-great grandmother Sarah's escape from slavery.
Includes bibliographical references.
ISBN 978-0-310-72763-7 (hardcover : alk. paper)
1. Race relations—Fiction. 2. Identity—Fiction. 3. Racially mixed people—Fiction. 4. Divorce—Fiction. 5. Family life—California—Fiction. 6. Great-grandmothers—Fiction. 7. Fugitive slaves—Fiction. 8. California—Fiction. I. Title.
PZ7.L56288Bl 2011
[Fic]—dc23 2011015208

Cover design: Gayle Raymer
Cover illustration: Natalia Kuchumova/Istockphoto.com
Interior design: Ben Fetterley and Greg Johnson/Textbook Perfect

Printed in the United States of America

---

12 13 14 15 16 /DCI/ 22 21 20 19 18 17 16 15 14 13 12 11 10 9 8 7 6 5 4 3 2

To all those who feel any kind of "otherness";
you do indeed live large lives.
May you expand your consciousness to fully inhabit them
and someday be grateful for the very "otherness"
that may plague you now.

CHAPTER 1

I'm furiously heaving it all into my green suitcase — the black Nike sweatshirt that I live in, my favorite Oakland A's T-shirt, underwear, jeans, charger — all because I *have* to go to Dad's place. It'll be my first time staying overnight, and even though I'm fifteen, he never even asked, just called and told me I was coming tonight. Period.

Wow. "Fifteen" sounds good. I'm just getting used to it since my birthday last week. But my parents still treat me like I'm twelve.

"I don't want to go," I mutter when I'm halfway to the front door. Mom is curled on the couch under the lamp, head bent over the *New Yorker* and petting Rolling Stone, our cat we hardly ever see. Normally he only comes out from who knows where when it's time to eat, but he's lying by Mom as if he knows I'm leaving and wants to comfort her. I've seen tears in her eyes a few times lately, since Dad moved out.

Everybody says I'm the clone of my mom — except I'm the tall, tan version with "mocha skin," as Dad calls it, and Mom jokes that she's the short, white original. But it's true: we've both got red hair (mine's curlier and darker, with red highlights), the same perfect pitch, the same guitar licks. My face is wider and my cheekbones higher, but we sound exactly alike. When people call and I answer, they start, "Maggie ..." I have to interrupt with, "No, it's Nina."

Aretha's singing "chain, chain, chain. Chain of fools," and Mom's humming along, peering up at me. "You know we agreed," she says.

"No," I moan. "I never agreed, I was told. Why do I *have* to go? Don't I get a say in this?" Ever since the day last summer when everything went crazy, Mom and Dad have acted like I'm a robot they can simply program. "I wanna stay home."

"Look, sweetie." She pushes Rolling Stone off her lap. "He's your father. Plus, you haven't seen Jimi all week." I can tell exactly how Mom feels by simply listening to her breathing. Right now she's holding her breath, so I know she's lonesome. But what am I supposed to do? "Bye, sweetie," she says softly and glides over. "Give Jimi a hug—you can pass this one along." She grabs me.

"Mo-o-o-m."

"Call me when you get there, okay?"

"*If* I go. It's so unfair." If I can't be home, I want to be with my friends, the only sane people on the planet lately. "I could go over to Jessica's if you're trying to get rid of me."

She presses her lips into a line and slouches back to the couch.

Since I can tell this is a losing battle, I start toward the front door, but suddenly I freeze. The air feels different; what is it? Then I see what's missing: Dad's pictures, the ones from the bookshelves and the piano, and even the ones on the wall. He took the Paris prints and the photos of his parents, leaving spaces where the paint is lighter. When did he come to pick up his stuff? When I look back at Mom, she's tiny under the high ceiling of the room, nestled alone in the far corner of the couch. I could help her, keep her company, but here she is shoving me out the door.

I slam out, trying to bang the front door, which is hard since I'm dragging my suitcase.

I walk fast, the way I do, five blocks to the number 62 bus. Everything feels strange today; even the sun is an odd red color from the fire, as if marking the end of the universe as I know it. Just as I'm coming around the corner I hear the bus roar up in front of the library steps, so I sprint through the smoky air and get there in time to see the green-striped bus glide past. I holler, only the driver doesn't hear or doesn't care. Since the light at the corner is still red, I dash over as the bus slows down, but it pulls away before I can bang on the door.

A few other girls are hanging out at the bus stop, laughing. I've seen them at school. One of 'em is shaking her head so her dreads wave around and the beads click against each other. I realize I'm staring, watching them strut and shoot each others' pictures, making silly faces, but they're not paying any attention to me. I wonder where they're going.

We all climb onto the next bus; they hop up first and prance to the back, talking and singing, clapping, taking up every inch of space with their giggles and loud voices. I sprawl out behind the driver, leaning back into the seat. I'm not there two minutes when something hits my shoulder and lands by my right foot: a wadded-up sheet of yellow paper. I whip around; the bus is empty, except for the girls laughing in the back.

"What are you looking at?" the smallest one asks with a wicked grin before she rolls her shoulder and turns her gaze out the window.

"You," I say, raising my eyebrows before I swivel my head back. But I add, *sotto voce*, "Don't do that again."

"Do what?" she snaps back at me.

"Throw stuff." I sigh, wondering if they're trying to be friends or only fooling around. While we roll along, I stare out the window. My neighborhood is so green it's like a park, with oak and maple shade trees, and lawns bordered by roses. Here, where El Camino Boulevard changes its name to Martin Luther King, storefronts sprout up. Cajun Fish, E-Z Credit, and Best Beauty Supplies. By the time I get to Dad's corner, everybody is black or Latino. Why did he have to move all the way to San Joaquin Boulevard, at the very edge of Canyon Valley?

I hop down at the corner of Muir Street—the three girls are still on the bus—and bump my suitcase down the steps. "Hey, good lookin'," a man calls out. He's old, moving slow. He doesn't look scary, but the three guys down the block do. They're leaning on a beat-up blue car, blowing puffs of smoke, with a radio blasting. I tighten my hand around the suitcase handle and cross to the other sidewalk, even though Dad lives on this side. The street is straight and broad, bordered by a few spindly oaks turning orange.

When the guys look over, I stride faster, holding my head up and shoulders back, trying to look cool. As if I'm just in a hurry to get someplace. "Hey ..." A shout, but I can't hear the rest of it due to the reggae. At the corner I almost run back two houses to Dad's, where a bunch of agapanthus, blue and white, line the sidewalk. I take the steps two at a time. Nine of them. That's my unlucky number, though it's Jessica's favorite. I shiver. When I look around behind me, the block is quiet except for the guys at the blue car and a truck rattling by. Dad's apartment is the top half of the house.

I press the buzzer over and over, but Dad doesn't open the door; he might be late since he had to pick up Jimi at school. Another reason I didn't need to come! Furiously, I dig into my pocket for his key ring. The first one, with the red-rubber cover, won't fit into the keyhole, no matter how I jiggle it, but the second one glides right in and turns. After I step into the hall, it smells different from home—the house that's Mom's and mine now, except when Jimi sleeps over. At home, as soon as I open the door, the sharp scent of ginger tea hits my nose. Mom slices up the root and steeps a pot of it every afternoon. This smell might be ham baking and—I sniff—something else I don't recognize. Strong, like garlic and onions. And cilantro. The landlady must be cooking downstairs.

When I get to the inside door I try the red-rubber key. It slides into the hole, but I can't get the lock to turn, even though I push, harder and harder. I stop and turn the key slowly, gently. The lock won't budge. I don't want to go back outside, not with those men, so I keep trying until my armpits are sweaty and my forehead is wet. "Take another crack at it," I can hear Mom's voice encouraging me.

Once more.

Finally, I sit on the floor with my back against a wall, unzip the suitcase, and retrieve my American History book and a pen. After a minute, though, I can't see the writing on the page. Everything's a blur. I have to wipe my eyes and sniffle. I hate American History, especially this unit on antebellum life. Why do we have to study something that happened a million years ago? All of American history's stupid. It's never about anything useful.

"Nina." I hear Dad's voice before his hand shakes my shoulder. "Don't you have your key?" I jerk and look up. Was I dreaming? We were home, snug and warm, all four of us squeezed on the couch: Mom, Dad, Jimi, and me. I shudder and try to retrieve the cozy feeling, but in real life I remember where I am, and don't want to wake up.

"Nina!" Dad's pulling on one arm, and Jimi's tugging on the other.

"Hey," I say in Jimi's direction, glad to see his skinny little self, with his stupid braces. I can tell by his grin that he's happy to see me too, even though now that he turned ten he's not throwing his arms around me like he used to. "Double-digit dude!" I call. He leans backward, straining to pull me to my feet. "Hey, little dude, what's up?"

Jimi grins bigger, yanking my shoulder practically out of the socket. "Not *little* ..."

"Okay, okay, let go."

"Are you all right?" Dad asks. He pulls me in for a hug, squashing me against his broad chest. I'm mad that he ordered me over here, but now that I'm here I like being near him, smelling his sweat and Old Spice lotion. It's a familiar mix. He looks different though. He always kept his hair short; now it sticks out an inch all over, like a soft black helmet. His cheeks are wide like mine, so his head seems huge. And he's wearing a loose blue shirt that I've never seen.

"Yeah, I'm okay." I rub my eyes. "I fell asleep."

"I see. But, sugar, what are you doing out here?"

"I couldn't get in. The key wouldn't turn."

"Oh," he says, rubbing my shoulder. "It's tricky. I thought I told you. You have to use a light touch, and then it turns to the right. Like this." He demonstrates. "Re-e-a-l easy. You try it."

Once I'm inside, everything's familiar but changed. The same pictures we always had are here, but not where they should be. That big red oil painting by the couch: at home it hung over the fireplace. The photographs of Grandma Bettye and Grandpa James sit on a sparse shelf here, but at home they crowded the piano. And now, as soon as we pull off our sweaters and toss them onto a chair, Dad hurries over and flips on the TV, which he hardly ever did at home.

The gas explosions again, and the flames that are still burning block after block of houses. Dad frowns. "If it were white people"—is it my imagination, or does he turn his head and scowl at me?—"the Red Cross would be swarming by now. See that!" He thrusts his hand toward the TV, as if I'm arguing. "Look! Don't people ever learn? Those poor folks in West Oakland are gettin' it this time. Of course CG&E upgraded the pipes in the rich neighborhoods. But not in Oakland. Eighty-year-old welds! No underground shut-off valves! Nope, save money on the blacks in Oakland." His face is twisted like he's about to cry.

The blacks? I've never heard him spit out those words before with that bitter tone. *Come on, Dad,* I want to say, *it could've happened anywhere. Two thousand people who lost their homes, lost everything; don't we see that in California after every earthquake, every fire?* But I hold my tongue, not wanting to hear more from this heartbroken man who's inhabiting my dad's cheerful body.

There's footage of dark-skinned people hobbling through rubble, trying to find their way to shelter, and others fleeing the fire, which is spreading. We hear more explosions, and gunshots. Rescuers are finding trapped people, some dead, some miraculously alive, under the smoldering wreckage. One little boy is pulled out whimpering. Heavy smoke shrouds every picture. Then the TV shows two black women with blistered skin on their faces squatting in a vacant lot, surrounded by a pile of belongings and a knot of white cops. "There *they* are, with guns and uniforms..." Dad gives a strange kind of laugh, not really a laugh at all. It's a sound I've never heard, more like a gurgle. "'Shoot on sight.' They should be digging people out, helping the fire fighters, not shooting innocent people." He shakes his head. Who is this dad? *My* dad always told me, "People are people." That we're all God's children underneath. The color of their skin is the *last* thing that's important. "It's the content of their character, like Dr. King taught us."

Since he's glued to the plumes of smoke, I plop into the brown easy chair that used to be in his study. If I sit still for a minute, my real dad will stroll through the door, place his hand on my shoulder, and say, *Sugar, let's later this joint*, and I'll hear his deep laugh, 'cause he loves to crack himself up with his tired old sayings. Even that lame joke would sound good to me now. Yeah, the fires are upsetting, even here the air is hazy, but why is he so mad? Accidents happen.

"I used to think I had enough Black Power to last a lifetime, before I was ten." Dad spins around, as if we were continuing a conversation. "Your grandparents..." —he shakes his head— "God bless 'em."

I know, I know, I want to say, but I don't dare. Last summer when my parents sent me to Atlanta for a week, like every summer, Grandma Bettye showed me a book she'd made for Dad when he was little, with a red paper cover. "Black is beautiful, like sisters, like brothers. Like night, like earth." She drew pictures too, of the night sky.

"I thought I'd had enough of that stuff," Dad says. "But it had its merits, and it might be time to bring it out again. This is unbelievable." He's pointing at the TV like it's evidence in a court case. "A white person at the front of a line"—his voice is strangled, as if he can't talk— "of hundreds of African American and Latino citizens waiting for two days for something to eat, for someplace to go. With no water! Old people, look at them. It's not like the gas company didn't have warning. They knew the old welds were vulnerable, everybody did. The *Chronicle* has been exposing it on the front page for the last five years. But CG&E didn't want to spend the money in Oakland."

He acts like I don't know about the explosions. I've seen the news. Everybody knows what happened. The newscasters are calling West Oakland a "war zone" with "unprecedented devastation" that will take years to undo. It's sad; of course it is. Nobody likes it, Dad.

Dad's grief-stricken eyes are glaring at me like I personally put that white woman at the front of the line. Where's Jimi? "Look at that," Dad repeats, as if that's all he can say tonight. He hunches over. "If I were walking down that street"—he points—"even Jimi and I wouldn't be safe, with those trigger-happy cops shooting at anything brown that moves." He grunts. "Fleeing while black."

"What's for dinner?" I ask, like I would at home, trying desperately to make this horrible new apartment, this scary, strange dad, feel like home.

He stares through me, mumbles something inaudible, and returns to the TV. "Look in the kitchen," he mutters. "They owe us, big time."

When I slink out of the living room, Dad doesn't even notice. I slip into Jimi's bedroom, crowded with two bureaus and a computer table. This room is gonna be mine now too, every other weekend. I can't imagine it.

I tiptoe up behind Jimi, who's staring at his computer, and land a good punch on his shoulder. When he looks up and laughs, with that milewide mouthful-of-silver grin, I figure I just might make it.

After an hour Dad bounds in, kind of twinkling in his old, familiar way even though he looks tired too, and all of a sudden the three of us squat on our haunches in a spontaneous huddle, hunched down with our arms tight around each others' shoulders, facing inward. After a long three-way smile, Dad shouts, "Go Armstrongs—here's to our new home," and we all burst up into a jump. Yeah, this is the Dad I know. Maybe I was imagining that other Dad. Though he probably did have a point. I never heard about a white neighborhood exploding and the fire department taking forever to get there so that blocks of houses burn for days, and hardly any ambulances arrive. And no food. I never thought about tragedies that way, about what town it happens in and how who lives there could determine whether people live or die.

Wow. That's deep.

CHAPTER 2

On Monday, my friends and I eat our lunches outside school, even though a rare, smoky fog is blowing in, thick, and my hands are freezing. The sun is still tinged by the explosion, a dim red through the sickly, burnt-orange haze. Twenty miles inland we hardly ever get this much fog; the east part of the East Bay is known for its hot, dry winds, whereas San Francisco is Fog City, but this crazy fall even the weather is changing up on me. The wind is whipping our lunch bags into the air so we have to hold on to every bit of paper, but we're having a good time. The four of us have been eating on the top steps of the amphitheater ever since the first day of high school last month. Everybody staked out a spot, it seemed, that first week. Other kids park themselves nearby, talking and howling. It's fun, like a big party every day. None of the teachers come out here; they're mostly in the food court, I guess, or the teachers' lounge, or who knows where. Honestly, I don't care.

I'm sitting on a cold step between Amy and Jessica, trying to ignore my icy butt. "Hey, Nina," Jessica says, "those are cool jeans. Would you care if I got the same pair?"

I shake my head and smile, relaxed in the comfort of sitting next to my oldest friend, feeling her shoulder rub against mine. Just sitting next to her makes me feel safe. Until I remember the quiz.

"I'm nervous," I admit to Amy, whose brown bangs fall over her eyes so that she has to keep brushing them back to see anything. She's shivering too, rubbing her arms through her lime-green jacket, which looks way too thin. Amy is the only one of us who invariably does homework. Before, Fran was the smartest girl in our group. Everybody knew that, and I felt lucky that she, Jessica, and I hung out together nearly every day at lunch. After school we carpooled to our soccer and field hockey games or track meets. I couldn't have imagined two better friends. We even babysat together when the parents would let all three of us sleep over, until some neighbors complained about our loud music. But now Fran's gone — moved away to San Luis Obispo, which I still can't believe — so Amy is our reliable scholar. There's an empty spot where Fran used to huddle next to me, so I was sandwiched between her and Jessica. Funny how an absence can feel like a presence, like that space practically glows with her outline and makes me notice how she's not here. Lucky I've got Amy though, to at least help me out.

"I just studied once this weekend for the Spanish quiz, is all, and it's going to count as part of our grade. Do you get how the punctuation is different?" I ask her. "Like the question mark is at the beginning." I'm listening for Amy's answer when I overhear Claudette say quietly to Jessica, "Did you see the looters on TV?" Claudette lowers her voice, but it carries clearly. "I mean, with the fires and all, those black people were like— "

My fist squeezes the foil around my sandwich until a piece of avocado slips out.

"—animals." Claudette brushes a leaf from the sleeve of her light blue sweater and flips her hair back. She's new in Canyon Valley this fall; she's tall like me, blonde like Jessica, and lives with her dad, like Fran does now since her mom flew to Italy to take care of her grandparents. Every day Claudette dresses to the max, and she's so popular that most girls in my class would crawl on broken glass just to sit next to her. Right from the first day, she latched on to Jessica. Now she reaches up, her blue fingernails flashing, and waves her hand in the air as if she's brushing looters away.

Jessica makes a face as if she smells something nasty. I know that look: disgust. "They were so—" Jessica grimaces, her tone an exact copy of Claudette's. It's amazing how she's picked up the voice in only a month: a high squeak that drips importance. Now that I see them together, I get why Jessica's not going out for track this year: it's not glamorous enough. I peek at Amy to see her reaction, but she's staring down at her gold leather Skechers like she never heard a thing.

"Wait—" I start to say, choking on a mouthful of whole wheat bread. Wasabi mayonnaise drips onto my lap; I wipe it with my napkin.

"Yeah," Claudette interrupts, as if I hadn't spoken at all. "It was gross. My dad says they should be shot."

"Shot?" I repeat, once my mouth is clear. "Who?"

Claudette leans over and studies my face for a minute, as if she just noticed I'm here. Her look says she knows I have no sense, but she'll deign to answer anyway. "The looters," she answers, rolling her eyes.

"Wait a minute." My mind goes blank in the face of Claudette's certainty. "They didn't have ..." I stop, trying to remember what Dad said after dinner.

"What?"

"Any water or diapers or food—"

"Nina," Claudette breaks in, exasperated. "The food was coming."

"But they were hungry."

"They were *stealing*," Jessica butts in, glancing at Claudette from the side of her eyes. "I don't think *TVs* are water," she says. "The looters didn't *need* TVs. Or clothes. The fires are an excuse." She gazes directly at Claudette, who nods.

"They're in gangs," Claudette throws in. "Like the ones in this school. Shoplifting."

"Yeah, thieves. Common thieves," Jessica says, with so much vehemence that the top of my nose gets tight and tingles. It's a warning: tears are about to come if I don't concentrate, so I bite my cheek. I've never heard Jessica talk like this. Is the whole world going freaky? First my dad has a personality implant, and now Jessica? Am I suddenly on some parallel planet, where everybody looks the same but they're strangers?

"It wasn't *stealing* if they didn't have any food!" I burst out, remembering what Dad said and unexpectedly agreeing. "When white people grab food, the news people say they're 'scavenging.' Like it's smart." I'm surprised to find myself on Dad's side, but this is so insulting I feel like protecting him. How can she say this, like being black automatically makes you dangerous? What does race have to do with anything?

"Nina, white people didn't break into any stores. My dad and I watched all weekend." Claudette has a funny look on her pointy face. Her eyebrows are arched way up over her blue eyes, and her nose is wrinkled. "We saw what happened."

"My dad says— " I want to tell them what he said about him and Jimi, how they could've been shot if they happened to get caught up in the fires, trying to flee, trying to find food to eat, but I know they wouldn't believe me.

"Nina! Your dad's crazy anyway," Jessica says, packing away the pasta-and-broccoli salad she didn't finish, wiping her hands on her paper napkin. "He said stealing is right? Why would you listen to him?" That comfort I felt five minutes ago in her mere presence has melted away.

And what she said is especially annoying because her mom really is mentally challenged, but of course I can't say so. Her mom has actually been in Contra Costa Regional Medical Center, after she stabbed herself all over her arms with a kitchen knife and Jessica had to wipe up blood from the floor. Another time her mom vomited from swallowing a whole bottle of sleeping pills, so Jessica had to stay at our house. At least once a week Jessica tells me about the scary things her mom is doing. And she calls my dad crazy?

I twist to look around at the other girls sitting near us on the steps. The preppy girls are all quiet, staring off in different directions. Were they listening? I glance over to the giant planters below us, where most of the black kids hang out. Some of them eat over by the science building too, except when it rains in the winter, I heard. Everybody else is inside at their own tables: the Asian kids, the Mexicans (at least that's what kids call them even though they're not all from Mexico—lots of them were born here, and some are from other countries too), the African Americans, the whites. I never thought about it that much before.

Jessica opens her bag of Milano cookies and pops a cookie into her mouth before she offers the open bag to each of us. She repeats, "Your dad's crazy," then she says to Amy, "How much does the Spanish test count for our grade?" as if nothing happened.

"I have to go," I tell them and pick up my neon pink backpack, feeling like I'm in a movie where everybody's working off a script I never received. Who *is* Jessica? We've been best friends since fourth grade, when we both fell in love, passionately in love, with soccer. Every afternoon we raced to the track and kicked a ball around. Jessica was so serious: she wore a red soccer jersey six sizes too big—Mia Hamm's number nine, of course—and she'd run like the wind for hours, passing, dribbling, shooting. That bright red jersey finally faded until it fell off her, full of holes, last year. Jessica was so wild about Mia, she framed an autographed Olympic calendar my dad bought for her twelfth birthday. It was her prized possession.

As I walk down the steps, I see Lavonn standing in a group of kids. Her mom, Saundra, used to drive our carpool in elementary school. Saundra's a fashion designer who creates awesome outfits, like the fancy black sweatshirt and hip-huggers Lavonn's wearing now. Once she made me an outfit too, pants with a matching purple top that was totally cool. I wore that until the pants were so high-water they looked like capris. Lavonn waves, so I stop, shifting my backpack to one shoulder. We used to sit near each other all the time in grade school, but it seems like in middle school we kind of drifted apart, even though she plays field hockey too. Once Fran and Jessica and I became inseparable, I'd usually see Lavonn with the black kids, but I never thought anything about it. She and I still talk sometimes after school, and we've always been friendly. I've even been over to her house, though not that recently.

"Hi," she says, smiling for a second before she spins back to this boy she's talking to. Her eyes are deep brown and huge, lighting up her round face. My face is all angles. Sharper. I'm also thinner and taller, with long legs and long arms like Anansi the wise spider, as Dad likes to tease me—"a trickster"—and my eyes change from green to brown depending on what I'm wearing.

Today, with her hood pulled up, Lavonn looks as if she's all eyes. At first, even though she's not talking to me, it feels okay standing here. The kids are pushing and poking each other, and nobody's noticing me. "Shut up, I do *not* like him. He is fine, though!" one of the girls says, laughing. After a few minutes I start to feel strange, with everybody ignoring me. I shift from one foot to another, trying to look casual, like I fit in, when I hear the boy Lavonn's talking to say something about "white girls" with a sideways glance at me and what sounds like a snicker. Maybe I'm making it up, but it looks that way. I start to sweat. The more I replay "white girls" and how he said the words, sneering, the lonelier I feel, standing on the edge of the crowd. I want to say something to Lavonn, anything, to get her to speak to me, but she can't take her eyes off that stupid boy. Then, before I can catch her eye, the bell rings. Everybody starts moving together like a pack, and we all herd inside, squeezing through the doorway. Cops block the doors. They've been slowing everything down since a gang of boys fought at lunchtime last week. This cop is a woman; huge, stone-faced, arms folded, with a black gun hanging from her belt.

The battle was more than your average fight; we heard a couple of kids had knives. All we knew for sure is that at lunchtime last Monday, two squad cars squealed onto the park by the school, where the skateboarders were doing flippy tricks. A knot of police jumped out with their clubs flailing, the word spread, and everybody rushed over to see the riot. By the time Jessica and I got there, the cops had pushed the boys together in a bunch, forcing their hands behind their backs and cuffing them. From the sidewalk I only recognized one of the kids, a boy in a hoodie named Dwight Jackson, who's funny and sharp. He's built like a beanpole, so he twists himself into silly Gumby shapes, and even though he only came to our school this fall, everybody likes him. Especially me, although I don't think he notices that I'm alive. I was surprised to see him in the midst of a brawl, and wondered how he got involved. You can tell he's not the kind of kid who'd fight unless he had to. In class he's a big compromiser, the student who summarizes discussions by weaving different comments together so they all make sense. The biggest shock came when another boy turned toward us, and I saw his face: he looked exactly like Dwight's ugly twin, with a scowl that could cut diamonds. Even Dwight's dimples were like slashes on this kid's cheeks. And whereas Dwight has kind of a ruddy complexion, this kid was so deathly pale he looked like a ghost. His washed-out blue eyes were dull, and the snake tattoo that wound up his neck around his ear added to the ghoulish impression. "Oooh, who's that?" someone had asked.

"Dwight's twin brother," Jessica said with a shudder. "Tyrone. He went to that school for truants." Later we heard that Dwight and Tyrone, along with a bunch of other guys, were suspended for three weeks, and Tommie Kennedy, one of the hills kids — some people call them preppies — got a week's suspension. Tommie claims he's related to President Kennedy, but I doubt it; he always lies. Anyway, they're all gone.

Soon I'm in Language Arts, trying to focus. I wonder about Dad and Jessica, what happened to make them change so fast. I'm kind of in a trance, half asleep, when a shadowy image flashes, just below consciousness, of Jimi being chased. It's a movie running just out of sight, one I barely see, but a feeling of dread creeps into me. That's how I stumble through the afternoon, in a daze, until I finally come alive last period. We call Ms. Pirtle, the Music Appreciation teacher, the Turtle, 'cause she's so slow, but on Mondays she plays CDs we can rap to. Some kids are really good. Not me. I'm a beginner at rap, even though I like it. Today I rap to myself, *Fire's coming, better get to shelter, everything's goin' helter-skelter.* When I shake my head and snap my fingers to get a groove going, I begin to feel better.

Usually I text Jessica first thing when I get home, even if we just ran around the track together. Or Fran, to find out if things are better in San Luis Obispo this fall than when she first got there, or I ask about her classes and how she did that day in field hockey. She's a star. But today I don't feel like texting. Instead, I run up to my room and stare at a sketch Jessica doodled last year of Jimi, with his braces and skinny legs, riding his skateboard, and me hanging on to him while we zoomed downhill. I peer into Jimi's room, where I picture him packing the day before school started. I sat on his bed then, but his eyes stayed on the floor while he picked up his million baseball cards. He pulled down his Harry Potter poster with the flying owl and Hogwarts in the background. He still didn't look at me when he ripped his red Jimi Hendrix picture off the wall and rolled it up, or when he jammed his clothes into black garbage bags and pushed them near the door. Then he was gone.

The room still feels empty, even though plenty of his things are left. He's supposed to come over later this afternoon, and I can't wait. Maybe he's the one person who's stayed normal through this whole insane time. Even though neither of us had any say over where we went—and why did they split us up this way?—the other day at Dad's he seemed like the same old Jimi to me: sweet, clueless, with eyes that gaze at me like I'm the best thing since hot chocolate was invented.

CHAPTER 3

When Dad and Jimi stride through the front door, I see they have a new way of walking together, swaggering in rhythm. Jimi's growing his hair out too, so he's even closer to the spitting image of Dad. They're like Dad and Little Dad. Jimi always did take after him — those full lips and jet-black hair — while I favored Mom's redheaded family. We used to joke about it, and it never seemed like a big deal before, when we were all mixed up: two kids, two parents, jumbled any which way. Dad would roll outside and we'd toss a ball against the back of the house, or he'd play a computer game with Jimi while Mom unraveled a badminton net with me. But now Jimi and Dad have this circle surrounding them. I can see it in the air, as if somebody took a brown crayon and drew a line around the two of them.

With Mom and me, it's complicated. Even though our friends say we're "light version, dark version," lots of people can't even figure out we're related. Once I heard Mom tell her mom, Granny Leigh, "On the ferry to Angel Island, a woman came right up and asked if they were adopted." Mom's face flushed and I could tell how angry she was. I thought it was strange that she was so mad, since the woman said how cute we were too, "like sweet little caramel candies." Instinctively, I walk over and put my arms around Mom from the back. She squeezes me. "Help with dinner?"

"Okay." I stare down at my arm next to her hands. Darker. How could that boy with Lavonn imagine I was white? I don't look like anybody in this family.

"Just give me a minute," Mom says. While I'm waiting, I sprawl in the living room chair, with its stuffed arms facing the bay, and watch the lights below sparkle like bright confetti. Jimi jumps onto one arm, squirming and leaning into me. I'm glad he's here for dinner; still, out of habit, I push him off and slap his hand when it touches me. Dad wasn't supposed to stay, just drop Jimi off, but since he's hanging around in the living room, I tell him, "Dad, at school— "

"Nina, I've got a lot on my mind right now. Later, okay?"

So I head into the kitchen where I pour water into a pot for spaghetti. The kitchen's so small that Mom and I bump into each other. We start butting our behinds on purpose, and all of a sudden we're giggling. When Dad comes in sniffing around the food, as if he'd like some too, Mom hands him a glass of red wine. But she doesn't say anything. They stand there drinking, neither one saying a word. They're not even looking at each other. "You won't believe what Jessica said— " I start.

"Look, Maggie, I'm sorry," Dad interrupts and kind of pitches forward.

"This new girl, Claudette— " I try again.

But Dad ignores me. "Here's to a good future, Maggie," he says and raises his glass.

I give up, jiggle the frying pan, and add a few leaves of oregano from the farmers' market.

"For all of us," he says.

Mom doesn't answer. Instead she lifts the pot of boiling spaghetti with two hands and pours the water into a sieve I hold over the sink while the steam rises over my face. Then she slams the empty pot back onto the stove. Loud. And she starts to curse.

Dad leans against the wall of the kitchen, pours himself another full glass, but a few seconds later he bangs his glass on the counter so hard, half his wine sloshes out, staining the counter red. "It isn't only me."

Mom makes a lot more noise with cabinet doors. "Not now!" she says, real sharp, and my insides clench tight as a rock. "Later." She nods her head in my direction.

"Look, I've *had* it with that martyr look." He tips up his glass. "The white-woman special," he mutters.

"I said, not now!" Mom turns her back. But I hear her muttering curses and see her shoulders shake while she stirs the spaghetti with a big wooden spoon. It looks like she's going to whip it into mashed noodles, she's beating it so hard.

I don't know what to do, so I ask Dad for the last, tiny sip, and after he hands over the wine, it warms my throat and opens my chest. I shake Parmesan cheese from its round green container. I keep shaking and shaking until it's all gone, and before we're ready to eat, Dad leaves. I never do tell them what Claudette and Jessica said at school.

On Friday Mom has to leave for a teacher's conference, so even though I'm old enough to stay by myself for the weekend, Mom insists, "Three days is too long, so you'll be staying at your father's. I'm not leaving you alone."

Friday night I ride the bus over to Dad's after an awesome field hockey game, where our Canyon Valley Cougars totally wiped out Walnut Creek. When I sit down to dinner in my black game shorts, I'm pleased to find him serving sweet potatoes, my favorite food, and "normally I'd have ham," Dad says, with a voice like honey, "but since you're a vegetarian now, I stir-fried tofu into the greens." He pulls his lips up, as if he's trying to smile, but instead he looks like he's about to eat rat poop. Jimi makes a face too. "Eeeww."

"Stop it." Dad frowns at Jimi. "Right this second."

Actually, I hate tofu. I don't know why everybody thinks vegetarians love it so much. It's too soft, like snot. I scoop as many greens onto my plate as I can without tofu, until Dad says, "Lilla Bit, you're not getting any of the good stuff." Now that I'm so tall, Lilla Bit is his joke, and since he cooked the tofu especially for me, I try mashing one piece into the sweet potatoes. But it's still slimy and gross. When he's watching a hummingbird at the feeder outside, I slide two more pieces into my hand and say, real politely, "Excuse me, Dad, may I go to the bathroom?" Jimi sees me and looks surprised, but I know he won't tell Dad.

After dinner I lie on the Deathbed to read. That's what Jimi calls the cot in his room that Dad put up for me. It collapses if you even think about moving. But it's nice to be in Jimi's room, even though he's not paying attention to me and I'm not talking either. Everything feels more normal than it's been in a long time, being near Jimi. He's slouching at his computer, playing a game with his back to me.

"Got any graph paper?" he asks over his shoulder.

"Yeah." I reach, moving carefully, until I manage to sit up and pull a notebook from my pack, tear a page, and hand it over. "Here."

After he grabs it he goes back to his game, while I lie down again and try to get comfortable. Pretty soon Jimi climbs into his bed, but I hear whimpering.

"What's going on?"

"Nothing," he whispers, sniffling.

"It doesn't sound like nothing." I feel like Mom or Dad, grilling him in the exact same way. Jimi never cries.

"Nothing." He stops and buries his head under the pillow, and I hear a muffled, "A boy . . ."

"What?"

"He's gonna beat me — "

"Beat you? Who?"

"Don't want to talk — "

"Jimi!"

Silence, until the image I had in class swirls up: Jimi running, chased by someone I can't see.

"Jimi." I clump over to his bed and shake him, but nothing makes him answer, even when I threaten to beat him up myself if he doesn't tell, and I give him a few sample punches. At last, trying to shake off my uneasiness, I get absorbed in a story for Language Arts, until Dad lumbers in with a pile of paper and stands between our two beds — if you can call the Deathbed a bed.

"Sugar, I'm writing," he says. His face is stretched into a big grin, so he's all mouth. "A novel based on your great-great-grandmother, Sarah Armstrong. She was amazing." He reaches over and squeezes my left shoulder. "I think you're going to like it. She struggled a lot, but she made it, and so will you — even if you have troubles now."

How did he know? At school, ever since the day Jessica copied Claudette when talking about the looters, it's been weird. We still eat lunch together, but I don't text her after school, and she hasn't texted me. Now suddenly my dad, who teaches accounting — B-O-R-I-N-G — is clairvoyant, and he's writing a book about some old woman who lived a hundred and fifty years ago. I knew he liked to read history, but now he's writing it? What planet am I on?

"A friend of mine, Helane, is helping with research," he says. "She's an African American History professor at Cal." He's smiling and sounds excited, which is not like him, believe me. He's always been Mister Mellow, at least until this recent incarnation as Mister Militant. "We even found an old journal in Grandpa James's attic that was Miss Sarah's! I want to read you the first chapter I wrote." He flashes another grin so big he looks as if he has chipmunk cheeks.

"I don't know," I say. In our family we read aloud a lot, but I'm not sure I'm in the mood. Plus, that seems like baby stuff. Nobody gets it that I'm fifteen now.

"Me, either," Jimi mumbles, following me like he does. He's already half gone, with his lids falling over his eyes. Dad reaches over, squeezes a one-handed hug, and tells him, "Go to sleep." Jimi turns his back, and in less than a minute we can tell by his breathing that he's out, snoring. He's so small, you wouldn't think he could make that big a noise. Five feet away, he's rattling the Deathbed.

Dad raises his eyebrows, like, *Yes?* They're thick and bushy, and whenever he lifts them it's a whole sentence. "I actually based her character on you," he says. "You know what they say: 'The best way to know a parent is to look at the child.' Well, I figured the best way for me to imagine my great-grandmother's nature was to take a hard look at one of her descendants, another feisty young woman."

I turn my head away, then shrug one shoulder. Dad drags in a chair from the dining table and props his feet on my bed. But he has to be careful not to lean too hard, even with me in it. That's how tipsy this so-called bed is.

"Your great-great-grandmother," he says in a soft voice, "died the year after Grandpa James was born, when she was ninety-nine. I only know a little about her. She never married, but late in life she had one child, my granddad, Albert. When he married, he and his wife had only one child: my dad, your grandpa James. That was pretty much all I knew until Grandpa James found this diary; it's just a few pages but it gives the outlines of your great-great-grandmother's story. We think she wrote it shortly before she died. And we've researched other slave narratives from the same time. Well, Helane has. They tell stories like Miss Sarah's." He stops and looks at me.

I can tell by how he's searching my face that he wants me to know about Miss Sarah, but I want to know about Miss Helane. Something makes me wonder: Is she the reason we're in this scary neighborhood that I have to ride a creepy bus to? How much of a friend *is* she?

"You're a lot like Miss Sarah, from what I gather." Dad's talking on, oblivious, smiling with his new alien face, until he tilts the light on the wall toward his papers. I can't imagine why I'd want to hear about an old lady, but I'm snuggled under my covers, so I mumble, "Yeah."

"First," he says, "I want to read you the end of her journal."

Yes, I was born a slave, but when I was fifteen years of age and heaven had been turned wrong side out, I ran for my life. The hound dogs chased me and the white folks were going to hell like a barrel full of nails tumbling over the falls, but I had a strong notion to own my own body. Couldn't nobody whip me or pen me then. I started out good following the old Pamunkey River north until

"Until what?" I ask.

"She stopped there. But listen, this is what I'm writing about. Here's the first chapter," alien-Dad says with an enormous, satisfied grin, and begins to read.

Hanover County, Virginia, 1853

"I'm never going back," Sarah vowed to herself. She had to keep saying it because her arms hurt from bramble scratches and her bare feet had more cuts than she could count. If she didn't keep up her chant—"I'm never going back, never ..."—she was afraid she would turn around and run straight home. Her feet knew the way.

"Sarah recorded that vow in her journal," Dad interrupted. "But of course I'm inventing the details."

"Stop it," Sarah said aloud when the devil thoughts, the ones that whispered, *You'll never make it,* crept in. "I'm never going back ..." she repeated, over and over again until her head was dizzy.

Following the path lit by moonlight, Sarah found little time to think about anything except going forward. She had to keep every sense focused on where she was going so she didn't trip on roots or vines, and she needed to be sure she stayed near—but not too near—the old Pamunkey. The river would split off into two streams, she knew, and when it did she'd take the right fork. She must stay alert, moving north with the aid of the river, the North Star, and her tiny compass. She gripped the small circle of metal in her sweaty hand; its cool solidity reassured her that the bird man's sudden appearance back on the plantation was not a dream. "Take this, child," the stranger had said.

Sarah jerked her mind to her present surroundings. "Don't think about the past," she told herself firmly. "No time to dwell," as Mama used to say. She had to listen carefully for the sound of bounty hunters or the distant barking of dogs set to track her. It was too early for anyone to realize she was gone, she thought, but who knew what ol' Master Armstrong had seen?

Awoooo! The hair stood up on her arms. The howl pierced the air again, and her skin quivered. Was that a hound dog? Her heart stopped then shuddered so loudly she was afraid it would wake the county.

Silence followed. It must be a wolf or a coyote. Or wildcat. She waited. No—it wasn't dogs. She set out again at a half trot, chanting a new mantra in rhythm with her footsteps. "I can't go back, I can't go back ..."

Every step took her farther from the Armstrong plantation. Yet while her feet moved north, her mind was split, chopped open like a melon cut in two by her father's axe. On one side, every bit of her brain told her *Go, run, legs, run for your life.* But the other side of her mind held one silent howl of NO. When Sarah let herself touch that scream, she wanted to turn, sprint, and fling herself onto familiar earth. Everyone she'd ever cared about in her entire fifteen years had been on that plantation. But now, it was hard to believe, all were sold and scattered.

The soles of her feet had touched every inch of dirt around the cabins; she knew the soil when it was dusty and dry, and when it turned to mud that squished between her toes like cool corn mush or sucked her ankles up to her calves. She knew where to find fat earthworms at daylight, wiggling after she tugged them from the ground. Every spring she waited for the red-tipped shoots that sprouted; later, when evenings grew hot, she knew to expect the sounds of crickets chirping in the night, lulling her to sleep.

A light drizzle started up as the past filled her head, both sides united now in grief. The memories rubbed sore spots in her heart, but still she sucked on them the way she'd savored hard, buttery twists of candy at Christmas, caressing them with her tongue, wishing they could last.

Awoooo! Her scalp quivered and the hair on her head stood on end. Yet her feet kept moving. She told herself that if she could get up to that giant mossy pine ahead, she'd rest there—shutting out the night's screeches and howls—and give herself in to remembering.

There. Just a few more steps.

"Coo, coo, coo," little Esther had called, chasing a squawking chicken through the yard. Sarah remembered laughing when she watched her sister clap her hands and run. Her brother Albert toddled along behind, weaving a silly line. Wherever Esther was, Albert, with his mischievous eyes and round cheeks, was never far behind.

Sarah thought of days she and Esther had observed baby starlings. The beaks looked half as big as the bodies they could see over the rim of the nest. "Cheep, cheep!" the babies never stopped shrieking, except when their mouths were full. She and Esther watched until the day the tiny birds fluttered off, one by one, on their first wobbly flights from home. The Sunday after that, the nest was bare.

Sarah had a lump in her throat that day. Four babies, two parents. The hurt felt like the one she had now, waking from a half sleep tucked into the crook of a branch low on the mossy pine, its needles prickling her. Only this lump was worse. It felt like a big cornmeal dumpling that wouldn't go up or down.

She lifted her head to make herself pay attention to the sounds of the night. Could that be a distant baying of dogs? *Stop thinking about the past!* she scolded, pulling a biscuit out of her pocket for one nibble. But with the familiar taste, her heavy heart flew open and a flood of memory washed in.

Little Albert could mimic the chattering of jays so well he'd fool them into thinking he was part of the conversation. Then she'd scamper up a tree and bring him down a warm bird's egg. Remembering her brother, heat swelled Sarah's throat and chest, and for a minute she couldn't breathe. She thought of how Albert used to climb into her lap and tangle his hands in her long hair, pulling and teasing. Then she and Esther would tickle him until he begged them to stop.

She forced herself to stand up and start moving again. The half moon was high in the sky. She had only a few more hours until morning, when she should arrive near a road and need to hide. She wondered if the bounty hunters were after her yet. If so, she couldn't turn back; they might kill her if they captured her. Or make her wish they had.

Now that she was walking, the best memory of all flooded in, the one that made her eyes swim with tears until she couldn't see the tiny arrow on the compass at all. The memory was about Sundays. Magic Sundays. For a sweet hour, until the moon dipped low on the horizon and the sky showed the first faint signs of pink, Sarah let herself sink into Sundays. Remembering was like being wrapped in a cozy quilt and rocked by Mama. On Sundays, she and her friend Ruth ran to a deep spot in the creek where they splashed and washed. Later they fished with a long strip of green wood, cut from just under the bark of a willow tree. They tied that strip, twisted like twine, to an old bent nail. Sarah forgot how sore her legs were now, after almost a full night of walking, when she remembered her excitement at the tug on the line—"Look, Ruth!" she'd scream—and how it felt in her hands, with the fish jerking one way and her pulling another. The spray was so vivid that for a moment she felt herself flipping up the line, and raised her hand against the water splashing over her head, until, shocked not to feel the drops, she dropped her hand. But she let herself breathe deeply, smelling the fish Mama cooked up on those Sunday evenings, all dipped in cornmeal, and she heard the sizzle in the pan.

When Sarah thought of Mama she thought of Papa standing next to her, giving thanks for their Sunday meal and another day together, and she missed them both so much her chest stung. Then, in the way that pain zigzags through a person like a magnet, one terrible thought triggered another, and she recalled the day that caused the first big crack in her world.

She'd been only six. Turkey buzzards circled high above, and she watched them, wondering. Ol' Master Armstrong used to tell her that buzzards gave birth to slave babies. "You're hatched from a buzzard egg," he'd say with a laugh, his great belly shaking while he swatted at flies. "The stork brings the white babies."

That day, like every other, Mama was out in the fields while Sarah chipped ice in the icehouse. She had to concentrate, not lose any of the precious, cold chips. Her bare toes dug into the dusty earth while her feet, long for a six-year-old, twitched. The air was always chilly with fear. Even on hot days, a sheer, invisible shadow made goose bumps on her arms. She could almost see it, like frozen screams.

At midday break she squatted, eating from the lunch trough Aunt Sally put out, sucking her fingers, savoring the flavors, tasting crumbled bread mixed with bits of cabbage, collards, and turnip greens, all made juicy with the pot likker poured over it.

Focused on licking her fingers, Sarah hadn't seen ol' miss until she was on them, flicking her cat-o'-nine-tails at the children. When they fled, scattering, ol' miss said quietly, "The more they scamper, the more they grow for market."

Sarah ran as fast as she could to escape the snaky lash that whipped through the air behind her, arching her back away from the stroke. She stumbled and bit her lip, hard. When she put her hand on her mouth to wipe the warm stickiness off, she saw the dark red blood. Ever since, her stomach had tightened when she caught sight of blood.

That night she waited outside until Mama stumbled home by the light of the stars and moon. "What did ol' miss mean, 'They grow for market'?" she asked. It sounded scary, the way ol' miss said the words.

Sarah saw her mother flinch. "Don't mean nothing, child. Hush." Her weary mother comforted her later, stroking her head while they lay together on Sarah's pallet. "Hmmm ..." her mother began as she hummed the familiar chant, "It's all right." Even then, Sarah remembered, she had a terrible feeling that in spite of Mama's words, everything was not all right. But she'd forced herself to burrow deeper into her mother, who hummed and rubbed her head until Sarah fell asleep.

Now, nine years later, her worst fears fulfilled, she was running for her life. When Sarah saw the sky lighten, she knew she had to find another hiding place, a spot to sleep until night gave her cover to walk again. Creeping under a thicket of tangled brush, she unwrapped her provisions. Sarah longed to crawl toward a creek she heard rushing over rocks nearby, imagining how the cool water would soothe her bruised feet. But she couldn't risk leaving shelter, even in early dawn. While mosquitoes buzzed and bit, Sarah forced herself to stay put, nibbling a corner of her biscuit.

Suddenly she heard a rustling nearby, the crunch of leaves. Her heart pounded. It came closer. She tried to flatten herself into the undergrowth, pressing into the ground. Twigs snapped. Something large was rapidly approaching. Closer, quicker, until two rabbits darted down the path, chased by a fox. After her heart quieted Sarah closed her eyes, praying no trader would find her while she slept.

While lying in the wet thicket, where she thrashed in spite of her determination to lie still, Sarah's dreams grew more vivid. The sun rode high in the sky while she slept and dreamt. Her past came swirling at her in dust clouds that covered her until she couldn't see anything else. In her dreams it was one continuous Sunday, a glorious day with no sound of the whip, and a chance to play or think. Everyone was in her vision: Mama, Papa, Esther, and Albert, just before—

But even in dreams she wouldn't let her mind go to that terrible day. Instead, she stuck to other memories, the happy ones, all jumbled up into one delicious stew of Sundays.

CHAPTER

4

I wake up to the smell of Sunday pancakes, and it wafts right through me, wrapping my gut in pleasure. Dad's cooking a batch of fluffy ones, his weekend specialty. After all these years, he still makes a deal out of frying an N for me, a J for Jimi, and an S for himself, and I still think it's cool that the pancake batter can form solid letters. It was always magic, how I could bounce down to breakfast and find a golden N on my plate. This morning at Dad's place, it seems strange not to have Mom's M in the pan, another of those where-am-I-now moments. I rub my eyes and wait for seconds, but even with that aroma tugging at me, I'm still thinking about Sarah.

"Why did she have to leave her family?" I ask Dad. "I mean, I know about runaways, but why couldn't they all go together?"

"Sugar, I can't tell you what's going to happen." He brings the second batch to the table. The smell is driving me crazy. "You'll have to wait to see how it unfolds."

"Well, you know, don't you? You wrote it. And it's a true story. You said it's our family history."

Jimi pushes against me, reaching for the maple syrup. "Don't chew with your mouth open," I tell him sharply. Jimi stares without blinking, like he's daring me, and stuffs his cheeks. A piece of pancake dribbles from his lips, but he grins right through it. Whatever he was whimpering about last night looks long gone.

"She was my great-grandmother," Dad says, not answering my question. "From what we know, this is how it happened. Not exactly with the details I'm writing, since I have to fill in the blanks, but the essence is true." His voice sounds scratchy, as if he has an allergy or cold.

"Tell me more about the chapter you read last night," I beg. "Why was she on the run by herself? What happened to her family?"

All of a sudden I want to race into Jimi's room and burrow under my blanket, grown up as I am. I'm so glad I have a bed, even the rickety one here at Dad's. But instead I ask again, and again he answers, "Wait for it to unfold." I do know one thing about my dad: once he says no, he means it. Not like Mom, whom I can usually convince to change her mind. So I ask something else that's bothering me.

"What did that ol' miss mean when she said, 'the more they grow for market'? Was she gonna sell the kids?"

"Well, in slavery times"—his voice goes all pompous, like I don't know anything—"masters did sell the children. Especially in the 1850s. The price of slaves had risen dramatically. And in Virginia, where Sarah's family was, tobacco land was worn out." He stops, and I see the muscles in the side of his neck twitching. "And they talk about stealing! Who stole who?" He's become livid.

"I know." Doesn't he think I learned anything about slavery at school? But why be furious about it now? It's the twenty-first century, Dad. The world has changed. I'm the living proof, aren't I? Nobody's growing me for market. And our family shows how different things are. "Why wouldn't Sarah's mother tell her about it? And hide her or something?"

Dad sighs. I smell burning, but he doesn't notice until Jimi shouts, "Dad! The pancakes!"

"Oh, yeah ..." Dad jumps up. When he comes back he says, "She couldn't. It was too painful. What could she say? She tried to hide the truth as long as she could. That was the hiding she did. Occasionally, mothers did flee with their children into the swamps, but it was very, very dangerous." He stops. Jimi and I are sitting still. Jimi's not even chewing. "Dogs were sent to sniff them out, vicious dogs. So, Sarah's mother—your great-great-great-grandmother—did her best by not delving into what was happening but simply keeping them all fed and as safe as she possibly could."

This sounds familiar, I think. Not delving. I wish somebody would delve into what's happening to Jimi. Or Jessica and me. We'd been like twins; the summer we were nine, before she and Fran and I started acting like triplets, Mom bought us matching yellow shorts and tank tops that we wore every day. When we were out in public, we told people we were sisters. I still smile when I remember what fun that was, even though it makes my head hurt too. We wore those yellow shorts until they tore apart. When the seat was full of holes, I still begged Mom to let me wear mine. When she threw them out, I cried so hard that she fished them out of the trash and washed them, and told me I could wear those shorts until they fell off my body.

Three years ago, on my birthday, Jessica and I even bought friendship rings at the mall. We pricked our fingers with a safety pin to put our blood on the rings, so we'd be blood sisters forever. "You are my true sister," we vowed, and swore we'd never take them off. I look down at the silver glinting on my finger. After all that, how could there be this strange barrier between us, like an invisible wall that I can't reach through?

All morning Jimi and I fool around, teasing each other, tossing a Nerf ball back and forth, until we tumble into playing our old childhood "bed football" on Dad's bed. Just as we did when we were small, we dive, and whoever gets the ball hangs on while the other one leaps on top, trying to grab it. Big as I am, it brings back a sense of normalcy, having fun in the same way we have for so many years. We pin each other to the mattress and laugh a lot. But once I hold Jimi down, and I'm pressing his shoulders back, I see tears in his eyes again. This is so not like him.

"What's going on?" I demand. "I didn't hurt you."

He watches me while I stare at him until he shifts his eyes away. "I know."

"So?" I raise my fist.

"It's just ... that boy," he says. "He's going to— "

"Going to what?" I'm tired of his cat-and-mouse game. "Who?"

"I can't tell you," he says. "He'd kill— "

"Kill? What's going on?" When he doesn't respond, I start to call, "Daaad." But after Jimi turns white—and that's a feat—I stop. "Jimi, you've gotta tell me. I'll take care of it. Nobody's going to hurt you. I'll talk to him."

"No!" he says. "He can't know I told you anything." He covers his face with his hands.

"Well, you hardly did," I say, disgusted again, but with a fresh seed of worry in the pit of my stomach. And no matter how I try to worm it out of him, even when I promise I won't tell Mom or Dad, Jimi won't say more.

That afternoon I ride the bus to meet Jessica and Claudette at the mall for a two o'clock movie. "Hey," I call when I see them outside. I wonder what they've said to each other about me. Before, it was always Jessica and Fran and me talking about everybody else. Nowadays, I always seem to arrive too late.

The three of us walk into the lobby, with its frayed red carpet and giant cardboard posters of coming attractions, and stand in line to buy soda and popcorn. It's noisy, with kids calling out to each other and a mass of kids pressing behind me. "Stop pulling on my backpack," I hear Claudette say to a boy behind her, and she starts lecturing him on common decency. Up a short flight of stairs I spot Lavonn with Demetre, who has all the answers in every class and lets everybody know it. When Lavonn waves, I motion that I'll go over after I get my Hershey bar.

Before I can get there, a boy—the one Lavonn was talking to at school—prances over to the girls, then other kids swarm them, the boys slapping each other, calling "Dawg!" and cracking up. They're loud; I watch a box of popcorn fly into the air and scatter.

Claudette looks over too and spins back to us. "Ghetto," she says, with a look I'm starting to recognize, while she arches her long back.

"Yeah," Jessica echoes, wrinkling her nose exactly the way Claudette does.

I stare at them. If Lavonn and Demetre are ghetto, and Jessica and Claudette are hills or preppy, what am I? Some kids say they're "mixed," but I'm not mixed, I'm scrambled—a bunch of separate pieces all jumbled in one body that hardly recognizes my best friend, shuttles between two homes, and has no idea what's terrifying my brother.

"What you want?" the kid behind the counter asks. A black kid. Before, I wouldn't have thought twice about that. Now I see how different he looks from Jessica and Claudette, with his huge black sweatshirt and backward hat, how completely different even his voice sounds.

"Large Coke, no ice," Claudette tells him in her bossy voice, looking away. Jessica orders "water, no ice, and large popcorn with butter" in the same imperial tone. I mumble, "A Hershey bar, please," and, since Lavonn has disappeared, I plan to wander into the movie with them.

"Hey," Jessica says, and her voice holds a tinge of the old warmth when she looks at me. "Let's not see *Prom Parade*," the romantic comedy we'd bought tickets for. She glances over her shoulder toward the ticket taker, then whispers, "We'll sneak into *New York Tango*." She points to a vivid poster for the R-rated movie, featuring a woman in a skin-tight red dress standing in front of a man crouching behind her with a gun, his face half covered by a cowboy hat.

"Yeah," Claudette agrees. "A thriller. It's supposed to be hot."

"Okay," I say nervously. "But how will we get in?"

"Nobody's looking," Claudette urges, her eyes swiveling around the lobby. "Come on."

We slide into the last row of seats, but the movie is stupid and there's so much blood I have to keep looking away. Plus, the man with the ridiculous hat, who's not really a cowboy, treats the woman in the red dress like dirt. All I can think is *I'm sitting next to Jessica Raymond, red jersey number nine, and suddenly I don't know her. Who wants to see this kind of stuff? What kind of person is Jessica if she likes this violence? Or is she faking to get in with Claudette, and if she is, what kind of integrity does she have?*

Once the horrible film is over at last, my stomach feels queasy. The three of us slouch against a wall outside, rehashing the movie: "Hey, what about when he kissed her for like half an hour? I think his tongue was halfway down her throat!" The other two girls scream while I try to enjoy the camaraderie, and my stomach settles down until I trudge by myself down to El Camino for the bus. It's lonesome in the fading afternoon light, with dry leaves blowing around. I'm chilly too. When I ride by the first corner of San Joaquin Boulevard, I glimpse a man on the sidewalk leaning against a gray wall where the paint from the Grove Liquor and 7-Up store is peeling off. As the bus moves on, I see a group of teens: girls with dreads wearing white tees and jeans, and two boys walking in that special way, rolling from side to side with their pants falling off. When we stop at a light I hear a car radio blasting rap so loud my temples pound, and I feel like a traveler from another land.

Dad's supposed to drive me home later that night, but I knock on the door of his study, a tiny room off the hall that's more like a closet. "Can I stay over again? I could go back home in the morning and leave my stuff there before school. I have my homework here." I stop and throw him my innocent look. "It's almost done."

He pulls his glasses down to give me his special, intense stare.

"The bus starts going at six. Six-o-five." I can't tell what he's thinking, now that he's back to being the old Dad, where his face doesn't show a thing. There's a minute of silence while I try to look like this is a great idea, until he smiles and grumbles, "Call your mother."

Mom asks softly, "Are you having that good a time?"

"Yeah. Jessica and Claudette and I went to the movies and hung around downtown. Dad's reading me this story he's writing. It's cool."

"Oh, that. I know about that." Her voice has a sharp edge. But she says yes, and when I hang up I throw a Nerf ball at Jimi, who's quiet, not like his old self at all.

After dinner I ask Dad, "How 'bout another chapter?" I lean over his shoulder at the dining table, where he's reading the *New York Times* and muttering.

"Dad . . ."

" 'Thieves,' they say! People left to starve. Or trying to get back a tiny fragment of the wages they've been robbed of for generations." He takes off his glasses, rubs his eyes, and looks at me. "Oh, baby, I'm tired." Yeah, me too, of listening to this rant. I know all that happened in the past, back in Miss Sarah's time, but it's over now, isn't it? Even if the people in Oakland did suffer a little more than white people might after an explosion, do we have to talk about it all the time? The sun is starting to get almost yellow again and the air isn't quite as smoky. I'm not coughing as much, and neither is Jimi, I notice.

"I know, Dad, but just one chapter?" I rub my cheek against his, trying to revive the old Dad.

"It's Sunday night, I have work ..." He glances back at the paper. "Look at that!" he says, pointing to a photo of people jammed into an old Oakland armory. "They're sleeping head to toe on the floor. Left to rot ..."

"Please?" I use my best-girl voice again, ignoring the photo.

He laughs. "You're like Sarah, relentless." Then he surprises me. "Read the next chapter yourself. It's in my study; you can read in there. 'Chapter Two — Did God Make White People Too?'" His dark eyes pierce me. "It's in the blue folder on my desk."

Whoa, Dad's never talked like that before. Usually he's "Don't touch my desk, don't go near it, don't even touch my chair!" Everything's changing so fast, minute to minute, it's hard to keep up. And that chapter, 'Did God Make White People Too?' I wonder what Jessica would say. Or Mom. Once, years ago, when our family was walking in San Francisco, a guy sitting on the sidewalk pointed at Mom holding hands with Dad and shook his fist, yelling, "Leave the brother alone!" I wanted to creep away, so he wouldn't think I was white and shout at me too. But I guess he could tell.

With a sigh I head to Dad's study's, which is neat, as always: stacks of paper lined up with the edge of the desk, and in the middle the blue folder marked with red ink, **MISS SARAH ARMSTRONG: ON THE RUN**. A photograph in a silver frame catches my eye. It's next to one of me and Jimi in the park: this shows Dad and a woman, laughing, with his arm around her. Suddenly I remember her. Helane. At the end of the summer she was in our house. It was freaky. After Mom came home from work one day and called from the front door, "Hi, I'm home," she stepped down to the den and scooted right back out like a witch was in there, like her hair was on fire. She slammed the front door, and Jessica and I heard her gun the motor on the Honda and peel out of the driveway. When Helane and Dad crept out a few minutes later, we watched them from the kitchen. Helane is thin, with a short Afro — almost bald — and she walks real smooth, like a knife cutting through butter. Dad had one arm over her shoulder, while the other was clutching a folder, and he hardly said a word before he opened the front door and blocked our view. Jessica and I stared at each other. We couldn't believe it. I promised myself then that if I ever saw Helane again, I'd cut her dead. And here she is, smiling out at me as if she ... belongs. I want to pick it up and fling it against the wall as hard as I can, but I don't dare. Instead I turn it facedown and shove it under a pile of papers. When I do that, a few pages flutter to the floor. I deliberately push more off, then a whole bunch. All of a sudden I want to scatter every paper in his study, create a blizzard, and laugh at the paper storm. But if Dad came in, he'd kill me. So I don't make more, but I leave the mess I made on the floor, open the blue folder, and begin to read, forgetting all about Jessica, Mom, whoever's tormenting Jimi, and those terrible fires burning up the homes of black people twenty miles away.

Did God Make White People Too?

On Sundays Sarah and Esther crept out of sight of the cabins. The long-limbed Sarah, thick hair tumbling in every direction, moved quickly. Her sister, lighter skinned, with fine hair cut close to her head, stumbled after, always managing to trip over a tree root, scraping palms and skinning knees. Sarah had to turn away if Esther's gashes were deep. Though she tried to be brave in front of her sister, she couldn't look at the wounds without feeling sick.

When the girls got to the creek, they'd walk all the way to the spot where it widened out and joined the Pamunkey River. They'd found a special grassy clearing where they liked to lie on their backs, stare up at the sky, and talk. Other children, gathering nuts in the woods, wandered by occasionally, but for the most part they were alone.

"Where is heaven?" Esther asked one time. She turned onto her side, wide hazel eyes fixed on her sister.

"It's high. Way, way up in the sky. Someday we'll be there." Sarah spoke authoritatively. Eight years old now, she took her big-sister role seriously. "It's good there. When we die and Papa dies, we'll get to be with him all week long." Sarah studied the clouds. Sunday was the one day they could be together as a family, before her father, Albert Winston, returned to the next-door tobacco farm, the huge Winston plantation where he spent the week. Sarah turned to face Esther, smiling, and tugged down her little sister's shirt. Like all the younger children, little Esther wore only a shift, slit up the sides.

Though her father was a Winston, Sarah's name was Armstrong, like her mother, Yasmine, and Esther and little Albert. They were all Armstrongs, her mother had explained when responding to Sarah's persistent questions one Sunday, "'cause Master Armstrong owns us." Yasmine had said this with a voice so sharp it made Sarah's mouth taste like metal. "We take ol' massa's name." Sarah had wanted to know more, but could tell by the frown on her mother's face that she'd get no more answers that day.

"Who's up in heaven?" Esther asked, rolling over and kicking so her shirt slid up again.

"Aunt Hannah says there won't be any massas in heaven," Sarah answered firmly.

"Where do the massas go?"

"Hmm." The question stumped Sarah.

"Did God make white people too?" The doubts seemed to tumble from Esther's six-year-old mind.

"God made everything," Sarah began. But try as she might, she couldn't reconcile the loving Shepherd her parents described with the evidence of his handiwork. Even Mama and Papa had to do everything white people said. "But there won't be any white people," Sarah repeated decisively, turning over onto her stomach.

Esther, appearing to be satisfied, tumbled and rolled down the muddy bank. A frog hopped out of the water and Esther chased it, her little arms stretched out in front of her body as she stumbled along.

Sarah stayed in the grass thinking about what Ol' Mister Armstrong preached on Sundays in their little African Baptist church. "Servants, obey in all things your masters," he shouted, apparently reading from the Big Book. "He that knoweth his master's will and doeth it not shall be beaten with many stripes!"

She'd asked Papa about this once. "Why do we have to obey him?" And "What are stripes?"

But Papa, picking her up and holding her tight, only said, "You're too little to be thinking such big thoughts, Lilla Bit." Then, big as she was, he tossed her in the air and caught her, swinging her by her arms so her feet barely scraped the ground.

Still, Sarah wanted to know. Over and over she heard ol' massa lecturing in the tiny whitewashed room. "Faults you are guilty of toward your masters and mistresses are faults done against God himself, who hath set your masters and mistresses over you in his own stead."

Why? Sarah wondered.

And ol' man Armstrong constantly warned, "Thou shalt not steal." Sarah puzzled over these words. She didn't know what to tell her sister about this. If she was hungry, as she so often was, and there was ample food nearby, was it wrong to eat?

Sarah thought back to her mother returning to the cabin one Saturday evening, saying she'd "found a stray chicken" and promised, "We'll have a broiling." The next day they'd roasted potatoes in the fire and burned rags to keep the white folks from smelling the cooking chicken. Sarah thought of the good filled-up feeling in her tummy with that chicken and potatoes in it. And how after they'd eaten that evening she'd chased little Albert back and forth in front of the fire, then around and around until they both fell dizzily onto the floor. Esther had fallen on top of them, tickling them both. They laughed so hard Sarah gasped for breath, and Mama started to laugh too.

Another thought plagued Sarah's thoughts: How had she come to belong to ol' massa? She tried to puzzle it out while Esther played at the edge of the water. Sarah didn't tell her sister about the whispers she'd heard. Mama's daddy. It didn't seem possible.

"Is it true?" she'd asked Mama. "Where's your mama now?"

For answer, Mama slapped her, hard. It was the first time she'd ever hit her firstborn. And she didn't say a word.

Mama had held her later and said she was sorry, but her face didn't look sorry. It was mad. And she didn't explain.

Sarah recalled her feelings were as hurt as her face. Why couldn't she ask that question? What was wrong?

Ever since, whenever Sarah saw ol' massa at a distance, she stared. Watching him move threw broken glass into her heart; when he bent his head to the side, cocking it in a familiar way to examine a fence rail or a broken wagon wheel, his gesture knotted her stomach. She thought then of Ruth's grandpappy, who teased her and brought her treats, candies he tucked away from the Big House and, once, a bouquet of wildflowers: yellow-and-white daisies, blue larkspur, and best of all, pink bleeding hearts, with their delicate bells.

Anxiety tightened Sarah's body too when she watched young massa and saw his eyes rake the women. Would he look at her that way now that she was growing up? She wished that every day of the week was Sunday, and she could stay by the river with Esther.

Late on Sunday afternoons, when the afternoon sky was latticed with ribbons of pink, she and Esther dashed off to gather firewood for dinner. Aunt Hannah sometimes came too, swaying and tottering, pointing out magic in the plants. "See, this one cures the arthritis, and that one, if I boil it, will get rid of the fever." She plucked a long, thin plantain leaf and held it out to the girls.

They nodded, then darted ahead to gather kindling for Aunt Hannah. Rushing back, they hurried to the corncrib to pick up the week's ration of meal—"A peck and a half." The foreman scowled, reaching out to Sarah. With a practiced feint she dodged him and raced to the smokehouse for bacon or middlin' meat, and finally on to the quarters to eat their cornmeal.

"Young fellow ran away from Winston's place last night," a friend of her mother's whispered one evening while she ate from an old blue bowl. "Young fellow, praise God, gone north."

Papa leaned in with a worried look. "Too many ..."

"A woman showed up in the quarters last night. A wild woman, coal black," Yasmine said and shook her head.

"With an iron collar," another said. "I heard she clawed at a window over there. Where is she now?"

Yasmine shrugged.

Through the chatter Sarah heard her parents speak harshly of the moods the foreman had that week, of the way tobacco was wearing out the land, and, always, of a time when their lives would not be so hard.

"Hold on a little while longer, hmmm." That was her mother's favorite song. She hummed it day and night, until late in the evenings when she switched over to "Am I born to die and lay this body down? And must my trembling spirit fly into a world unknown? Oh, am I born to die?"

But over and around their anguish her parents laughed. They teased their neighbors and boasted of transgressions: stolen apples or a chicken, a quickly broken hoe or rake ("Can't work no more right now, boss, sure am sorry."), a feigned illness, an instant of privacy free of surveillance.

Too soon Sunday evenings ended, and the week was ready to bare its fangs. Sunday night signified Papa's return to the Winston place. Sarah had only heard about his tiny room, the windowless one he shared with two other men, a room that was the fifth from the front in a long row of rooms. Each week, his leave-taking made her cry. From the adults around her she understood that Papa might or might not be back—always depending on the master. Rumor whispered that ol' Winston had gambled away all he had and needed cash.

But on Sunday nights before Sarah's father left, he sang to his children. The music, he told them, "carried from my father's father," who'd remembered a youth "far across the water, before the men with turbans came." Papa told sorry stories about captured people, yoked with long, slender logs and forced onto big ships. Some jumped overboard and their bones, he said, walked back home. Hearing the tales, she shivered. Then her father would lean over to warm her in an embrace. His big arms enfolded her, and despite the dread that bruised her days, for that moment the world was good.

CHAPTER 5

What's the matter?" Jessica waves her hand in front of my face. Today when we were hurrying inside after lunch she asked, "Do you want to come over after school?" When I said, "Soccer?" she looked as if I'd proposed deer hunting, so here I am, sitting on her bedroom floor under the Hawaiian poster. Last winter she found a palm-tree spread for her loft bed and two shaggy green pillows, and painted the window frame yellow. Even the cup on her desk is a coconut shell.

"Nothing." I shrug.

"I said, 'What about ice skating on Saturday, with Claudette and her brother at the West Hill rink?' Her dad's gonna take us." Jessica scratches her pink tee, scraping off a microscopic stain.

Wasn't it Claudette's dad who proposed shooting "looters"? A nasty lurch unsettles my stomach. "I might be at Dad's on Saturday."

"You haven't heard anything! Before that I asked, 'Do you want to walk to Fat Slices and get fudge?' You didn't even answer!"

She shoves a pile of books away and pokes her head into my face. "Nina?" She scootches closer.

Despite biting my cheek until it's raw, tears dribble next to my nose until I wipe them with my sleeve. "Everything's different," I blurt. "I'm reading this book my dad's writing, about my great-great-grandmother running from slavery. It was horrible — dogs were after her ..." I freeze. Jessica's pinched, pink face, radiating disdain, could be the spitting image of ol' miss flicking her cat-o'-nine-tails. It could've been *her* family's ancestors who owned Miss Sarah; her dad's family is from Virginia. Suddenly I can't wait to leave, but to where? At Dad's I don't even have a room, only the Deathbed in Jimi's corner. At Mom's — wow, it's strange to call it that — everything's too quiet. The silence is driving me crazy. We haven't seen Rolling Stone for days, and Mom's as different these days as Dad is. She's grouchy, for one thing, in a way she never used to be. And even more clueless, like her mind is somewhere else. The mom who used to cook great dinners or offer me rides now simply waves toward the fridge, like Dad does, and kind of stares past me vacantly. Not that I'm eager to hang out with her, but she's so out of it she makes me nervous. When I see her in the living room I mumble "I'm busy" and head up to my room, which is lonely too without Jimi nearby.

"I've gotta go."

"Why? What's — " Jessica asks, arching her back like an exact replica of Claudette.

"Nothing. I have to." I'm on my feet, hoisting my backpack.

"Nina, we just got here." She leans forward and yanks my wrist, trying to pull me down, but I shake her off. Then, before she can grab me again, I tear out into the hall, run downstairs, and burst through the front door. But where to go?

I wander over to the Cougar track and run around a couple times, trying to figure out my mixed-up life. But it's hot, even for October, our hottest month; the wind burns and the dust chokes me. Everything's brittle and dry. We haven't had rain since March. As I wander off the track onto the street, a red bike whizzes by, chased by a screaming boy shaking his fist. After the blur passes, I do a double take. Was that Jimi on the bike? His head was tucked, no helmet, and he was pedaling fast, but I recognize his Afro, which is growing wide like Dad's. Jimi's bike is an old brown beater, though. This couldn't be Jimi or his rust bucket. Funny how it looked like him.

The scene of them whirring by and the shouting lingers. It sounded like *"Thief!"* and the other boy looked like Dwight Jackson — or his evil clone, Tyrone. But that couldn't have been Jimi.

I wipe my face with my hand to clear away the vision and head over toward Sierra Street. I hardly know where my feet are leading me, but by the time I look up I'm passing Fran's old house, which makes me catch my breath. Why did her parents have to separate? They were both white. If you call Italian white, since Fran's darker than me. She says her parents fought because her dad wanted another baby — a boy, he insisted, after four girls — and her mom refused. And then her mom had to go to Italy when her parents got sick, so Fran doesn't know if they're ever gonna live together again.

Maybe Fran would understand some of what I'm going through — or at least listen if I called. But first I need to get home. My feet just don't want to go there yet.

All of a sudden I'm standing at the corner in front of Lavonn's, banging the brass knocker. The sound startles a blue jay from a perch on the porch, and its cry as it soars off, screechy and scratchy, sounds like my jangled nerves.

"Oh, Nina." It's Lavonn's mother, Saundra, who looks pleased to see me. It's been months since I've been here. "Lavonn's not home, but you look thirsty. It's so hot outside. Come have something to drink." She's seriously dressed. Cute, like always. Today she's wearing a black dress with a crinoline, so the skirt sticks out in a triangle. She leads me through the living room. It's always been soothing, with dark wooden statues and carvings and beige woven baskets. A strip of orange kente cloth on the back of the couch is the only color. Saundra guides me to a counter that separates the kitchen and living room, and clears away a basket of yellow gourds. The polished wood and African art remind me of Dad's apartment, where he's hung masks, and last Saturday he brought home a giant wooden giraffe with swirls of black for the living room.

"Do you want a soda or iced tea? Water?"

"I don't know," I say softly. I've known her since I was a kid, but I've never talked to her alone like this.

"Oh, sit up here; give your feet a rest." She motions to a high stool at the counter. "How about some orange soda?"

"Sure," I say, still quiet. "Thanks." I don't know how to leave, now that she's offering me soda. And it feels good, for the first time in weeks, to have an adult actually take an interest in me. When she returns with my drink in a glass clinking with ice, she asks, "What's up? How's life treating you?"

I don't know what to say. My life couldn't be more confusing.

"Or how are you treating it?" She smiles and I remember how kind she was to us when she drove carpool. Seeing her watch me the way she is now, as if she cares, I feel those rotten tears start behind my nose, but I choke them back and mutter, "It's okay."

"Nina, I was sorry to hear your parents split." She sucks her teeth. "It's tough, I know."

You wouldn't.

"My parents divorced when I was your age." Saundra gives me a penetrating look, as if she's deciding whether to say more. "We lived in South Central LA."

"Oh," I say politely. *You don't have a clue about what it's like for me, being scrambled. Or all the other stuff going on.* But then

I really hear what she just said. "South Central. Wow. I've only heard about it. What was that like?"

She becomes very still before she bends forward. "Oh, any neighborhood kids grow up in is 'normal' to them. The community was okay. It was my family situation that was so tough."

I thought she meant the divorce until she added. "You know, my mother's black and my father's white."

"Whoa," slips out of my lips. I thought Lavonn was black, plain black. "Lavonn is biracial too, then," I say, before I realize I'm voicing my thought aloud.

"Most African Americans are. But it's not always acknowledged."

I'm stunned into silence.

"More white people have a touch of the brush than they want to admit. Or even know. Everybody wanted to deny it back then. My father's parents disowned him, so I never met my white grandparents or cousins until I was grown. One aunt—my father's younger sister—broke the family rule and contacted me, years ago, after he passed. That broke the ice."

I'm totally uncomfortable, wondering how to absorb this personal information, when she adds, "Sometimes the white folks who are most vociferous about keeping us down are the very ones who've got some hidden great-grandma themselves, some ancestor they can't bring themselves to accept."

Claudette's face flashes into my mind. Could that be the case with her? Then I wonder, if that's true, what does being white mean? I remember Mom telling me that Jews like her mother's family weren't always considered white, right up to today in some places. Irish people too, on her dad's side. My mom told me about the "No Irish need apply" signs that used to be around. Is *Mom* even white? How do people decide who's what, and why does it matter anyway?

Saundra breaks into my spinning thoughts. "So I do have an

inkling of what you might be going through. More than the average kid coping with divorce."

I don't even have words for how crazy I feel, so I'm not sure how even Saundra would get it all. Divorced parents. A dad who's changing into another person right before my eyes. Two homes. And this insane race stuff that I never even noticed before. Why do I have these humungous issues when all other girls have to worry about is how good their hair looks? Or what jeans to wear? Or what boy likes them? It isn't fair. Even when Fran got so upset about moving and ran away, coming back to Canyon Valley for a couple days, she didn't have to deal with all this other stuff.

Just when I'm feeling like the unluckiest kid alive, Saundra says, "You know, Nina, biracial kids signed up for a big life." She smiles again. Her face is narrow, not like Lavonn's, but when she grins they look the same. "A big life," she repeats. What does she mean? "You might feel fragmented now—especially with Silas and Maggie on such bad terms—but, in the end, you'll see. If you can pull it off, you'll have access to two complete, fascinating worlds." She laughs with a big, deep laugh. "It's a trip."

I take the last sip of my soda, my mind exploding like the Oakland fires. I wonder if the chair I'm sitting on will dissolve and I'll tumble to the floor. My science teacher says matter isn't solid anyway; it's all energy. I believe her. Nothing feels solid right now.

"The culture will call you African American—that one-drop rule still reigns—yet you get to choose. It's complicated, but you can play it all!" She throws her head back and laughs again. The sound is like a musical line, dipping up and down. "Listen, I've got to run off to a meeting, but I wanted to talk for a few minutes with you." She pauses and gives me that stare. "Lavonn said—" She stops again. "I'm so glad you dropped by. Why don't you call her?" On the way to the door she says casually, "Lavonn's rehearsing for the *Black Nativity*, at the James Baldwin Theater. She's over there now with Demetre. They could use more black kids."

More black kids. Despite her talk of "playing it all," of getting to choose, that's how she thinks of me. Why does everybody want me to choose?

"It's the Langston Hughes play, you know? The black Christmas story." She laughs. "It's great, gospel."

Oh, music. I've never heard of the play, but I nod as if I have. "I don't know," I mutter. "I might not have time. But I'll see."

Afterward I tear down to El Camino, kicking shriveled leaves, hardly noticing where I am while I stare at parched, yellow grass bordering the sidewalk. I'm not a black kid: I don't watch BET, I sing white folk songs with my mom, who I suddenly feel, in the oddest way, is the one person I'm closest to. And she's white. Or so-called white, Jewish-Irish white. It's hopeless.

Before I know it I'm at San Pablo. Without thinking I turn right and head down toward the lower flats. A strong, sour garbage smell hits my nose. *Eeeww.* I look around. The shadows are long. I'm not used to the shorter days yet. My mom would murder me if she knew I was here by myself on the corner of San Pablo and Central. Well, that would get their attention, wouldn't it, if I got mugged. I'm cold and it's grayer by the minute. When I see two drunk guys weaving toward me, I turn and start to trudge back up the hill, thinking about Sarah. Did I get my name from her owner, Mr. Armstrong? Is that why I'm up front when we sit in alphabetical order?

Finally, when I can hardly take another step, I stagger up my block, and there's Mom on the top step of our porch, playing her guitar. It's so embarrassing. She looks like a wild, red-haired elf, with a raggedy sweatshirt under a huge guitar. But still, I'm glad to see her. More than glad.

Her face lights up like it always does when she didn't expect me and I swing into view. By the time I get to the foot of the steps she's beaming. "Sweetie, I'm glad you're home. I thought you were at Jessica's." She looks puzzled but she sings a ditty she wrote when

I was little. "Oh Nina, you're the one. Your face glows like the morning sun."

She's so happy that I join in on the chorus, and for a minute the world spins back in its orbit. Yeah, this is my mom, and this is me. When she beams the way she is now, everything that's tight inside melts and I want to hum along, in harmony. *Nina, Nina, you're the one.* It's a baby song. I'm sure everybody in the neighborhood has heard it by now. After we finish she strums the chords to "Union Maid": *There once was a union maid, she never was afraid.* We belt out the chorus, "Oh, you can't scare me, I'm stickin' to the union, I'm stickin' to the union." When my mom and I sing that song, we totally blend into one. We both sing soprano; hers is higher than mine, but we've sung together so much that our voices wind around and it's special, not like anything else. Mom and Granny Leigh, her mom, sing together too. This time, though, just when everything's normal for a minute, a sharp thought pokes in: Mom's voice sounds tinny and thin. Real *white.* And these union songs that are brave, like, "We're standing up to the bosses," well, my American History teacher told us unions didn't let black people join—for years. They had to be scabs if they wanted jobs. Why am I singing like unions are so great? Okay, I admit that unions were good for white working people, and I feel the tug to Mom and Granny Leigh and G'a Milt, but I can't believe Mom would keep singing this racist stuff. Can't she see what she's doing, pitting herself against African American history? The warm ripples swirling in my body spin into my stomach, until I'm nauseous, just like I was at Jessica's. The steps are crumbling, and God just tumbled out of heaven. Gravity might be loosening its hold too; nothing makes any sense again.

"Oh no," I mumble, putting one hand on my tummy.

"What?" she asks.

"I don't want to sing." I stand and race up to my room, where I lie facedown, rubbing my bedspread between my fingers, scraping the bumps in the material against the pad of my thumb until I hear Rolling Stone scratch on my door, and as soon as I let him in he plops on my back for a few minutes. When I roll onto the floor he rubs against my legs, like he's my best friend and where have I been?

The two of us settle down to homework, which I can hardly do because Rolling Stone is walking on top of it and waving his fat tail in my face. The more I push him away, the more he insists on sitting on the book. No way can I do homework. Anyway, my mind is as mixed up as my ancestors are. I give up and send a quick text to Fran, asking how it's going for her, and telling her to call me. Soon.

Later, when I can't avoid Mom, because I have to go to the kitchen to eat, she hands me a brown envelope and stares as if she's trying to penetrate my soul. "Your father left this for you."

Your father again. *Can't you say Dad, or even Silas?*

I grab the package and zoom up to my room; as soon as I tumble into bed I rip open the envelope and read a note clipped to the front page: "Lilla Bit, let's talk about this all after you read it. Notice the curiosity (smile). Sound familiar?" Riffling through the manuscript, I find three whole chapters of **MISS SARAH ARMSTRONG: ON THE RUN**. Sarah, who might actually be the only person on the planet I can relate to. The only problem: she's dead.

Reading: Don't You Dare

Even though she'd turned nine—too big for a Lilla Bit, as Papa proudly teased her—Sarah still waited all week for Sunday. But now it was for the after-hours preaching. On Sunday evenings, late, after Papa left, she would hear the singing start, sweet and low, "Steal away ..." and her heart leaped. She knew what the music signified.

She'd follow the voices to a prayer meeting deep in the woods, held whenever Preacher Thomas could organize the secret gathering. The rail-thin preacher had a gift for reciting long Bible verses he'd committed to memory. These nighttime services had a different message than the ones she heard in the chapel during the day, the ones ol' massa preached. On full-moon nights, eyelids closing, Sarah loved to burrow into her mother's lap and hear the old preacher talk about Jesus, who suffered for her and offered rest. Or Moses, who led his people to freedom. Sarah pictured her whole community walking in a group, their few bedraggled belongings on their heads, marching up to freedom. She imagined great gates bursting open. Gates to that heavenly place called Freedom, which seemed so far away that she could only picture it in another realm. Laughing, people would change into fine, new, shiny clothes before settling down to eat all they wanted: biscuits, butter, pork and chicken, gravy, vegetables, three kinds of pie. They would sleep right past first light. At Freedom there would be no field work, no beatings, and shoes for everyone. Shoes that fit, that didn't pinch or rub her ankles. And her father would stay all week.

At the camp meetings people shouted and prayed, "Didn't my Lord deliver Daniel? Then why not every man?" *Why not?* Sarah wondered. Would she be delivered? And Mama and Papa and Albert and Esther?

Early one morning, Tamra, a sixteen-year-old heading to the field while carrying her baby on her back, whispered, "We got a secret school, out in the woods. On nights when the moon is full."

"School?" said Sarah.

"Yeah, reading and writing. Aunt Rachel— " She broke off when the overseer passed by and, lost in a crowd, Sarah heard no more that day. But soon she learned that a few brave people met for lessons in the evenings. Everything in her hungered to go, though she knew Mama would never allow it. The danger of prowling at night, with the bloodhounds ready, would drive her mother wild. No, Mama would say. Absolutely not.

Sarah tried to forget all about school, and reading. But every time the moon shone brightly, she couldn't sleep. No matter how tired she was, her mind raced, wondering what it would be like to read the Good Book for herself. Surely all her questions would be answered there. The more she thought, the more she wanted to go, and she had to force her mind to concentrate on her mother's heavy breath, in and out, in and out, until she put herself to sleep.

One moonlit evening Sarah lay on her pallet listening to her mother's nighttime chatter: Aunt Hannah's antics in the Big House, and Sally's thirteenth baby, white, blond, and blue-eyed as could be. The next morning Sarah called out to her mother, "I heard Aunt Sally say, 'He made him some more dark babies. Like shelling peas out a pod. But I've a mind to drown them all.' Why did Auntie say that?"

"She's just mad at ol' massa," Mama said, redoubling her concentration on her mending. Whatever she was doing when Sarah asked questions like these seemed to become doubly important.

Sarah paused, her mind grabbing and prodding the unruly idea until she could wrap it in an answer. When Mama kept her silence, she ventured to ask, "Why?" The unanswered thought hung in the air. Still Sarah waited, hoping her mother would volunteer more.

"She just is." Mama turned away, shushing her daughter. Mama, who was so kind when Sarah got hurt or scared, never seemed to answer the deepest questions. Whenever Sarah brought up anything about ol' massa, Mama simply flushed, wiped her hands on her apron—even when her hands looked clean—and looked away.

What did that mean, "He made him some more dark babies"? How could Master Armstrong make babies, when the turkey buzzard hatched them? He wasn't a buzzard, was he? But all Sarah heard for an answer was the familiar humming before her mother's prayers. "Hold on a little while longer, hmm hmmm."

Soon, thinking her exhausted mother had fallen asleep—though she didn't hear the customary snore—Sarah began to creep toward the door.

"Girl, don't go down there!" She heard the muffled cry from under her mother's covers. "A storm is coming, I can feel it. Master'll catch you; he'll whip you. Daughter, don't you dare go or I'll whip you myself!"

But Sarah bolted out the door. She had to find answers for the questions that were burning holes in her brain. And since Mama and Papa wouldn't—or couldn't—explain what she saw in the world around her, she was going to find out another way.

She'd heard that deep in the woods Wilbert and Tamra, with Aunt Rachel, had dug a giant hole, working for weeks on the underground cavern, and then covered it with branches and vines. As Sarah approached what she imagined was the secret area, she spotted Wilbert, a stocky twelve-year-old. Sarah's heart jumped, and together they pulled back the boughs. Sarah, always agile, easily leaped down into the pit, while clumsy Wilbert tumbled after her.

The smell of damp dirt and moldy leaves hit Sarah's nostrils. Then she inhaled the smell of a torch. Smoke scratched the inside of her nostrils. So this was pit school.

She watched Tamra and Wilbert struggle to hang a wash pot bottom up. Aunt Rachel explained that it would catch the sound of their voices. Sarah reached out to help them hook the pot onto two cut-off roots sticking into the pit. On this night, no overseer would hear them talking. For good measure, Wilbert had carried water in a bucket from a creek nearby. The water too would muffle their talk, she learned. Finally, they hung a quilt over the opening.

Secrecy was essential. In this pit, Aunt Rachel, her lined, oval face lit by a stolen candle and a torch, taught reading to her few courageous students. She'd learned the illegal skill years before at another plantation, where she worked in the house and kept a schoolbook hidden in her blouse. When white children came home from school, Rachel said, she'd asked questions about what they learned that day. Because she was so proud of every scrap of book learning she picked up, the white children taught her how to read and write. Whenever she found a chance, she passed it on.

Learning to read, Sarah knew, was a crime. She'd heard of masters threatening, "If I catch you learnin' I'll chop off your hands." Though they didn't usually follow through—for, as Papa said once grimly, a man with no hands couldn't work—she'd heard that young Master Phillips over by Richmond cut off a finger when he caught a girl trying to "git learnin'" from a Bible.

"Hell," that white man said while he chopped, as people in the quarters told it, "you don't need no learnin'. You'll never be free. And you ain't got sense enough to make a living if you were free." No judge punished him, it was said.

But in spite of everything she heard about the danger, Sarah burned with a passion to decipher the Good Book herself. Was it as Preacher Thomas told them: that they'd get to heaven no matter what they did, and the sooner they got there the better? The masters were going to hell for sure. "Better yet," Preacher Thomas said, "go on and run to freedom! That's what ol' Moses did!" And he'd recite a verse.

Or did it tell, as ol' massa said, "Any of you see anybody stealing Mistress Armstrong's chickens or eggs, go straight up to her and tell her who it is and all about it." How could the Book say that when Mama, who loved the Lord, taught her never to tell white people anything? Aunt Sally and Aunt Suzy, who both cooked in the great fireplaces at the Big House, brought food back to the quarters at night. They'd reach under their aprons into the pockets of long gingham skirts and pull out big pieces of ham, or a handful of white-flour biscuits. Was that wrong?

Sarah vowed she'd learn to read, and she promised herself that the next night when she came back to school, she'd bring Albert and her friend Ruth, who was always ready for an adventure.

Finally, when the moon had moved across the sky, almost touching down, Sarah crept back to the quarters, worn but exhilarated. Aunt Rachel had given her a tiny Bible to keep, so long as she kept up with the work. Yasmine, with a drooping body and lines in her face, looked as if she'd sat awake half the night. "Daughter, don't go out in the woods again at night!" she screamed, and brought her hand up. But Sarah ducked before her mother could hit her, and tumbled into bed, glancing up to see Esther and Albert poke their heads up out of their pallet, likely hoping to see the commotion. "That man won't spare you, don't think he will, just because— " Her mother stopped. She stood silent, her fury spent, then lay down beside her daughter and flung a heavy arm over her back.

"Because what?" Sarah asked.

"Means nothing to him," Mama murmured. "Fact is ... meanest of all." She spit out the garbled words, putting her forefinger to her lips. Her voice was a whisper, harsh and bitter, before she fell into a deep sleep.

What did that mean? Sarah lay puzzling it, her tired mind whirling.

In a moment quiet snoring filled the room.

Too soon the driver blew his horn, signaling time to get out to the fields. But slipping out into the dark morning, Sarah knew even at nine that in reading she had found a precious light, one she would need to untangle the mysteries of the world around her. She hoped it wouldn't cost her a hand, or a finger. When she thought that, she balled up her fists and put her hands behind her back.

CHAPTER 6

I'm sauntering home after school, kicking leaves, when I see Jessica and Claudette ahead, arm in arm. "Hey," I yell, and run to catch up.

"We're going for candy," Jessica calls back. "I know you want some, double-triple chocolate to be exact." When she laughs it's comforting. Yes, she knows me inside and out.

After we walk into Fat Slices, next to the dry cleaners, Jessica and Claudette giggle and wave their arms—weaving, twirling, kind of dancing—but the aisles are so narrow you can't get by without brushing against the toys, perfume, and stationery piled on the shelves. Dusty old stuff. Suddenly Claudette tumbles into a metal stand of birthday cards. They fly everywhere, scattering and knocking a shelf of colored pencils, pens, and markers onto the floor. In the commotion I see Claudette scoop something up and jam it into her back pocket. I blink my eyes and convince myself I must have imagined it. Claudette might be snooty, but I've never heard of her stealing. She and Jessica start laughing at the mess then, so I join in. We're still kind of chuckling when Alvin, the old guy who's the owner, heads toward us. He's paunchy and balding, with a stringy gray ponytail that hangs down past his shoulders.

"Don't move," he growls, before he turns back to lock the door. No one else is in the store, except for the three of us. "I know your tricks," he mutters, and I'm scared that he's going to finger Claudette. Until he limps toward me. "You think you can have your friends divert me while you stuff everything you can get your cotton-pickin' hands on into your clothes. Well, girlie, you're not getting away with it today! Old Alvin's not quite ready for the grave yet. The old eyes still work pretty well." He inches in and repeats, "Don't move." Up close I see his blue eyes, cold, glittery. Hard. Why is he picking on me when I didn't take anything?

I don't say a word, though.

"Let's see what you've got in here." He reaches toward me. Instinctively, I step back. "Not so fast," he says, seizing my arm; he thrusts his meaty, disgusting hand around my back, then tells me to empty the pockets of my jeans. I have my small Afro pick in there. "Humph ..." he snorts. "Let's see what's in this bag. Dump it." He points to a shelf. One of my books bumps down the shelves until it hits the floor; my papers float.

"Hey!" I say, when I see my schoolwork scattering like that.

"Don't you 'hey' me, missy. I've seen what you people have been doing in Oakland, using the fire as a cover." His eyes bore into me. I don't want to rat out Claudette and tell him she took something. I figure he'll find out soon enough, once he searches them.

When I bend to pick up my papers and books, my hands slide on the paper; my arms splay out and I'm on my stomach, like an idiot. I scramble up, expecting to see him cornering Jessica and Claudette next. But he doesn't. They're standing, watching, real quiet, with a strange expression on their faces. Like they're scared too. Claudette's eyes are narrow, as if they're saying, *Don't you dare tell on me.*

Alvin doesn't apologize. Not a bit. Instead, while he unlocks the door he turns his head back to me. "I'll let you go this time, but this is a warning. No funny business in Alvin's store, got it?"

"Uh-huh," I tell him, keeping my head down while we file out. Once we're on the curb Alvin calls out, staring at Jessica, "If you're in on this gang, you better think twice or you'll end up in juvie right along with your friend here."

The three of us don't say anything until we're half a block from the store.

"What was that all about?" Claudette asks me, her cheeks burning.

"Are you kidding?" I'm shaking. "You knocked over the cards. *You* put something in your pocket."

"No way. Are you crazy?" She arches her eyebrows. "He must have seen you steal something! What was it?"

I kick a pebble as hard as I can. "He's a creep."

"Come on," she persists. "We won't tell."

"I didn't take anything, Claudette. But you did."

Claudette tosses her head. Jessica doesn't say a word. I expect her to be furious at Alvin and to follow my lead in questioning Claudette, but she's totally quiet. She and Claudette are walking next to each other, in step, hogging up the whole sidewalk. I'm dancing to the side.

Claudette looks at me long and hard, her eyes like slits.

I shrug and shake my head. The only kid I know personally who steals—well, before Claudette—is a girl a year ahead of us who brags. She says she uses her "honest face" to get away with it. It's true: she looks like she's in *Swiss Family Robinson*. She shoplifts cashmere sweaters and jewelry from the mall on weekends, stashing it in a giant leather tote she carries, then sells the stuff to kids at school for half price. I've heard of another kid too, who supposedly shoplifts on a regular basis, but I don't know if it's true.

While I'm thinking about this, Claudette starts talking about the movie she saw last night. Jessica talks with her, acting like we simply bought chocolate exactly the way we'd planned, and nothing else happened. But I can't join in.

At school the next day, Lavonn's caught up in the hall behind a mass of other kids. She's ambling along—until she spots me. I see how much her movements are like her mother's: they both have a style of walking that, even if it's quick, looks relaxed. Once she's with me she matches my long-legged pace, as much as she can, with the crowd pushing around us.

"My mom said you came over." She pulls at her backpack strap, black like her jeans and boots.

"Yeah. I needed someplace to go and ..." I rub my forehead, which is aching. I keep striding next to her, shouldering my way through masses of kids, and lower my voice. "My dad's got a girlfriend, I think. And my mom's clueless."

"Your moms is kinda cool," Lavonn says.

"I never see Jimi anymore." Words are tumbling out. "And he's in some kind of trouble. Big trouble, as in somebody's after him." I wonder, abruptly, if I'm imagining that, because of Sarah's story. "At Fat Slices ... Jessica and Claudette, they— " It would sound crazy if I told it all; there's nothing I can prove.

Lavonn shakes her head as she pulls open a classroom door, but before she steps in she turns her head back. "The way I remember it, you used to complain about Jimi, that he was a pest." And she flounces into the room, with her head high, leaving me standing alone. Even Lavonn doesn't get it; nobody does.

I rush off to Biology and watch the clock, then at lunchtime, feeling totally lost, I wander over by the basketball court to see if Lavonn is there. This week she's been hanging out there to check out the guys. Sure enough, she and Demetre, whose gold hoops are the biggest I've ever seen, are huddled on a ledge with a couple of others. "Hey, girlfriend," they tease, wrinkling their noses when I unwrap my rice cake with almond butter and sprouts. "What are you eating?" They talk to me exactly the same as they do to each other. "What do you have?" they ask, peering into each other's lunches, giggling and joking. "Did you catch the awards last night? It was so good."

"Off the hook."

"They were kickin' it," another girl chimes in. She jumps up, lifts her arms, and shakes her tiny body, real graceful.

"Hey, what about Algebra?" Demetre asks, squinting her eyes, and all of a sudden we're discussing one of my favorite subjects: math. She brings up logarithms, and then we're off, throwing around sets of new words: quadratic, polynomial, trigonometric, exponential, and rational functions. "Let's get basic. What are real numbers?"

We all get into it. "They can be written in decimal notation," Lavonn recites. "The set of real numbers includes all integers, positive and negative, all fractions, and the irrational numbers."

"I'm scared of you!" Demetre says, lifting her index finger high in the air.

"Picture them as points on a line or something like that," I tell them, remembering what Dad told me once. I draw a line on the back of a notebook and mark it up with negative and positive numbers. Soon my head is spinning with numbers, fractions, and ratios.

The bell rings. We stand up, brush off our clothes, then Lavonn says, "Nina, come to rehearsal tonight. It's hecka fun."

I shake my head.

"You should try it out. And if you don't like it, you don't have to come back." She tugs on my arm.

I'm tempted, I really am, but scared. What if I go and someone says, "Hey, you're not really black; you don't belong here"?

"Not this time," I say and shake her off. "Thanks anyway, though." I smile. "I'm gonna think about it."

All week I bounce back and forth between eating with Lavonn and Demetre and with Jessica and her friends. Now I'm calling them *her* friends, because actually they are: Jessica follows Claudette like a puppy trailing its mother. She's even begun to toss her hair back in the exact same way. On Thursday, after lunch, Jessica pulls me aside as we scamper to class. "Come here," she whispers and jerks my arm, pulling me away from the crowd until we're hanging precariously on the outside of the stair railing. It feels good to have her seek me out again and try to get us into a private space. Maybe I've been blowing everything out of proportion. Mom says that can happen in new situations, and everything around me sure is new.

"What is it?" I look around eagerly to see what she wants to show me.

She turns her back to the steps, so nobody can hear. "Nina, what are you doing?" she hisses. Her pale green eyes are cold, like a frozen lake.

"What are you talking about?"

"How come you're eating with *them*" — she waves her arm toward the bottom of the stairs — "like every other day? Is that who you want to be friends with now?" Her face is getting red.

"Are you counting? I didn't know you were keeping score. Can't I eat with whoever I want to?" I'm mad too. "Since when am I your property? I didn't think you'd give a ...!" And I start cussing.

"Oh, now you're talking like them too!"

"Them?"

"You know," she whispers, "those ... kids. *Lavonn*."

"My mom is the one who swears, Jessica! You know that. My *white* mom." I take a deep breath. Does this mean she *does* want to be friends? I'm too angry to care. The second bell is ringing and kids hurry by, so we push in too. The little bit of sturdiness in my world—the bits of the old Jessica that were left, the Jessica I knew—just collapsed.

That weekend I'm going to Dad's again by myself on Saturday afternoon. The neighborhood that seemed so scary when I first came is familiar now; I know old Mister Hannibal with the shaky hands who hangs out on his step next door and tips his hat to me, and the little girl who jumps rope in front of the blue house on the other side of Dad's. She's a double Dutch whiz. Everyone knows who I am too—"Mister Armstrong's girl"—and they stop to comment on how "mighty proud" my dad is of me, or the need for rain after all this smoky air, or sometimes, shaking their heads, people fuss about the "six foot" potholes pitting the street, "big enough," they mutter, "to swallow a car."

Once inside I'm getting cozy, curled up in Dad's big brown easy chair, when the phone rings. "Hey, little sister," a woman purrs. Her voice is syrupy, as if she knows me.

"Who is this, please?"

"Helane Douglass. We met last year. Over at . . . your place." She sounds like she's smiling so hard her face could crack.

"Oh, yeah, I might remember." I try to make my voice cold enough to put her in a deep freeze.

"Well, I'm going to be over soon, so hopefully I'll have the good fortune to see you again, *ma chérie.* Is Silas there?"

"No." And what's this *ma chérie* crap?

"Would you please tell him I'll be coming by about three?" If I were an ice-cream sundae, she'd be hot fudge, oozing all over me.

"Okay," I mumble, whipping a chill around the word.

"Have him give me a call when he gets in, okay? Bye-bye, see you soon."

"Bye." I thought Dad and I were going to get a chance to talk about Miss Sarah Armstrong. Not Miss Helane.

Dad and Jimi burst in with a smell of sunshine and fresh air. Dad's arms are full of grocery bags, and he's sporting baby dreads, a new look since I last saw him. Jimi too. I stare until Dad says, "Nina, give us a hand, will you?" While I help put food away, lifting cans from the bag and handing them to him, he asks, "Any calls?"

"No," I lie. No way am I going to give Dad that message from *chérie* herself.

Outside the window I catch a glimpse of someone who looks like Tyrone, slouching on the sidewalk across the street from Dad's. Just standing there. What's he doing in this neighborhood?

I shoo Jimi back into his bedroom, force him into the corner, and confront him. "What's going on?"

"Going on?" He exposes his teeth in a gap-tooth smile, like Mister Innocence, except his silver braces shine like a gangster's grill.

"No good," I say, pushing him against a wall. "The red bike?" I take a gamble. "The bike I saw you riding. Where'd you get it?"

He blanches. "Bike?" he echoes, while his face crumbles.

"Jimi, tell me. Something's going on. You haven't told Dad, I see, since you're still alive."

But he doesn't laugh. Instead, there's silence, until I twist his arm behind his back.

"Tell me."

"Okay, okay." I feel his arm tremble. "I took it," he whispers. "Don't tell Dad. Please . . ."

"You took it?" I repeat numbly, hanging on to his arm, tight. "You *stole* it?" Jimi was never a thief.

"Uh-huh." He nods. "I was only going to borrow it. But he saw me— " Jimi's whimpering and tugging on his arm, trying to free it. "Dad says they *owe* black people!"

My body blocks his escape, and I tighten my grasp, twisting the skin on his arm. "*Owe* us! What ever happened to you that makes anybody owe you anything?"

"Dad's telling me about it. It's compen … compen …"

"Jimi, you can't go around taking other peoples' property as *compensation*. That's ridiculous." I stop for a minute, keeping my grip on his arm. "You're in big trouble, boy."

"I didn't think …"

"You're right, you didn't think. That's the problem. Where did you find it?"

"In a garage on Cedar Crest," he says, quietly. "It was open, and the bike was in front, just laying against the house. With no lock."

"Back in the old neighborhood." I roll my eyes.

"The kid is going to kill me." He starts to cry. "I didn't know the bike was his. Last week he saw me riding it up by Martin Luther King."

"So that *was* you. Do you realize what you did? The bike is Tyrone Jackson's." My heart thumps as the facts solidify. "The whole high school is scared of him, Jimi! He's crazy." I relax my grip on his arm and try to think. My head is pounding. "What was the point?"

"I wanted it," he whimpers. "I didn't know it belonged to Tyrone Jackson!" He's shaking. "You heard Dad, the way white …" His snot muffles his words. "They owe—"

"That's not about you, Jimi. Two wrongs don't make a right." I let go of his arm. "Besides, how did you know the owner was white? And didn't you think he'd find you?"

He shakes his head no and lifts his arm to wiggle it. I see the burn mark my fingers left. "Tyrone doesn't know where I live."

"It's not like you moved off the planet." Even though it feels that way. "You're still in Canyon Valley. In fact, he's standing across the street!"

Jimi shakes again, desperately.

"Where's the bike now?"

"In the yard." Jimi points. "Out back."

I cross to the window, but there's no view of the backyard. Instead, what I see are shoulders, crouching, half-hidden by a pink azalea in the side yard. "Jimi," I whisper, and duck behind the faded yellow curtain. "Is that Tyrone? Be careful he doesn't see you." I hold up a book and cover his face from the eyes down. "Here, peek for a second."

His entire body shakes twice as hard. "Yes," he whispers.

At that moment, we're interrupted by the doorbell ringing, over and over, with a squawk. "It must be him," I say to Jimi. "Let me go. You stay here." I hurry into the front hall, trying to get there before Dad, who's in the bathroom. *I can't let him find out about the bike.* But instead of Tyrone, I see Helane strut in. She looks as bad as ever with her nappy hair, short skirt, and big grin.

"I used my key." She smiles and walks into the living room like she owns the place. "Rang the bell to let you know I was here." She calls out, "Silas." In a flash, he's by her side.

"Hi, honey," he says. *Honey?* It's one thing to see a photo, but this word cuts right into my soul.

"I was waiting to hear from you." She looks puzzled.

I want to break in so she doesn't tell Dad she left a message, but at the same time I'd like to ice her, to let her know she doesn't belong here. My relief at seeing Helane, instead of Tyrone, wore off the second Dad called her honey. "Hi, Helane," I say as coldly as I can.

"Hey, little sister." She grins and raises her hand. *"Ma chérie."*

I ignore her and turn toward Jimi's room, so we can plan what to do about the bike. We've got to get rid of it. I could simply take it back and explain that it was a misunderstanding. But would that help? Not very plausible. My mind is calculating all this when I hear Dad's voice before I'm fully out of the living room.

"Nina, you remember Helane." A pause while he waits for me to return. "She's consulting at the Oakland Museum during her sabbatical, and she's helping me with the research on Miss Sarah."

I don't turn and I don't say a thing. Instead, I stand still, with my back to them.

"Helane hasn't seen you for a while," Dad says, his voice rising.

I know, and why should she? I mutter words under my breath, wishing daggers could shoot out the back of my head, slicing her into pieces. At that moment Jimi walks out of the bedroom and bumps into me, but sails on past. I turn and watch while he runs to Helane, slaps her a high five, and stretches his arms to give her a . . . hug?

"Hey, my man," Helane says, squeezing him back.

That's it. Why should I help that little traitor? Who cares if he gets beat up? Killed, for all I care. I've had it with this crazy family. I march into the bedroom, throw my clothes into the stupid green suitcase I'm tired of living out of, pack my books, and stalk to the living room. They're sitting, jawing, Helane blowing smelly smoke rings and Jimi watching as if those fading circles are the coolest thing. Yeah, we don't know anybody else who smokes, but is it really that fascinating? He's watching the smoke curl up like it's the latest show, acting as if he hadn't been crying to me one minute ago about how scared he was, as if a tough teenager weren't outside waiting to attack him, as if I weren't racking my brain to save his sorry butt. "I'm going home," I tell Dad, not looking at anybody else.

"You're supposed to stay 'til tomorrow afternoon, until your mother gets back." A frown descends until his face doesn't look wide; it droops, all lines and creases.

"I'm ready to go now." I hold my books tightly, wrapping my arms around them, trying not to scream.

"I'll drive you over," he says, surprising me. I honestly never thought he'd agree to let me stay home alone. I don't say anything while he slips on his brown leather jacket. "It's getting nippy out, Nina. Where's your jacket?"

"*Dad*! I think I'd know whether or not I need a jacket." I'm so steamed I don't even think about Tyrone outside. When we pass the front door I remember and jerk my head to the right. We make our way down the steps onto the sidewalk, where I force myself not to stare at the bush around the corner of the house, although I sneak one more peek. Yes, it's fluttering. And it's not the wind, because the air is dead still.

Once we're on the street Dad takes my suitcase from my hand and drapes an arm over me. I harden my shoulders. "What is it, Nina? Something at school, baby—" His deep voice wraps itself around me, and I have to keep my body rigid so I'll keep in mind what a rat he is.

"School?" I whip around. "No, it's not school, even though nobody talks to me anymore, because who am I, a black girl or a white girl? School I can stand. What I can't stand is that *slut*—" And I add a curse. It's out before I can stop. I put one hand up to my mouth, but the awful word hangs in the air. I want to reach out to grab it and stuff it back into my mouth, but it's too late. Dad hates swearing.

"Nina Armstrong. No, you didn't—" He's shaking his head, as if by shaking it enough, the word will float out of his ears and fly away. "You didn't ... don't you ever, don't you ... ever—" His eyes are bulging, his teeth are clenched, and he's turning the strangest purple-black, like a bruise. As we stand in the driveway a truck rumbles by and an old woman with a shopping cart hovers, bent over, waiting to cross at the corner. She's watching us, scowling. Does she think Dad is going to hit me, which I wonder about too?

"Dad—" I start, but what can I say? Who does Helane think she is, coming in and saying hi like she knows me, and high-fiving Jimi, letting him hug her like she's his *mother*. "Young lady, don't you ever— " He's so furious, I can tell that for a second he still believes he didn't hear me right. Cursing's always been a big deal for him. Dad used to reprimand Mom, "Not in front of the children, Maggie," and throw her a dirty look. Now he's sputtering. "Respect ... Helane— "

"Dad, I'm sorry." I'm crying. "But what about Mom?"

"Look, Nina, your loyalty to your mother is admirable, but you have to understand ..."

Understand what? If he can stop loving Mom, does that mean he can stop loving me? What's next?

"And I am seeing Helane. Whom you, young lady, will respect." He stops and grabs my shoulder. "I saw how you cut your eyes at her. That will *not* happen again! You will treat her with respect. The respect that she is due."

If I ever see her again. Which I intend not to. "She's not— " I start to say, *She's not my mother*, but somehow the words come out different. "She's not a woman I respect." I hear a voice that sounds like mine speak those words. Out loud. Honestly, it's like the devil's got my tongue. I wish I could run away right this second and disappear forever. I'd never come back.

Dad looks like he's gonna lose his mind. Grounded for life, he's gonna say. He's turning totally blue and purple, and his eyes aren't bulging anymore. Now they're slits. I'll be locked in my room forever. No food, no water.

"I will deal with you when we get back to my apartment, where you will apologize to Helane. Immediately," he snarls, before he spins around.

"But why should I apologize to her? I didn't do anything to her," I protest.

He keeps moving, with me in tow.

"She doesn't even know what I said!" Now I'm righteous, as Dad would say. "So I don't see why I should apologize." I'm practically snapping my fingers. I don't know where my courage is coming from, but really, I *don't* see any reason to say I'm sorry to somebody who doesn't even know there was a conversation about her.

He drags me away from the car, growling, "You *will* apologize, young lady." His lips are tight. "You showed disrespect by leaving abruptly. Rudely. Helane's no fool. She can put two and two together." He glares.

I feel like rolling my eyes, but even in my newfound state of bravery, I don't want to commit suicide.

"And the things you said to me ..." His eyes start popping again. "I will not have it, Nina Armstrong. You will apologize for being rude. To her. And to me. You will ask forgiveness from us together."

Together. Ugh. The thought makes me so sick I shake.

But he tugs me back to the staircase in front of his building. When we get there he takes the steps two at a time, pulling me up, and turns his key in the front door. While I'm being dragged up the steps I glance at the azalea bush. It's motionless.

In the mirror built into one wall of the hallway, I see how scared I am. Paler than Mom. I put my eyes down and stare at my feet, hoping I'll dissolve into a puddle on the floor, like when Jimi and I used to play the bad witch—"I'm melting, I'm melting"—and sink down.

How did everything get so bad so fast? Three months ago I knew who I was: Nina Armstrong, with no color that was important, with one mom, one dad, a pesky brother, and one best friend left after Francesca moved—Jessica Raymond. And there was no scary thug chasing Jimi.

Dad opens the door and pushes me into the living room. Helane is sitting alone, grinning like an idiot. Jimi must be in his room. When she sees us storm in she looks up and says, "Baby, what's wrong?" But she's not talking to me, she's talking to my dad. Sweet like honey. It would make anyone gag.

"Nina has something to say." Dad thrusts me in front and moves back, like I'm a puppet who talks on command. He stands there, arms folded. Waiting.

I'm numb. It's as if all the words in me have flown away. I've never felt so speechless. I couldn't talk even if I wanted to. Which I don't.

"Nina!" His voice rises.

No. I am not going to apologize. Not to her. Suddenly I know that if I say even one word, all the tears inside will gush out, like a fountain. I'd probably cry for the rest of my life. I am not going to do that in front of Helane. I hold my breath.

Dad lunges toward me.

My feet sprout wings, all on their own, and before he touches me I've bolted out the door and I'm sprinting toward home. All I can think through the fog of terror is, *At least I've got more Sarah Armstrong to read about. I hate my dad, but I do care about her.* All I want to do when I get to my room is bury myself in the pages and forget about everything else in my rotten, crummy life. I race home as if my life depends on it.

Horses Reared, Horses Pitched

Whenever Aunt Rachel gave a sign that she'd teach that night, Sarah stole back to pit school, leaving her mother, she knew, anguished with worry. Soon Sarah made the torment even worse. She wanted to take Esther.

"No," Mama screamed. "One is enough. I won't risk you both."

Sarah persisted, her mind swirling. "Why?" she asked. "Why is he mean? Why does he hate for us to read?"

"Why, why," her mother echoed. "There's not a reason for everything. He is what he is. Seems like they're put on earth to peck at us poor colored folks, the way a buzzard pecks at a dead man's eyes. Peck, peck, they won't leave us alone. Like you won't let me be for two seconds without your questions. Reading is trouble, that's all. Ol' massa is trouble. Put the two together, it's like dry wood and a match."

So Sarah began to tug Ruth along, as she'd originally intended—Ruth, who was as outspoken and agile as she. That night and for weeks afterward they pored over the alphabet. Yet Ruth grabbed the concept of words before her friend.

"Listen," Ruth labored, reading a verse one dark night. "It says, 'And God saw every thing that he had made, and ...'" She had to sound out the next word. Finally, she got it. "'Behold, it was very good.'" Ruth turned to Sarah and smiled so delightedly her entire body seemed to shine, leading Sarah, instinctively, to want to cover her up. Every nerve was on edge, attuned to secrecy. "And behold," Ruth repeated. "It was very good."

Sarah's eyes smarted. "How can it be?" She gestured around their schoolroom of dirt, pointed at the flickering candle, and began to cry. "I'm afraid ol' massa is going to find us here and cut our hands off."

"No, he won't." Ruth looked sideways at her friend. "Don't think about that. Think how we're reading." Ruth touched her friend's arm and squeezed it. "Dwell on good, like the Good Book says."

And so it was. During that one long summer, with its warm nights, the two friends grew into what they'd heard was a most feared possession: property that could read. Now they could decipher scraps of newspaper with writing on it, bits and pieces that fluttered from carriages entering the plantation. Now they'd be able to work out Bible stories for themselves. "There must be another Bible within that white peoples' Bible," Sarah had heard the old folks say. She was going to find it.

Sarah often stole away at night now to read. She pored over the stories, looking to see the parts ol' massa quoted. She couldn't find anywhere a story saying that buzzards hatched black babies. Was it true? And look though she might, Sarah couldn't find a passage that said if she saw someone stealing chicken eggs, she should run and tell ol' miss right away who did it.

Instead, she read about Moses leading his people out of bondage, going to a promised liberation. And the Day of Judgment swore justice. When she read this, Sarah, who habitually stooped, pulled back her shoulders and lifted her head. "Hold your head up, daughter," her father told her. She'd ignored him before, but after reading the Bible, something inside thrust her shoulders back, yanking her upright.

One windy winter night, while Sarah struggled to decode murky words in the dank pit school, she heard shouting, then the pounding of hooves. Terrified, she clutched at Aunt Rachel. "I don't want ol' massa to find me here. He'll whip me, or cut my fingers."

The woman held Sarah close for a moment, whispering, "Remember our plan. And run as fast as you can."

At that moment Sarah heard the distinct sound of a gang of pattyrollers thundering in on horseback. Three voices, the voices of white men hired to patrol roads and woods around the plantation, echoed in the clearing, and Sarah imagined their lashes flying. "You got no time to serve God," one of the men shouted, no doubt supposing they'd stumbled on a camp meeting. "To bed, so you can serve!" The sound of whips tore through the air and the horses' hooves beat a deafening sound, lending violent noise to the fury.

The five students and Aunt Rachel jumped out of the pit, scattering in all directions, zigzagging to escape the lash and confuse the pattyrollers. Only Wilbert and Tamra ran together down one broad path, clearly visible, choosing the route they'd long planned should their underground school be discovered. In the ruckus Sarah and Ruth scrambled through a thicket, as they'd been instructed, until Sarah heard great cries and stopped to listen. "Ow!" "Help!"

She could tell by their screams that the pattyrollers had ridden into their trap. She and Ruth, only yesterday, had stretched a line of grapevines across the wide path. Wilbert and Tamra had led the men that way, where vines tripped the horses and bucked the men directly into a briar patch. Now they howled and begged for help.

Sarah sprinted with the others back to the cabins. They tore through the woods as fast as they could, but went the long way around, not wanting to meet any more of ol' massa's men. Sarah ran so hard she thought her lungs would explode. Bursting into her cabin, she stopped short, out of breath, and froze, gasping, in the middle of the floor.

"What happened?" her mother asked, hand to heart.

"Pattyrollers," Sarah panted.

"Oh no." Mama instinctively reached out to pull her daughter close.

"But we got 'em." Sarah took a deep breath.

"You can't go again. Promise me."

"I will go," Sarah said, hardening herself against her mother's pleading face. "I have to."

"Headstrong girl. Trouble." Mama turned her head away, muttering, but Sarah felt a teardrop on her arm.

Early the next morning a new song flew among the cabins. "Horses reared, horses pitched, throwed them pattyrollers in the ditch." By afternoon the verse tucked neatly into a long chant, sewn so subtly it sounded as though it had always been there, a classic stanza hidden among other rhymes of rebellion, bracketed by the constant reassuring refrain, "Yes, Lord, Oh, yes, Lord." Every time Sarah heard people sing it, she tried to picture the pattyrollers, stunned and terrified as they hurtled through air, headed for the briar patch. She sang along, chuckling at the memory of the pattyrollers' cries, but underneath the chuckle, a cold fist of fear clamped itself on her heart.

CHAPTER 7

"He was so mad, I thought he was going to die right there on the spot." It's Monday noon and I'm on the lower school steps. The fog has rolled in again; it's suddenly cold for mid-October, which I associate with blistering heat. Could the Oakland fires have anything to do with this strange climate? The Halloween decorations sprouting all over school look odd in this freaky weather, black cats looming out of the billowing fog. The wind blows hard, biting into my neck, and I'm shivering. Lavonn sits next to me, looking totally unfazed by the abnormal chill while she unwraps her disgusting roast beef sandwich. The meat is practically bleeding into the rye bread. I'm trying not to look, but it's so nasty I can't keep my eyes off it.

On her other side is Ayanna, a large girl with a white shirt that's way too small, who's following us around. It's annoying. Lavonn's *my* friend and I need to talk to her. "I mean, he almost died of a heart attack. I've never seen him so furious. It was like a nightmare."

"What happened?" Ayanna grills me, leaning over Lavonn.

I keep talking, munching on chips. "He was screaming, 'You have to apologize to Helane!' No way. Then I ran away from him."

"Who's Helane?" Ayanna butts in.

That girl is driving me nuts. But I answer her, with a mouth full of chips. "My dad's, uh, girlfriend, I guess."

"Your dad has a girlfriend?" Her eyes grow round and she leans toward me. "Whoa. My moms would hit my dad. *Whack.*" She makes a smacking motion and laughs.

"Forget about it," I say to Ayanna, and turn back to Lavonn. "Can you believe I ran away from my dad? I left him standing there. 'Disobedience.' That's the thing he hates the most. 'Showing out in public.' It makes him wild. But I'm not going to apologize. Why should I? She's the one who should apologize to me."

"Yuh." Lavonn's mouth is full.

"Dad called my mom before I got home. She said he sounded out of his mind. It was horrible. He told Mom he's going to deal with me, after I 'ponder my transgression.' And he's not playing. I know my dad."

Red juice from the meat drips down one corner of Lavonn's mouth. When she sees me stare, she picks up her napkin and wipes it. I continue, "Next time I'm supposed to be at his house, and Mom thinks I'm going there, I'm gonna have to hide."

"Girl, you're crazy. Where you gonna hide?" She puts her sandwich down and looks at me like she's about to call for a straitjacket.

"Hide?" Ayanna echoes.

My heart's beating fast. "I've gotta find somewhere." The bell clangs behind us.

I want to tell Lavonn about Jimi and the bike he stole and Tyrone looking for him. Now Tyrone knows where Jimi lives, and he saw me too. I wonder who he's told. The bell rings again and everybody's scrambling up, crumpling papers, tossing them into a big can near where we sit. A wax-paper wrapper lands in my lap, with bits of gummy food. I brush it off; some sticks to my pants. "Missed the shot," someone calls over, laughing. When I whip around I can't tell who in the crowd did it. Could it have been Tyrone?

"We have to go." Lavonn stands up and looks at me expectantly.

"I have to think of something." I don't move. "I'm supposed to go to Dad's on Friday. Four days from now."

Lavonn simply pulls me up. I follow her and Ayanna into the old brick building, the unrenovated part of Canyon Valley High, where I squeeze into Government class one second before the door slams shut behind me. I take my assigned seat in the front row and prepare to be bored stiff for the next forty-five minutes.

Mr. Apuzio is pacing back and forth, like a caged animal. "The Thirteenth Amendment is the one that did what?" he asks. Like I care. Government is not my favorite subject. Music and math are my two best, and I like history too, but this class is so dry, all about federal, state, and local regulations. Like who cares? Today we're on the Constitution, I think. The teacher's voice drones on, putting me to sleep. I slouch in my seat, trying to figure out where I could hide until Dad forgets. Ha, like never. I'd have to stay hidden for the rest of my life.

"The Thirteenth Amendment?" he asks again. No one answers. I wonder if anyone's even listening. Why are we studying this stuff? He holds up a piece of paper and begins to read. I barely hear him. "Section one," he starts, and I know I'm in for a long nap, which I'm perfecting in this class. Already I've learned how to nod off with my eyes open. I peer up every few minutes—that seem like an hour—at the clock on the wall. When I'm sure I haven't looked for ten minutes, it's only been two.

"Neither slavery nor involuntary servitude ..." Mr. Apuzio's voice punctures my trance, and I sit up in my chair, " ... except as a punishment for crime whereof the party shall have been duly convicted, shall exist within the United States." He stops. "So what did this amendment do?" Hands shoot up now. He peers over his glasses and points at Claudette, sitting in the back of the room. "Claudette, can you tell us?"

"Freed the slaves," she mouths mechanically, as if this ancient history is the most boring subject in the world, as if it has nothing to do with her.

"Yes," Mr. Apuzio says, "the Thirteenth Amendment did something remarkable. You remember that in 1863 President Lincoln had issued an Emancipation Proclamation. Which . . . ?" He pauses and looks out again over the top of his glasses.

Moeisha shoots up her hand. "Freed the slaves too."

"Right, but *which* slaves?"

Silence. Mr. Apuzio starts to talk while my stomach churns my lunch. "The proclamation declared that, based on the president's war powers, in states *in rebellion* against the United States, 'all persons held as slaves . . . within designated States, and parts of States, are, and henceforward shall be free.' The proclamation didn't address slaves in the loyalist states." He stops and stares over his glasses at us, in a way that's supposed to be significant, I guess. "Plus, there were questions about whether the proclamation was even *valid*. Did the president have the power to issue the order at all?" He stops again. "In fact, most people were convinced it wouldn't hold once the seceded states came back to the Union. So, to end slavery, we needed a . . . ?"

Two boys in front call out in unison, "Constitutional amendment."

"And that gets passed how?" Mr. Apuzio asks.

Now I raise my hand. "By Congress," I say.

"If the House of Representatives can muster a two-thirds vote, it does," he says, nodding. "But this one didn't. It had to go to . . . ?"

"The states," Demetre calls out.

Mr. Apuzio nods. "In December, 1865, it was ratified and is now the law of the land. A Supreme Court decision affirmed in 1883 that it applied to every class of citizens, when it ruled that it 'forbids any other kind of slavery, now or hereafter.' "

Wow. Too bad Sarah couldn't have been born a little later. She wouldn't have had to run away by herself. But if she hadn't headed to Washington, D.C., she might not have survived, and I wouldn't be here—which might or might not be good, considering the way my life is going. The bell clangs and everybody stands up, even though Mr. Apuzio keeps talking over the din: "Read pages twenty to thirty in your books." Most of the white kids chat and laugh; all I hear them say is the usual stuff about themselves. Don't they get it? Tommie Kennedy is even mimicking a "yassa, massa" voice. Some of the black kids don't appear to be taking it seriously either. Brandon is pulling Paris's hoodie, and Paris is grabbing Jeezy's baseball hat. But I see a couple of African American girls look really solemn. At this minute, I am completely, one hundred percent, one of them.

Before I know it, I'm walking out of class next to Mei Ying, and she says something. I have to bend to hear her, with kids jamming the doorway and yelling in the hall. "There's a lot of slavery still," she's saying to me. "It wasn't only then. In China and Korea, girls are sold, smuggled out. It's awful. My mother's cousin ..." Her words trail off. "And over in Berkeley, remember that guy that was arrested who owned the Indian restaurant? He had teenage sex slaves from India. Like girls our age."

"What happened—" I ask, but Mei Ying drifts away in the crowd.

After field hockey practice, where Fran's absence hits me with a pang, I kick leaves, which seems to be my new favorite pastime, and kind of jog around the school, not sure where to go or what to do with myself. I'd try calling Fran, but she still hasn't answered my text. As I round a corner of the plaza, I find Jessica and Claudette lounging on the ledge of a huge planter overflowing with petunias. It's a riot of purple. Jessica matches; she has on her pink Abercrombie & Fitch T-shirt, exactly like mine. We bought them last summer when her dad dropped us off at the mall to shop, and afterward we gorged on shrimp dumplings at P.F. Chang's. Amy slumps next to Jessica and Claudette. I keep jogging, near enough so they can see, but no one calls out to stop me.

I'm nearly home when Tyrone and Dwight lope up East Hills toward me. Now that we've seen each other, there's no way to avoid them. My legs are long, but so are theirs. My first idea is to dash into the driveway next to a brown-shingled house; even though the red Prius there isn't very big, I could duck behind it. But it's too late; they've picked up their pace and are only half a block away. And why should I run? What do I have to be afraid of? So my brother took Tyrone's bike. It's not the first one to be stolen in Canyon Valley. Happens to kids all the time. Big deal. Plus, we're going to return it.

"There she is." Tyrone points and charges toward me. This close he looks even more menacing, with that strange scarred face and the permanent scowl. He's bigger than I'd realized too. "I'll bring the bike back today, dudes, if you'll give me a chance," I want to shout. But on instinct I bolt into the drive past the Toyota and directly into the backyard, slamming the gate closed behind me, and race as fast as I can, crashing through brush as I break into the next backyard, and then the next. Hopping over a trickle of a creek that runs behind the houses, I fly to Calusa and make a series of switchback turns, hardly letting my feet touch the ground, until I come out on Oak Hill. Panting, I finally let myself look back over my shoulder. There's no sign of the boys.

"Mom!" I puff when I get home, dripping sweat and gasping for breath. My voice, winded as it is, reverberates off the high ceilings. "Mom!" My stomach aches. "Mom!" The house is empty. Without thinking I begin to text Jessica, but once my fingers touch the keys I realize that by now the whole school probably thinks I stole some stupid thing from Fat Slices, thanks to Claudette's version of what happened, and Jessica could have heard about the bike too, which might be why she's hardly talking to me. She must think we're a whole family of thieves. What's the point of telling her that Claudette was really the thief, and how Tyrone's chasing me, how terrified I am? She'd probably say I deserved it. Even though I didn't do anything!

At last I hear Mom downstairs opening the hall closet before she kicks off her shoes and pads over to the couch. "Nina," I hear her call up. I know her routine: she always lies down to listen to music for a few minutes, then asks me to help her make supper.

"Mom." I rush down. "Mom." Yeah, she's on the couch under the window, listening to Aretha. "R-E-S-P-E-C-T." Mom's singing along, *Sock it to me, sock it to me.* I want to tell her how lonely I am, and how frightened, more than I realized, about the cops shooting black people in Oakland, the so-called "looters," after the fires. Twenty-six people died, not all of them from explosions or flames. A couple of teenagers had bullet holes in their backs, and so did one ten-year-old girl. A commission is investigating. What if I lived there, or Jimi or Dad, like Dad said? Would we be safe? The class on the Constitution scared me too. "Mom," I blurt, "if it was only an *amendment* that freed the slaves, couldn't they pass a new one? And make slavery legal again?"

She looks at me and draws a big breath. For a second I forget how clueless she is and how grown I am; I wish I could burrow into her, the way I did when that used to make everything all right. Then all I had to do was hear her voice and everything was okay. "If they did pass a new amendment, Dad and Jimi and I could be slaves. We could be bought and sold, like furniture." I'm shaking.

Mom leans up and holds her arms out. "Come here, sweetie. Slavery's not going to be legal again." She scootches up so she's halfway sitting.

I drop onto the couch and lean into her. "How do you know?" I search her face.

"I'd never let anybody take you away."

"You let Dad take Jimi."

Her shoulders tighten. "Nina, Jimi is not enslaved. This is completely different— "

"Not that different. And if amendments get made, they can get unmade. All it takes is votes! Mr. Apuzio told us that today." I'm itching for a fight.

"Nina, there's a whole international understanding now about human rights that didn't exist two hundred years ago. Nobody's going to reinstate slavery."

"But there's slavery in the Sudan. There was a show on it. And a girl at school told me girl slaves are smuggled from China, and there was even sex slavery in Berkeley." How can I be sure slavery couldn't come back here? I bet the people in the Sudan didn't expect it. I never thought my family would fall apart either. I never thought a bully would call my brother a thief—or that Jimi would steal. I never believed Jessica—*Jessica!*—would stroll by and act like she didn't even know me. My feelings about my mom are so mixed up, I'm gonna explode. She's always been my confidante, because she could understand what I was going through and help me out when nobody else could, except maybe Fran and Jessica, but now it seems like she's standing across a wall from me—this wall called race—and suddenly I'm on the other side.

I'm exploding too because I don't dare tell her about Jimi and the bike and the boys—Dad would kill Jimi before Tyrone could get to him. It's hard to keep it in, when normally she would help me figure it out. I'm trembling, I feel so scared and lonely. I try another hot subject, to see if she understands. To see if she can help me through this thicket of confusion. "Shouldn't African Americans get paid back for all the years our ancestors worked for nothing? If anything can happen, and there's no safety anywhere … We built this country; we even built the White House. Did you know they had slave pens in sight of the White House?" I frown at her the way Dad frowned at me, with that fierce, penetrating look.

Mom is staring back, as if she's trying to see inside me. "Nina, what's wrong? You're acting so strange. I know the separation is hard on you, honey. I'm so sorry." Her lips are tightening; she looks like a tulip closing up at night.

"Why did Jimi have to move too? How could you let him go?" I can't stop accusing her, stop wanting to know.

"Oh, sweetie." She lets out a big gulp of air. "Is that what's bothering you?" Mom bores her green eyes into my face, like an X-ray.

"Why did Dad only take Jimi? Didn't he want me?"

"Oh, sweetie, that's not it." She sighs. "Not at all. Of course he'd love to live with both of you, but … Nina, what's going on? You're leaving your clothes and your schoolbooks and dishes scattered all over the house. I'm picking up after you every minute, you won't talk— "

"Who won't talk? I ask you about Dad. I ask you about slavery. I ask you why you let Dad take Jimi. Everything I ask, you don't answer. And now he's got a girlfriend!"

Her eyes fill. "Nina, that's not what this is about. There's a lot you don't understand."

Right.

"I wish I could explain, but I'm trying to understand it myself. The world is hard on mixed— " She stops and takes another breath. "We've had a rough time lately."

"I thought race didn't matter. That's what you always said. 'You're you. With lots of wonderful heritages, all mixed to make a perfect you.'" I hear the sharpness in my voice as I mimic her. "What if Jimi were a looter?" She looks at me strangely, but my words tumble out. "He could get shot. And Jessica's been avoiding me ever since I started eating lunch with Lavonn and her friends sometimes."

"Is that what this is about? Eat with whomever you wish, Nina," she says primly, as if I haven't just told her my world has exploded under my feet. "Claim every bit of who you are."

Right. Tell me how! Should I claim the thief part too? Did you know your precious little Jimi—that you abandoned—is stealing? And speaking of abandonment, why did my own father abandon me?

"If someone is treating you badly, you know what my dad says: you're wearing a Kick Me sign. People will treat you the way you expect to be treated."

"That's not true! It's all about race at school. You have to be one or the other. You don't understand at all." My voice is tight with trying to hold back sobs. How could my whole world have erupted exactly like Oakland did, from one day to the next: everybody at school hates me, plus my own family doesn't even want me, and then this insane stealing thing ricocheting between the bike and Fat Slices.

"Race doesn't matter," Mom says. She gets a glassy look in her eyes. "Yet it does too. It's paradoxical. Your father and I grew into different ideas—about what you kids need, about life—and it's not only race. Though it's partly based on our different backgrounds." She's rambling and stumbling. "We do love each other. But your father got to a point—" She stops. "Hon, you're growing up—"

This is making no sense. Not only does Mom not take my

problems away, these days she makes them worse, acting like everything that happens to me is my own fault.

Suddenly she sits up and says, "Nina, you've lost your center. You can't keep making excuses, blaming other people about what they did or they didn't do. You've got to listen for that still, small voice that tells you what to do. You know, the voice I call intuition." She gets a funny look on her face, a mix of sadness and love that I can't read. "The inner voice your father calls the connection to God. Whatever it is, you know you're disconnected when you feel this bad. You need to get quiet and look within so you can hear that voice. It's always with you."

What? This is so not helpful. "Mom, there's a lot of stuff going on that I can't control. This isn't about any voice inside," I say sarcastically. "This is about mean kids ..." And mean parents.

She gives me a frustrated look and shakes her head, and then she says, like it's part of the same conversation, "Jimi's coming after school tomorrow. To stay for a week."

"Why? It's not his turn. I'm supposed to go to Dad's this Friday."

"Oh, Silas is going to Oakland for a week with a friend. They're driving a truck over with food and clothes, and they're going to stay for cleanup."

A "friend"? I bet I know who. Why didn't he tell me?

Without warning, I hear my new harsh voice drill into her, as if she's the person who's turning my world upside down, as if she's the one who stopped gravity and kicked God out of heaven. As if this mom I counted on had jumped over to the other side of that stupid race wall on purpose, to leave me alone. "If slavery comes back, you'd be Miss Ann," I snarl, to let her know for sure that I don't care about her one bit. Then it's like it was with Dad: I can't believe what I said. I've heard a few people sneer about *Miss Ann*—a stuck-up, bossy white woman, like the female Mister Charlie—and I know it isn't nice.

"Miss Ann?" Mom repeats, as if she can't believe it either. For a whole minute she stares at me. "Miss Ann?" She sounds confused. Her voice tightens. "I am hardly Miss Ann, Nina Armstrong. All my life I've been *fighting* racism!" She stands up and raises her hands to the ceiling, like she's gonna scream. "Why ... why did you call me that? It's that book your father's writing, isn't it? Well, that's enough of that book. You've gotten more and more withdrawn. And now this obsession with slavery. No more reading that nonsense! It's not helping."

She stomps into the kitchen. "I bust my butt all day long, and I am not going to come home to *you* telling me I'm Miss Ann!" I hear her banging around. "Oh no," I hear her raving and cursing worse than I've ever heard. "Not from my own flesh and blood." She's wild. "You, Nina Armstrong, are not a slave." I've never heard her like this before, crashing dishes. I think something broke inside her. She's insane. I sit on the couch, paralyzed, until I realize I've had a reprieve: Dad's going away. I won't be scheduled to go over for a week. That'll give me time to dump the bike, and put off my reckoning. At least with my dad.

I creep to my room and it sounds like Mom doesn't even notice, she's so mad. Finally I hear her calling from the hall, "I have to run out to the store for a minute. We will talk about this when I get back, young lady!"

Mom doesn't know it, but I've got two more chapters of **MISS SARAH ARMSTRONG** stashed in my room. There's nothing else to do, since I don't care about my homework, and anyway, if she doesn't want me reading it, that's reason enough right now. I find a note Dad pasted on the next chapter, a note he wrote Before I Called Him Out and Wrecked My Life: "Miss Sarah was one persistent reader, like you! ☺ Love, your papa."

I can't wait to dive in. Now that my parents both hate me, I feel like the only person who cares about me is this girl from long ago.

~

Papa

Even mesmerized by reading, Sarah noticed that everything around her was changing. The land was giving out. No matter how many oyster shells they crumbled and spread for fertilizer, crops weren't growing the way they used to. "Oh yeah," old-timers clucked, "I remember when tobaccy was this high," and they'd stretch their hands. "But now ..." Their hands lowered and they shook their heads.

Ol' Master Armstrong, she heard, was gambling like his neighbor, losing money. His slaves had started calling him Master Tipsy behind his back, "because he looks too long down the whiskey glass." In a bad mood more and more, he swore and threw dishes, lamps, anything close to hand—or rained blows on anyone unlucky to be within striking distance.

For the first time, too, he made plans to sell his "family," as he called them at church. "At the highest prices ever!" Cotton way down south needed more pickers, or so she heard. Traders began to travel out to the plantation, holding auctions in the wide, grassy spot on the side of the Big House, with its huge white columns covered by purple clematis, the selling platform bordered by sloping lawns and pink magnolias. The scent, which Sarah used to breathe in deeply, began to sicken her. She didn't go over there much; but when the auctions were held on Saturdays she held her hand to her nose and watched from a distance.

Soon Aunt Sally was sold off, with three of her children, shaking and trembling. Sarah heard they were "going down with the gangs to the cotton fields." Unfamiliar places were on everyone's lips now. The first she heard was Georgia. "Yes," said Rachel, sucking her teeth, "That's right, I had a baby once in Georgia. Far, far away." *Like the look in her eyes,* Sarah thought, until you got closer and understood it wasn't a faraway look; it was right up close, with agony burning inside her pupils.

A new place, Alabama or Alabamy, was repeated over and over, each mention filling her with dread. Louisiana, Mississippi. The long words had a fearsome sound. Once Aunt Sally left, no one heard from her again. It was like that with everyone who got sold away. They were sucked into some indescribable place, and all you recalled were the last-minute tears, the expressions on the faces — terror or anger — and maybe some happy moments before that. Or a curious incident that you remembered, like why did Aunt Sally say she'd a mind to drown her little blue-eyed babies? That's what stuck with Sarah, along with the warm feeling of Aunt Sally feeding her by hand when she'd been a tiny girl.

One Sunday morning Big Albert didn't show up as he always did, week after week and year after year. All day she and her family waited for Papa.

And the next day.

It wasn't until Monday afternoon that they got the news, from one of the foremen. "Over to Spotsylvania County. Sold to a Mister Jackson, I heard. Small place." That was the next county.

After that Mama worried about everything, all the time. She cuffed Sarah for no reason, and hollered at little Albert when he played under her feet. It was two months before they saw Papa again.

Sarah spotted her bedraggled father walking into the yard that Sunday morning, his feet dragging but a big smile on his face. She flew straight at him, and pasted herself against his chest. He scooped her up. "Lilla Bit! You're Big Bit now." He swung her back and forth, laughing and kissing her.

"Yasmine, Esther, Albert!" he called. They tumbled out of the cabin, and Papa pressed them all close. "I walked all night," he said, his arms around them all. "Charley, on the Jackson place, forged me a remit." He couldn't stay long. The pass expired

Monday morning. "Glad to have it," he said, patting his pants. "In black and white. And you know black and white will talk." Papa laughed, looking at them and slapping his pocket.

That was one of the glorious Sundays, but it carried a pain in it too, because they didn't know for sure when they'd see Papa again.

Ever since, Mama had berated Sarah about her tiny Bible. "If you're troublesome, keepin' up with that book readin', massa might sell you. Be careful, daughter. Don't you get caught."

"I won't," Sarah said.

"Put that thing away."

Sarah slid her book under the quilt on her bed.

Yet one dawn, after almost-nightly school lessons, Sarah woke to hands pulling her up. Before she was fully conscious a driver grabbed her, told her to run fast, and rushed her into a clearing that already held Tamra and Wilbert, lashed to a tree. Sarah searched for Ruth's face, and was relieved not to see her. At least Ruth was not among those seized.

The driver ordered them to strip. Hands shaking, Sarah unbuttoned her thin cotton shirt, and once she removed it, unwrapped the scarf she'd kept around her neck while she slept. She unbuttoned her skirt and let it drop, now naked in the cool morning breeze.

The driver ordered Tamra pinned to the ground. Another man tied her, spread-eagled, to four small stakes, wrists and ankles lashed with rope. He muttered while he bound her, "The driver's crazy. Don't stay quiet, holler as loud as you can. He'll stop sooner."

First, the driver brought the leather strap up and down, as hard as he could, on Tamra's bare back.

"This will teach you to take up white-lady airs! No good comes of reading!" the black driver shouted. Tamra moaned, then shrieked as the whip struck thirty times.

Sarah saw blood. Her stomach tightened and she turned away, but still gagged and vomited.

The driver then laid into Wilbert, striking and cursing as he brought down each blow on the silent boy, who looked as if he might be dead. His fluttering eyes proved otherwise, however, and Sarah struggled to decide if death might be the better fate. "Ain't got time for this nonsense. Reading!"

Sarah closed her eyes and tried to keep breathing, though the stench of her vomit gagged her again.

Only once before had she seen such prolonged lashing. She'd hidden behind a poplar tree while Uncle Jeremiah took sixty bloody lashes for stealing a chicken, so ol' master claimed. Jeremiah too had cried out as the leather strap hit again and again. Watching now, Sarah remembered the high-yellow foreman swearing at the heat and "lazy field hands, who only want to eat."

But now he cursed their book.

By the time the driver finished with the second scholar he said he had no arm for Sarah. But morning, he promised, would find him a man refreshed, ready for this work.

"I've got to get to the farthest field," he said. "But tomorrow morning ..." he swore.

All day Sarah shivered. Mama's face seemed permanently streaked with tears. Loping back to the quarters before dusk, they found Wilbert and Tamra, tended by Hannah and another old woman. Mama rubbed her own ointment onto their torn bodies.

That night Sarah huddled with her mother, her sister, and her brother, waiting miserably for the sound of the driver's horn. She thought of running, but Mama begged her to stay. "They won't kill you," she pleaded, eyes tearing yet again. "You're young, you're strong. You'll have children. But if you go, they surely will be your death."

Mama was always practical. "Girl, you got to make your way," she often told her daughter. "And here is where you are." That awful night she reminded Sarah again, "It's too dangerous to run. You got to work with what you got. What you got is here."

It was true. What Sarah had was her tall, firm body and reflective mind, her brother, her father—when he could come—and mother, her "uncles" and "aunties," Ruth and other friends, like Amely and Wilbert. And her life. That was too much to risk for a chancy escape, one that could easily end in death, ripped apart by dogs. Or sale to the terrors of the deep South, to those unfamiliar, scary-sounding places: Georgia. Alabamy. Louisiana. Mississippi.

"Pray, daughter. Pray for deliverance."

Before dawn the family tried to eat their biscuits, but no one could swallow the mealy pulp. At the last possible moment her mother ran to a field where new land was being cleared. Albert and Esther ran behind, holding on to her skirt while they looked back, wide-eyed, at their big sister. Sarah had to stagger off alone to meet her fate.

There was no escape.

When she arrived at the soaking wet lower field, as the sky lightened behind the silhouetted trees, the driver unfurled his great whip. But this was a new man, one Sarah had never seen before. He flicked his lash with a sound like unfurled lightning.

Sarah trembled.

"I'll tear the hide off your back," this new head slave roared, rearing back. Yet, astonishingly, the snake of leather never touched her skin.

The driver hollered, and Sarah and two others screamed when he told them to, "Please no more, oh, please, Lord, no more!" But every droplet their owner would see, should he happen by, was berry juice mixed with the blood of an unlucky squirrel.

On this day, far out in a distant field, no one came to inspect. The screams carried far enough.

Sarah could not believe that she'd escaped—but she knew it was a sign. This was a miracle like one of the many she'd read about, like when Moses wandered in the wilderness with his people, so thirsty, and he smote the rock that gushed forth a great stream of water for everybody to drink. Or when the Red Sea parted and the children of Israel walked through in order to escape the Egyptians. God was her Shepherd, and had given her the signal. She wasn't born for this life, no matter what Ol' Master Armstrong said. One day she would no longer be enslaved. And she would never, ever, let herself be whipped. Before that happened she'd run away. No man would ever tie her down like that.

CHAPTER 8

For once, even my purple-striped comforter doesn't comfort me, and no matter how far I pull the covers over my head, I'm shaking. Sarah was so brave. I don't know if I'd have that much courage — to face a whipping. I only know I need to find out what happens.

Just when I open the next chapter, "The World Explodes," which sounds like a perfect description of my universe, I hear Mom's footsteps charging toward my room. I jam the papers under a pile of books on the floor and reach up to turn off my light, so I can pretend to be asleep. No way do I want to hear her screaming at me now. But it's too late: she'd hear it click or see it flash out under the door. Instead, I grab my American History book, prop it on my stomach, and half close my eyes, doing my best imitation of sleepy reading.

Mom sails in and plops on the side of my bed. No apology, no invitation, nothing. Not even any rage. "Oh, Nina," she starts. "I'm sorry I got angry. This is a tough time for me."

Mmm-hmm, you're not the only one. And why are you opening up to me now? You know, I'm the kid. I'm the one who needs you; it's not supposed to be the other way around.

"I know you didn't mean it," she says. "And I didn't mean to react like that, either. It's just the school budget's being cut again and I'm writing grants like mad, applying for funds from every foundation under the sun." She settles in, raising her hands to her forehead. "But I want to be here for you."

All of a sudden she's smiling. I've got my real mom back, we're on the same side of the wall, and a cozy feeling creeps through my chest until tears sprout in my eyes. If I don't tell somebody soon about how *my* world's exploding, I'm gonna burst. *Mom,* I wish I could say. I want to lay my head on her lap and let her know about Tyrone, how he's so horrifying and vengeful, and about Jimi and the bike—how could he steal it?—and ask her to get it safely back into Tyrone's yard. I want to tell her about Sarah Armstrong and the terrible suffering she endured, to share that pain I'm feeling with my mom. And then I want to hear her say I don't have to be black or white, and help me figure out how to hang out with everybody and not have to choose. I need her to remind me, like Dad does, that "faith is the evidence of things not seen" in the soothing way he says it, assuring me that everything will work out all right even though I can't imagine how. God's got it covered.

"What, sweetie?" she asks, reaching out her hand to rub my forehead. She strokes me, right where the hair starts, and keeps pushing my curls back, over and over. Her fingers are soft, and make my back tingle. This is how she used to put me to sleep, along with singing the songs she wrote. As if she can read my mind, she starts to sing, softly, "Nina, Nina, you're the one ..." She sits on my bed like that for a while, humming, and I feel myself being lulled into a drowsy mood.

"Mom," I burst out, all set to confide.

"Tell me, sweetie, what's on your mind? If you talk about it you'll feel better."

"At school," I start, relieved to let it out, even to her, "the biracial kids mostly hang with the black girls. But I still want to be friends with Jessica too. We used to do everything together, you know that, and now she hardly talks to me—"

"Nina." She looks straight at me, while her hand keeps stroking my forehead. "People may look at you and see an African American, but you're white too. Whatever that means; you know it's a construct, about as scientific as a flat-earth theory. And even if you *weren't*"—she smiles—"you can be friends with anybody you choose."

"White kids call everything they think is bad 'ghetto.' Jessica's starting that too. And she's not interested in Dad's novel, even though it's based on my real great-great-grandmother! You know, Sarah's family; something terrible happened, so she's running away ..."

Mom's hand freezes.

"It's so sad," I say. "In the night I imagine she's knocking on my window, and I wish I could help her."

Mom jerks her hand back from my face. "Nina, I told you." Her voice is steely; right before my eyes she turns into a stranger. "Your father ..." Her mouth moves as if she's chewing something nasty. She spits it out. "I told you not to read that book. It will poison your mind. Your father ..." Her teeth are clenched. "In the last year, he's changed."

"Mom, stop!" I've never heard her talk like this.

"Your father ..."

"Dad."

Tears come into her eyes. "I am not the *man* ... You know, there are good white people too."

I sit up and, out of habit, I wrap my arms clumsily around this creature who's invaded my mom, even though that's the last thing in the world I want to do.

"Being white isn't a bowl of cherries, either. These days the whole world hates us." She looks straight ahead, at the purple wall. "Race is … it's not actually real, Nina. Honestly, white people made it up to keep people separate."

Look at the steps of Canyon Valley High at lunchtime. Race is real.

"I'm not even totally white," Mom says like a robot, with a voice as glazed as her stare. "Not with you and Jimi as my kids." She stands up and pulls a tissue out of the box by my bed. "This is tricky territory, sweetie. But remember, you get to be friends with anybody you want, with Jessica and Claudette and Lavonn or anybody else. Even if it doesn't seem like it." After she blows her nose, she says, "Your generation might actually have a chance of figuring out how to do it."

"How?"

"I don't know, exactly. But ninth grade is rough no matter what. I remember when I was a freshman, there was a snooty group — the popular girls who wouldn't talk to me because my dad was a union organizer, and he wore overalls, not a suit."

"That's nothing like this!"

"Exclusions like that are just different versions of the same thing, Nina."

Mom totally, totally does not get it. Why do I ever ask her anything? I'll never again confide one solitary thought to her; I'll never let myself get lulled into believing she knows anything. She's a fool.

"And I know something about being mixed. I had the Irish-Jewish split in my family, and believe me, in Boston forty years ago, that was something."

"This is so, so different." I have heard that story a million times and it was nothing, absolutely nothing like what I'm facing.

"Not as different as you think." Mom checks her watch, and all of a sudden she flips back to "normal Mom," like this pathetic conversation never happened. "Ten forty-five! You better get to sleep. Everything will look better in the morning. And next year, in tenth grade, things will start to settle down."

Next year?

"Turn off your light, sweetie, as soon as I'm out the door." She leans over to give me a kiss.

After she leaves, my mind jumps around. What did she mean, "Being white is not a bowl of cherries" and "I'm not white"? Yes, she is. Her mother's white, even if she's Jewish, her father's white, her sister's white, she's white. No problem. Not like me, who's half everything.

For hours my mind swirls. Race didn't used to matter, in our family or with my friends. What happened? How could Jimi have gotten us into this mess with — of all the kids in the school — that maniac, Tyrone? Who is weirdly the brother of that cute guy, Dwight, who probably hates me now too, if he even knows I exist. And what's gotten into both of my reliable parents; have they been taken over by aliens so neither of them has a clue what it's like to be me? When I realize long after midnight that I'll never fall asleep, I reach under the pile of books by my bed for the next chapter about Sarah Armstrong. I flip on the light, crawl deeper under my comforter, and lose myself in reading about a girl who faced even bigger problems than me.

The World Explodes

The day dawned like a normal day, with a scarlet sky and rain clouds. Roosters crowed, dogs barked, the overseer blew his horn, and kittens mewed. The sounds, the familiar smell of pigs' feet boiling, the everyday noise of people running to the fields, and the feel of the rough blanket against Sarah's skin gave no indication that day was to be different. The air burned as hot on that July day as on others.

There was no warning.

Sarah shifted on her pile of rags and straw, forgetting for a moment that her leg was fractured, broken from a leap into the pit school weeks before. It was starting to mend with the help of a crude splint fashioned by one of her aunts and the good health of a robust twelve-year-old.

Abruptly, she heard shouting. She hobbled across the small wooden floor, pushing past laundry drying by the fire to exit the door of the cabin in time to see two white men, jackets flying, running, shouting, and grabbing people on their way to the fields. The way they yanked arms decisively and threw on shackles made it clear their targets had been marked. For a moment it was bedlam, screams piercing the air.

Then, too quickly, the momentary silence of shock.

Sarah, wide-eyed, immediately picked out the familiar figure of her mother among those seized and roughly told "Run!"—to gather a change of clothes.

Freed from the irons, Mama had a moment to collect a bundle, then wrap and tie it in a large square of frayed orange cloth. She'd been sold, and they hadn't even known.

Yasmine, sobbing and trembling, rushed to pass Sarah her own small, forbidden Bible, folded in a white cloth. This and a few bone buttons were all the objects her mother had to pass on. "White folks going on to hell like a barrel full of nails," she said, shaking. "Master Armstrong's the evilest ..." She seemed unable to finish her sentence. But she left Sarah with a critical admonition, whispered as she was shoved outside. "Take Esther and little Albert and run, girl. Go north. Pray for guidance—"

In the six months since Papa had been sold, they'd only seen him once. But short-tempered as they all were these days, Mama and Sarah had developed an even closer bond. "We're cut from the same cloth," Mama often said. Though she could be rough when she needed to, cuffing or reprimanding her firstborn for "foolish dreaming," she always promised, "We will be delivered," and every night she crooned songs whose words and tune fused together to etch hope deep into Sarah's brain.

Now, as Sarah limped after her, Mama forced a muffled hymn through her sobs. "Nobody knows the trouble I've seen, nobody knows but Jesus." This Jesus, she told her children, could be counted on, lifting high their tribulations until burdens had no weight at all. But where was Jesus now? Before Sarah could fully absorb the blow, she saw her mother, orange bundle on her head, ordered into a wooden cart with five others.

"Get in the buggy! Ain't got no time for crying and carrying on!" The trader in a high top hat stood, one foot up on a brown leather suitcase, cigar in his mouth, chuckling and chatting as he handed over cash to Ol' Master Armstrong and received slave papers in return.

People swarmed the sides of the two-wagon caravan, calling out to those inside. A woman Sarah knew well, whom everyone called Auntie Mabel, sat rigid with dignity and shock; a teenager who'd only recently come to the plantation slumped against a grizzled man, disbelief and terror in his eyes. The older man, with a trembling hand, patted the younger one's shoulder.

When Mama laboriously climbed up into the cart, her former owner—her daddy, Sarah thought, allowing herself the realization—slapped her good-naturedly on the rump.

"Farewell, Yasmine," he said with a laugh. "You'll make some man— "

Sarah lunged for him until Mama, as if able to spot her daughter's move before she made it, motioned her back forcefully. "No!" Sarah screamed, and the words left her mouth as the trader's boot sent her reeling. Master Armstrong only glanced in her direction before he strolled away. Sarah then saw Mama stand up in the open cart, tears marking rivers in her cheeks where the sun glinted on the drops. "NO, NO, NO," Sarah shouted, stumbling after the cart.

The trader pushed her back with a shove, and drew a pistol. "If you come one foot closer, I'll shoot."

Her mother screamed, "Stay back!"

Sarah staggered backward. She and her mother had seen this scene too many times in recent months. To plead for mercy would only bring a kick or the offered shot.

The horse began to pull the creaking buggy along the rutted dirt road.

Sarah strained to capture the last sight of her mother: the dark-green shawl; her face partially covered by her old white bonnet; the familiar torn and stained light-brown dress, with the sleeves pulled down almost over her hands to protect her from the burning sun.

As shock took over her body, Sarah heard the screech of the large wooden wheels and her mother's alto voice, choked with furious tears, singing—almost screaming—"Hold on a little while longer."

Sarah stood, bent with grief and fury, holding wailing Albert's hand on one side, silent Esther's on the other, until the wagon and her mother's precious voice were completely out of range. Later, all the driver could tell her was, "Girl, she's gone south. Don't know where. Don't think about her anymore."

Yasmine, she learned later, was twenty-nine years old.

CHAPTER 9

In the morning I wake with the words *Run, girl* rattling in my head. And all of a sudden that's what I'm tempted to do: run away to Fran's house in San Luis Obispo, like she did after her dad took her away from Canyon Valley. She ran back here for a couple of days to "figure everything out," she said, and landed at Jessica's house. The first night Jessica's mom didn't tell Fran's dad she was there, after Fran threatened to go out on the street if her dad discovered where she was. They made a twenty-four-hour deal: Fran had to call her dad at the end of the time. Which she did, and then he let her stay on over the weekend before he drove up to get her.

That's what I need to do: get away to sort everything out. I need time when I'm not looking over my shoulder for Tyrone, worrying about Jimi every minute, dealing with Jessica and her idiot friends, and wondering if Lavonn's friends think I'm really black. *And* last but not least, Dad. When he gets home he'll come by here first thing to pick up Jimi, I know he will, and unless I'm ten counties away I'll catch every kind of hell he can unleash on me. That man doesn't mess around, either. Old-school dad; he doesn't have any patience at all with kids who talk back, which is how he still views me, even though I'm fifteen.

I have six days to make a plan before he gets home, to get out of here and save my sanity. Crawling out of bed, shivering, I open the pink jewelry box Grandma Bettye made and check the secret compartment. Unfolding the bills, I count them and sort them into piles, all the crumpled ones and fives and tens and twenties I've collected over the last couple of years from babysitting and birthdays. Same as last time.

"What's wrong?" I'm walking next to Lavonne, with kids pushing and squeezing past us. Since it's drizzling outside—our first fall rain—the million kids in this school are packed into the cafeteria, a big rotunda where every sound echoes. What stupid architect came up with this design: an echo chamber for a high school cafeteria? I can hardly hear what Lavonn is saying, but I know by the way she's looking at me quizzically, with her eyes big, that she's asking me something. Finally I make it out: "Hey, I asked you to check out my new sneakers. I got them yesterday."

Yeah. Cool. Silver leather, rhinestones.

"Did your dad make you apologize?" Now she's shouting. "What did he do?"

"No, he's gone. To Oakland to help clean up the fires and stuff." We push through a crowd of screaming kids 'til we find a corner of a table over by the windows. I unwrap my avocado and sprouts sandwich—same old thing—while Lavonn snakes over to the line at the burrito stand to buy lunch. As I settle in to eat, my Hershey bar falls out. As soon as I get a whiff of the candy, the smell is so sweet I have to unwrap it and start chewing. I can't stop. Chocolate seems to be my only real pleasure lately; well, that and reading about Sarah. Every day I buy one chocolate bar, and there's a certain way I eat it. First I bite off one corner, slowly, and taste the sweetness on my tongue as it dissolves. Then I bite off another corner, and another. I nibble my way around the edges until there's only a sticky center. Hersheys melt too fast, that's the only trouble. Once I tried a chewy bar, like Snickers, that would last longer, but unfortunately I hated it. The melting's actually part of the enjoyment, even if it's quick. I could eat candy bars all day. How many could I buy with all the money I've saved?

"Dad's away for six days," I start, when Lavonn comes back with her tray, carrying a chicken wrap and a juice box.

"Girl, you better have your apology ready when he gets back." She picks up the dripping wrap. "He's gonna kill you."

What can I say?

"Eeeew, this is terrible." She squishes up her face. Red and blue paint is smudged on her fingers.

"Art?"

"Yeah, it's messy."

"I hate that class with Miss Williams. The art projects we have to do are so ugly they make dirt look good." We crack ourselves up. I'm about to tell her more when Demetre comes over. The three of us joke around until Jessica and Claudette stroll past, gliding by with their faces turned away.

"What's up with that?" Lavonn asks. "You used to eat with them every day."

"Used to." I wish I had another Hershey bar.

"Aren't they, like, your best friends?" Demetre says.

"You mean *were*."

"White girls. You can't trust 'em." She squints her eyes until her small, usually pretty face looks mean. Her nose gets even thinner; suddenly everything about her is pointy, sharp, like Snoop Dogg. She looks like she could slice me if she leaned forward.

"I'm part white!"

"I know." Demetre laughs. "I'm gonna keep my eye on you! You might turn *all* white. We got to watch out." She cracks up.

"What's that supposed to mean?"

"Oh, 'white's all right, but I'm down with brown.'" She wiggles her neck and shoulders to a rap beat. "Yeah, I'm down with brown."

Funny how now I feel like defending the white part of me, the white part of my family. My mom, my grandparents. Even the white part of Jimi. Before I can think of a quick comeback, something that will calm my pounding heart, the bell clangs and we rush off to class. Then it happens. While a million kids push their way behind me, I hear a whisper behind my neck: *"Thief."* I whip around, but nobody's looking my way. A shudder ripples through me. How can I answer an anonymous insult? Or is it a threat?

In class, while the words ring in my ears, I watch the time on the clock tick slowly by and fantasize about living someplace else, even for a little while. I've never been to San Luis Obispo, but I know it's halfway to LA, because my family camped at Montaña de Oro State Park a couple summers ago. And Hearst Castle is near there too, I think.

At last, school ends and I'm out in the fresh air, jogging home alone, my pack slapping against my back. The sky is a clear china blue, and the sun is out now, warming the back of my neck. I'm soaking it up, and dawdle next to a wall of jasmine just as a hummingbird buzzes me, zooming inches from my head. When I hear the sudden *whoosh*, I leap. Wow, I didn't know I was so jumpy. Ever since lunch, when Jessica dissed me again, I've been on edge.

"Nina!" I turn and see Amy running awkwardly, holding her glasses on with one hand while her pack thumps against her back.

"Hi," she says, out of breath. She bends her head down when she talks. I never realized she was so shy.

"Hola. Buenas tardes." I respond. *"¿Qué pasa?"*

"Buenas tardes. Nada." She smiles, keeping her face tucked down.

"Donde está . . ." I hesitate, then smile back and try, *"¿Donde hay un . . ."* I pause and try to think of the word. *"un . . . persona que habla ingles?"*

She giggles. "Right here!"

"Gracias. Habla solo un poquito espanol."

"No." She laughs again and asks, *"¿Donde está el baño?"* We all know that one.

Now that we've exhausted my knowledge of Spanish, I don't know what to talk about. Amy wears hecka cute clothes, but I can't think of anything to say about that. "Are you still hanging out with Jessica and Claudette and everyone else in their little group?" I try.

She looks more embarrassed than ever.

"Sí."

"I don't see them that much." I immediately want to undo the words. "Well, sometimes," I lie, with a sick feeling in the pit of my stomach.

We fall into step. "You know they're saying bad things about you."

I nod, not wanting to hear the details, and we walk in silence until we get to the corner; she turns left and I head right.

At home I drop my pack, gulp milk from the container like I'm not supposed to, and feeling out of place in my own home, I run back to school where I race around the track fifteen times, leaving me soaked. When I'm about to leave, I catch sight of him: Tyrone, swaggering with that tough, slow walk. His unnerving eyes, with their terrifyingly blank expression, rove from side to side, as if he's looking for something. Or someone. His hands are in his pockets, where I wonder if he's clutching a knife. He glances toward the track. Does he see me?

His pace picks up, and I spin back, race halfway around the track again, and sneak out the back entrance. Is he mixing me up with Jimi somehow, or is there another reason he's after me? But he's too scary to talk to, and I'm too upset about everything else to try to reason with him. I've gotta get away to Fran's so I can calm down. But first, if I return the bike, I won't have to worry about Jimi so much when I'm gone.

Once I make it safely home, panting and shaking, I count my money — same as before — and open my green suitcase, staring into its emptiness as if it's going to give me the answer. Should I go or not? Fran texted me, apologizing for not getting back sooner and saying it would be perfect to come now, since her dad won't even be home for the weekend because he's going to a conference. A next-door neighbor will watch them from her house, and seeing as the neighbor doesn't have kids, we could pretend I'm a local friend. My parents would never have to know where I was for at least a couple of days. Let them worry — that would serve them right after all the grief they're causing me.

That night I talk to Lavonn on the phone, but it's hard to concentrate on anything else except my runaway plan, and I don't dare tell her. She might let her mom know, and that would be that. Instead, I'm so nervous I spill out, "Jessica and Claudette are saying I'm ghetto. I know they are."

"I think you need to set them straight, if they've been talking smack about you. Don't let *your best friend* talk about you behind your back."

Now how am I going do that? And is she my best friend anymore?

"White people will turn on you, if you let them. Girls especially. They're backstabbers. It's ingrained in them from their mothers. You better stick with your own kind, girl."

"What's *my kind*?" Does she mean my mother ingrained something in me?

Lavonn keeps going as if I hadn't said a word. She sounds angrier than I've ever heard her. Usually she's the most laid-back girl I know. "And what's wrong with ghetto? You don't want your snotty little preppy girlfriends calling you black. Is that it?"

"That's not it!"

"For real?" She's furious. "I don't think you want dark skin. You wish you were *all* white like your precious Jessica. Or your mom."

"*What*?"

"Demetre's right. No wonder you don't want to be in *Black Nativity*!"

"Why do I have to be in *Black Nativity* to prove I'm black?" I stop. "I'm thinking about it, though."

"*Thinking about it, thinking about it*, forever, and never doing it. That's so *white*!"

"What? Why can't I be both? Your mom is both."

"And look who she married! Look who her friends are! She lives black, she's not ashamed of black."

"Neither am— "

She hangs up with a sharp click and I hear that eerie dead-line sound.

"That is so wrong!" I say into the dial tone, and for a moment almost forget my plan to escape. A few minutes later I open Sarah's story, wishing I could lose myself in the whole rest of the book. At least I have one more chapter.

Aftershocks

Fall on the plantation came and went, and the cold rains of winter fell. It was all a blur in Sarah's mind. After an eternity the buds of spring burst out, though she hardly noticed. Miraculously, a full turn of the seasons cycled. How could the world have gone on spinning, with Mama taken away?

Sarah stung with longing and red-hot anger. Why did Mama let this happen? Why hadn't they all run away together, Mama and Papa and she and Esther and Albert, when they were still together? Mama had always said, "This is your place. This is where you are. Make the best of it here." Well, she'd been wrong, hadn't she? And left Sarah to care for her siblings. Albert cried every night in his sleep, and so, she imagined, did she. Esther had stopping speaking altogether; rigid, she moved through the days like a ghost. Sarah's heart ached as if it carried stones, weighing her body down. Even her arms felt sore.

Some days her anger spit itself out at the foreman and Ol' Master Armstrong. She glared and threatened them with axes and shovels behind their backs, brave when they couldn't see her. Day and night she raged, incredulous, at the man who had ruined her world.

Like Mama, she swatted Albert if he didn't jump to her commands quickly enough, and lashed out at Esther: "Speak!" Fury blanketed her world, until she couldn't see anything but meanness and badness all around.

Ruth, Old Hannah, even Tom, her mother's childhood friend—all bore the brunt of her anger. People tried to stay out of her way, as her hot temper seemed to burn even the grass where she walked.

Then, spring flowers poked up. Daffodils opened and closed, white roses and lilacs budded. It was a glorious spring. Ample sunshine, the smell of jasmine and blue skies that could burst open most any heart. Ruth had tried to get Sarah to chase her ever since Sarah's leg healed, and the change in the air caused her to redouble her efforts. "Come here, slowpoke," Ruth called out, attempting to get a rise out of her friend as she took off in the mornings. "Catch me if you can." She tagged Sarah, who stared angrily ahead.

On Sundays Ruth swatted at her friend's matted hair, giving a tug for good measure. But Sarah waved her away.

Old Hannah, who'd moved into the cabin with Sarah and Esther and Albert, regularly cooked up special broths, tempting Sarah to eat. But she refused all enticements. Sarah had always been thin, but now she heard murmurs of "down to a bone" whenever she passed, often paired with the shaking of heads.

All that tethered her to this world were her brother and sister. Though only thirteen now, Sarah—when she wasn't cross—cared tenderly for her forlorn baby brother and mute sister, bundling them into bed on the floor at night, looking out for them in the field. What Sarah couldn't do others did, passing on a piece of maple candy that made its way from the Big House, or offering a rough caress.

But increasingly, familiar faces on the plantation fell away. Aunt Rachel was sold along with one of her two young children. Tamra and her baby. Wilbert. Gone. Sales were at the courthouse, Sarah heard, when they didn't happen right outside the Big House. The more the auctioneer's hammer rang, the more people on all the plantations stole away. They ran from the Winston place, from Armstrong's, from as far away as Jackson's. The whole area fell under a twenty-four-hour watch, women who worked in the Big House reported. Pattyrollers guarded the roads and searched every northbound boat. Rumors of runaways dominated every conversation. Most were captured, but a few, everyone believed, made it north.

One June day Sarah, through her haze, saw a notice fluttering, its corner blown up from the ground. The paper, which must have fallen from a wagon and lodged on the ragged prong of a root, beckoned. She snatched the circular and read the heading: RUNAWAY.

Her interest aroused, Sarah glanced over her shoulder to make sure no one saw her, and slipped the notice into the deep pocket of her skirt. Back in the cabin she held the paper near the fire and put her fingers on the words. Still she couldn't see well enough. She walked over to a tin cup filled with grease, lit a wick of wool, and slowly made out the words: "Runaway, young NEGRO fellow, Robert, middling tall, thirteen or fourteen years old, has one finger cut off at the middle joint, black complexion, wore a negro cloth jacket and took an axe. He may be gone toward the river. $200 REWARD if he is given to me, or lodged in jail."

Her breath catching, Sarah sank to her knees and begged whatever God existed for Robert's safety; she knew him from the Winston place, her father's old plantation. Don't let the dogs get him, she prayed, her heart skipping a beat. Carry him safely to the North. Please. She wiped sweat from her forehead. Keep him safe. Keep my mama safe too.

As times got tougher, more fled. Every time traders came, Sarah tried to keep Albert and Esther out of sight. When she saw horses raising dust one Saturday afternoon before they were unhitched at the Big House clearing, she rushed her brother and sister back to the cabins and pushed them behind a building. Anything to keep them hidden. Often she remembered Mama's words, "Pray for guidance," and tried to follow the injunction.

But not long after Robert ran away, the entire world tipped sideways. Sarah was out late one Saturday afternoon gathering firewood when Ruth came running with terror jumping from her pores.

"Auction ..." she gasped.

"What?" Sarah's heart froze.

"Little Albert ..."

Sarah flew to the yard around the Big House and positioned herself behind a hedge. Her breath hitched: a short white man, dressed in a suit, had stripped Albert and thrown him onto a scale.

Sarah watched, horrified, as the man poked out his chest and called, "Forty pounds! The bidding begins!" The auctioneer lifted Albert up onto a box in the yard as a small crowd of men gathered around.

"Boy, can you count?" the white man asked in a booming voice. The man tapped his fingers together, waiting.

"Yes, sir," said Albert, whimpering.

"Let's hear you, boy."

"One ..." Albert's lip trembled. "Two ... three ..."

The man laughed. "Let me see you jump!"

Albert hopped.

"Folks!" the trader called out. "Look what a fine, strapping boy stands before you. If I was buying I would give ten dollars a pound for this little buck."

Sarah felt as if someone had hit her in the stomach. Hard. Her brother paraded like a prized pig to market.

"Show us your teeth." The man yanked at Albert's mouth.

"Your eyes." He rolled Albert's eyelids back.

Sarah looked away. This couldn't be happening. Should she charge the auction block? Or scream?

"Look at these big bones. By the time this little one's eighteen, he'll be worth a thousand dollars," the auctioneer called out in his singsong voice, tapping his fingers together.

Sarah looked back, only to hear a broad-shouldered man call out, "I'll take him! Three hundred dollars."

No one else bid. The auctioneer pointed his pencil. "Sold to the gentleman from Washington, D.C.!" The gavel rang down, reverberating in Sarah's ears like a clap of thunder.

From her place in the bushes, Sarah caught some of the buyer's words as he bent down and spoke softly to Albert. The boy stood, immobile, with only the single trail of tears trickling down his cheeks showing he was even alive. "Come here, I'm not going to hurt you ..."

She'd never heard a white man speak that way before.

"I'll take his sister too," the man yelled to the auctioneer, pointing to Esther. Sarah had been so riveted to little Albert, she hadn't noticed her sister was next on the auction block. She put her hand over her mouth and slumped to the ground. How had he known that was Albert's sister? While she'd been picking up firewood, Mister Armstrong must have told the man about her siblings. A flash of hatred blazed through her: first for ol' massa, but then the fire zigzagged in and hit her heart. *I shouldn't have left the children alone.*

"For three hundred more, this little girl can sweep the house and help my wife." The strange white man reached out and put a hand gently on Esther's arm. Esther bolted toward the woods behind the quarters. Sarah knew exactly where she was headed.

But the auctioneer raced behind, running faster than his short legs indicated he could, and grabbed her heel; Esther pitched face forward into the dirt. The man shook her upright, slapped her face, and shoved her roughly at her new owner.

Sarah scrambled out from her hiding place, shrieking. But before she could reach her sister, the two children were already in the buggy of the Washington man, sweeping down the driveway.

Why did he want Albert and Esther? Sarah's quick brain had slowed to a crawl. It couldn't process anything she was seeing, but questions flitted though her mind. Why had this man come all the way from Washington? And why didn't he take her too?

Sarah was too stunned to cry. Right in front of her eyes, they'd rushed away the little family she'd cared for since Mama had been taken, and they'd never even let her say good-bye.

Days went by, and it all still seemed impossible. Her heart, swollen in her chest, hurt more than ever. She hardly knew what was dream and what was real. Ruth pulled her to the field in the mornings, then hunched low by her side and instructed her, "Lift your arm, chop. Cut the leaf." At night Ruth lay with her, holding her friend close.

Still, Sarah hardly cried. Her brown-specked, hazel eyes were glassy, blankly fixed on the horizon. She didn't answer when people spoke.

Over the next few months, more sales and auctions occurred, but mysteriously Sarah was spared. Each time traders came she had an injury, or was laid up with fever, or for no reason she could divine was never put up for sale. She knew her price, that she would be a prime offering: young Negro female, a breeder, $700. Yet somehow she was protected on this Hanover County land where she'd lived her entire life.

As the plantation—and she—began to fall apart, others cared for her, especially after their own sons and daughters were sold south one by one. Suzy, the short, wizened seamstress with a face that could "freeze hell," as Mama used to say, mended Sarah's clothes or cooked her a broth when Old Hannah couldn't. Jeremiah whittled a whistle for Sarah, and prodded the phantom she'd become to pluck his fiddle mechanically while he slapped a rhythm.

Aunt Suzy spent hours on Sundays with her, teaching her to sew, while Ruth leaned in next to Sarah, warming her friend's ever-chilled body. Grief had sucked all the fire from her core, and she shivered, even in bright sunshine. Ruth and Aunt Suzy sat Sarah between them, and together the three stitched the community's tattered shirts and shifts.

Sarah's body automatically put one foot in front of the other and walked stiffly toward the fields in the morning, with the overseer's shouts dimly penetrating her daze. But she hardly cared. She returned woodenly at night and dropped off to sleep, thinking only vaguely of her family. Everything was indistinct. Papa, she believed, was still nearby in Spotsylvania County, but only barely near enough to get occasional third-hand word of, not to see. Mama had vanished to Southern cotton, into those places with the forbidding names. And now Albert and Esther taken north to Washington, D.C., a city so far away it might not be real. Sarah stopped praying, the habit of a lifetime, because she knew God had given up on her. Or she'd given up on God, it didn't matter which. She was alone.

Evenings, Sarah hummed sorrow songs, murmuring the words without thinking. "Oh, Mary, don't you weep, don't you mourn." Sarah felt the music work its way into her veins like water trickling down a hill. When she started to sniffle she spoke out loud to herself, mouthing the words Mama would tell her: "Hush up, sister, you've got to bear it. You've got to go on, keep your faith, work with what you've got. Can't sit here staring into space all your life. My spirit's here with you."

Over that summer, the old songs slowly breathed life into her paralyzed lungs, while her friends' efforts began to break through her wall of shock. She felt the slightest tingling of life.

"Pharaoh's army got drowned, Oh, Mary, don't you weep," she and Ruth sang together. If Mary wasn't supposed to weep, Sarah thought, she wouldn't either. And Pharaoh's army would get drowned. It was a promise.

As she hummed to herself in the evenings, Ruth or Amely or Old Hannah sat by her. The energy in the music picked her up and flung her into God's great universe, one creature spinning among many, each in their orbit. Even with her heart cracked into pieces and her anger at a burning point, she'd find a way to live.

And a way to go.

CHAPTER 10

God's great universe, one creature spinning among many, each in their orbit. How could Dad write this? How could he believe *each in their orbit,* when our family got flung apart like Sarah's family, even if it's not as bad as hers — is that the point he's trying to make to me, that she had it worse? *It's not God's* great *universe, Dad,* I'd like to tell him; *it's filled with a bunch of mean kids who divide everything into black and white, and nothing is going to turn out all right in the end.* There is no harmony in this chaotic universe. Only one friend far away who might understand me. Maybe. I haven't seen her for five months.

I'm standing in his living room. Dad would never expect me to be here alone while he's away. I can only stay a minute 'cause Jimi will be at our house after lacrosse practice, and Mom made me swear I'd be home. I step into the living room, my heart beating fast, and wonder if I'm crazy. Just as I'm ready to tiptoe into Dad's study, the phone rings and the sound echoes. After a few rings I hear Dad's deep voice cut in. His answering machine — yeah, he still uses one; he says he likes to screen calls—is turned up, and I hear that he's actually trying to rap, which is a joke. Dad even halfway singing is like a frog croaking. *Click*. The caller hangs up.

When I open the door to Dad's study and peer in, I find everything as neat as always, which I counted on. But when I scurry over to Dad's desk, I don't see what I came for. The blue folder should be right on top where it was last time. When I reach out to poke under a stack of papers, my hand is shaking as if it's got a life of its own, and I have to struggle to control it. Did he take the manuscript with him? I lift up a pile of papers and start to sort through them, caught up in my task until I hear a noise in the living room. I slap the pile down and take a step back. If Dad came home early from Oakland after only two days, or if he dashed back to pick up something and found me here, going through his papers—wow. No one, not even Mom, could ever touch his stuff.

What was that faint banging? A door opening? I stand completely still—except for my legs and hands, which are shivering—and listen. The wind is the only sound. Could it have been a tree branch thumping against the house?

Knock. There it is again, coming from the door.

Who could it be? My breath is starting to catch, and I can feel my palms getting clammy.

Knock. Knock. It's louder, more insistent.

With my heart thumping against my chest, I walk toward the living room and step into the room, ready to run if I have to. I look through Dad's peephole, the way he and Mom have trained me, and practically hit my head on the floor falling back. It's Tyrone Jackson! I hope he didn't see me come in. Or is it really Jimi he's after?

I freeze and listen, trying to quiet my pounding heart. He must be as motionless as me, because I don't hear any sound or footsteps retreating, and no further knocking. My heart is beating so loud I'm sure it will give me away. I put one hand on my chest:

Calm down. I try breathing deeply—but silently—and still, no sound from outside the door.

After at least two minutes, I hear him creep away. My relief only lasts a moment, however. He must know I'm in here. Otherwise he wouldn't have stood so quietly when no one answered his knock. How long will he wait outside?

Suddenly I'm drained. But I know I have to get out of here: I tiptoe back to the desk, and this time I see the blue folder sitting off to one side, with **MISS SARAH ARMSTRONG** across the front in red. Now I really better scoot. If Dad knew I was here, stealing his book ... But if I go outside—my brain balks. I part the living room drapes just half an inch and peek out. No one. Wait, there he is, walking away, up the block toward Prince Street.

Allowing myself a couple of deep, noisy breaths, I force myself to sit on Dad's couch for ten full minutes, watching the clock, just like school. Then I grab my helmet, dash out the front door, and jump onto my bike. Only losers ride bikes, Claudette says; Jessica has stopped riding hers. But at this moment, I don't care. Since Tyrone will be taking the bus along Martin Luther King, I head the other way, toward Redwood Road, where I speed along with the wind in my face. Pink roses are still in bloom, and the delicate smell gives me a lift. I turn up Cedar Crest and left on East Hill, enjoying the breeze and the huge old oak trees. But when I see a girl up ahead on the sidewalk, alone, I skid to a stop.

"Jessica!"

Her eyes go from my green helmet to my bike, and then she says—like she's picking up a bug—"Hello."

Here goes. If Jessica despises me, that's just one more reason to go. I take a deep breath, my specialty lately. "We've been best friends ..."

She looks over my head and doesn't answer.

"I heard you don't want to be friends anymore. How could I go from being your best friend to nothing, so fast?" I'm straddling my bike, and I jerk the wheel for emphasis. "Tell me," I shout. "What kind of traitor are you?"

"I never said that." Her neck gets red and splotchy, and the color spreads up her cheeks in big patches until she looks like a strawberry with yellow hair. Jessica never could tell a lie without blushing. Too bad for her we know each other so well. "But all you ever do is hang out with— " She pauses. "You know . . . you're starting to talk that way. I don't even know who you are anymore."

"That way?" I say, squinting my eyes.

"You know, your clothes, they're changing. More— "

"How?" I can't believe she's critiquing me like this, especially when I haven't changed my style much.

"It's not only that— " She stops again, as if she's not sure she should go on.

"What? What?" I'm fierce.

"The stuff about you stealing at Fat Slices that day. I don't know, it made me kind of uncomfortable, with him searching you and all . . . It was so embarrassing."

"Made *you* uncomfortable! Embarrassing! You sure did a lot to help me out. Gee, thanks. And what makes you believe some store owner instead of *me*? You were *there,* Jessica. You saw what happened! Plus, what about your fairy princess, Claudette? She put something into her pocket that day, I saw her."

"Oh, you can't deflect the crime away from yourself by lying." She spits the last word. "And your brother's a robber, I heard." Her voice rises, shrill with venom. This is a Jessica I've never seen. The girl in the red jersey, flush with the joy of kicking a soccer ball to me all afternoon, has been replaced by this cardboard facsimile. "Your father thinks stealing is right—oh, excuse me, depending on who does it—and your brother evidently thinks the same, so what should I believe about you?"

"That I'm an honest person, the same one you've known since

we were in first grade. And don't you dare talk about my dad or my brother that way." I lift up my fist.

She doesn't say anything in response, and I can tell by her look that she doesn't believe me about what happened at Fat Slices. When she raises her hand to flip back her hair, I notice her ring finger is bare. I hop on the seat and peel off, pedaling hard in spite of the tears clogging my vision. After a minute I call back over my shoulder, "I hate you!" I don't think she hears, but I don't care.

At home, Jimi's in the kitchen. "Nina!" He sounds excited.

"What are you making?" I call in, dropping my backpack, which contains Dad's folder, on a living room chair.

"Scrambled eggs."

I stomp into the kitchen. "You know Mom said not to cook when nobody's home."

"I'm here. I'm not nobody."

"Very funny." I give him a look, the kind that used to shrivel him. His eyes would dart away, but now he looks back steadily.

"And you're here." He's triumphant.

"Yeah, and that means you can make me some eggs. Thanks, bro." I put an arm around his shoulder, then charge upstairs to hide **MISS SARAH ARMSTRONG** in my closet. As I do, the memory of Tyrone's face in the peephole comes rushing back. Before I leave for Fran's, I've got to go back to Dad's and get the bike, then ride it across town to Tyrone's house without him beating me to a pulp. I can't take Jimi with me to Fran's—he's too young, there's no way he'd come without telling Mom, and I need to get away by myself to think. Ever since the world fell apart, things are spiraling down, getting worse every day, and I don't know how to fix them. Jimi will have to show me where Tyrone's house is. Then I definitely need to split.

Thoughts of the bike lead me to something else I need to do as well.

I race out the back door alone, carrying a small envelope. A few garden tools, rakes and shovels mostly, lean against the deck, so I grab a shovel and carry it into the back corner of our yard, then jab at the dry dirt over and over, leaning all my weight onto the spade. This clay soil, full of tangled roots, is tough; in ten minutes I manage to dig a hole just big enough for me to slide in the stupid package. "You are not my blood sister," I whisper vehemently. "This is a reverse vow. I bury you and break our vow forever," and with those words shovel earth over Jessica's ring, stamping it down while I repeat, "I bury you, I bury you."

When I return to the kitchen I try to put on a normal face, even though inside I'm churning. A mountain of hard eggs fills the frying pan.

"How many did you put in?" My voice sounds stern, like Mom's. It's weird to hear it come out of my mouth.

Jimi's face pinches, and he backs up. "What do you mean, how many?" His voice is small.

"I mean *how many*? One, two, three— " I open the door under the sink and look in the garbage. A dozen egg shells, at least. "You put them *all* in?"

"I thought— " His eyes tear up.

"Oh no, Mom's gonna get you. There are none left for breakfast."

He doesn't say anything. I see a tear roll down one cheek until it's hanging off his chin.

"Never mind, I won't tell. Let's eat." I lean down to drape my arm around his shoulder and we carry our plates to the dining room. When I do leave home, I'm gonna miss Jimi more than anybody. I wish I could tell him I'm leaving, but I don't dare say good-bye. Instead, I ask, "Where's the bike?"

He blanches, but swallows the mouthful of eggs and chews

until he can finally get the words out. "Under the back porch at Dad's. I shoved it way, way back under."

"After we eat, walk me over and show me the house where you got it. I'm going to return it in the morning." Before I leave.

When Jimi sheepishly points out the large gray house with white shutters on Cedar Crest, and shows me the exact spot where the bike was leaning against a wall, I promise him, "It will be back there next to the garage when Tyrone gets home from school tomorrow. Won't he be surprised?" And won't everybody? I don't think I'll hear Jessica talk about robbers again — if I ever do come back to Canyon Valley. Maybe Fran's dad will let me stay a long time. What's one more daughter when you've already got four?

When I come shivering out of the bathroom after my morning shower, Jimi's already left for school. Probably just as well; I couldn't have said good-bye to him without crying, and that would give everything away.

"Hurry up," Mom calls from the bottom of the stairs. "Get dressed. I have to leave, and I want to be sure you have breakfast."

"I will, I will." She didn't notice the missing eggs, so this must be an oatmeal morning. She makes it with these gross sunflower and pumpkin seeds, pouring some kind of strange "natural" sweetener over it and stirring so it's one hideous gooey mess, like mucous in a bowl.

"Bye," Mom calls up. "I've got to leave. Right this minute, sweetie. Are you ready?"

"I'll be down in a minute," I call back. "Bye, Mom."

Silence. Until I hear feet coming up the stairs, and she rushes into the room. "What on earth is taking so long? I have to leave right now. I want to see you eating breakfast."

"Can't you leave me alone for five minutes?" I bend down and tug on my socks. "I told you I'd be down in a minute. I'm getting dressed!"

She hurries toward the door with a parting "Now!" But when she doesn't hear me behind her, she stops in the doorway. "Nina?" She turns and stares, like she senses something, and I can feel the tension in me snap.

"Leave me alone!" I explode. "You are always on my case, every second. Can't I have some privacy?"

"Nina Armstrong, stop screaming at me!" she shrieks. "I have to go. I'm running my staff meeting in one minute, and you will get downstairs and eat your breakfast. I am not going to have you going off to school on an empty stomach." She puts her hands on her hips. "Now!" I hear a curse.

"Stop telling me what to do," I shout. "Don't you trust me to eat breakfast by myself? You treat me like a child. You can't order me around. I'm in high school now!"

"Oh no? Watch me." Her face is tight and she's tapping her foot. "Nina, this is not the time for this. Just you wait until tonight—your insolence has gone too far. First with your father, now with me. But if I don't leave in one minute I won't catch the bus to BART and I'll miss my meeting. Oatmeal's on the stove." Then she's gone.

I grab my suitcase, throw in my jeans and my Oakland A's T-shirt, plus a blue ceramic bowl Jimi made me in kindergarten; I scoop the money out of my jewelry box and race downstairs. I have got to leave. Not one person, except maybe Jimi, understands me, and even he has no idea what's really going on. I have to leave now, at the same time I always go out the front door, so no one will suspect I'm not on my way to school. But first I scoop out a handful of cornflakes—I will not eat her oatmeal!—slice a blackened banana, pour vanilla soy milk, and wolf it all down.

I crack the front door just enough to listen outside. It's quiet. Tirza, the next-door neighbor, must have left for work. The air is nippy today and the days are definitely shorter now, but the morning sun feels good on my face. I breathe deeply. From the corner of my eyes Mom's silver car sparkles in the driveway and an inspired thought flashes: Why don't I drive it? Even though I haven't taken Driver's Ed yet, I've had lessons from Mom. She was amazed how, after the first couple of times we were out, the car hardly lurched when I started up. And I parked on a hill once. In five months I can get my driver's permit. That would be *so* much fun, to float down Highway 1 in the car, instead of riding on the stupid bus. I know I could do it.

But a faint voice in my head says, almost as if it's real: *If you think you're in trouble now, look out. What would your mom do when she discovers the car missing? You could have the whole California Highway Patrol after you, as well as your parents.* Stuffing down the glorious vision of myself flying along the coastal road with ocean waves crashing below, I sigh and put my attention on locking the front door. Mom hates for it to be left unlocked.

Just when I've released my happy fantasy and feel safe with the relief of knowing I'm in the clear with no one seeing me leave, I hear a clunk. It's Tirza, in her bathrobe and slippers, pulling a dark-green garbage bag off her front porch, bumping it from step to step. Her white poodle is yelping from inside the screen door. "Good morning, Nina," she calls. Her Israeli accent's so thick I hardly understand her. She peers at me. "Going on a trip?"

"No." I shake my head. "To school."

Her eyes go to my feet. "With a suitcase?"

"Yuh . . ." My mind is blank. "We have a science project— " Oh no. She's a scientist.

"Really?" She drops the garbage bag and shuffles over, looking up into my face, all curiosity. "What's it about?"

"Um . . . germs."

"Germs?" She looks fascinated, like she could stand here all day.

"I have to go. I'll tell you about it—later." I grab my green suitcase and hurry to the sidewalk.

"Germs?" I hear her behind me, sounding puzzled. "Why a suitcase?"

I'm starting to sweat, and I haven't even gotten off the block yet. "It makes sense, trust me." I flash her my best grin, the one people say is a million-dollar smile. My face feels like it's going to explode, I stretch my mouth so wide.

"Nina— "

I'm trying to act normal, but what is that? "I can't be late!" I shout and flee down the street with my suitcase rolling against my heel. Jimi will be waiting for me when he comes home from school and unlocks the front door to discover an empty house. Should I have left him a note? But I can't risk going back. I've got to keep going now.

I bump my suitcase up the steps of the number 62 bus by the library, ride along Martin Luther King to Dad's, and run around to the back of the building. Yup, there's the red bike underneath the porch, shoved way in the back like Jimi said it would be. I look around: no one in sight. After I crawl under the gross porch, with spider webs tangling in my hair and leaves sticking to my knees, I manage to balance my suitcase on the handlebars and zoom back up to the hills. With all my attention and one hand on the green bag, I have a narrow miss in traffic: at the corner of Upton and Martin Luther King a car swipes close, terrifying me and tipping the suitcase, but I manage to get the bike stable. There, I make a mistake. Without thinking about my route, I turn automatically, and before I realize it I'm riding past the back of the high school, where lots of kids hang out. And who should be swaggering toward me but Tyrone, looking meaner than ever. The sun glints off the ointment from his newest tattoo, there's a fresh scar on the side of his face, and even from a distance his eyes gleam with a hard look. He must be cutting school.

I spin the bike around, balancing my ridiculous suitcase with one hand. I wish I hadn't packed my favorite books and that ceramic bowl Jimi made me; they make the load so heavy. When I turn the bike it wobbles, the whole thing flips on top of me, and my luggage crashes, splitting open. Tyrone keeps strutting toward me, fast though not running, but I'm able to scoop everything in—except the blue bowl, which smashed into a million pieces—and jam the faulty zipper shut before he gets to me. While he's lunging, I hop on, with one foot just out of his grasp, and pedal away as fast as I've ever ridden.

"Stop!" he yells. "That's my bike!"

I don't dare turn around long enough to tell him the truth: that I'm taking it to his house. And it suddenly hits me that my fear is only making the situation worse. Now I definitely look like a thief.

He's running behind me, screaming and swearing, but even with the bag I move faster than he can. Pedaling furiously, I'm grateful for my strong legs, made powerful thanks to my daily run. *Thank you*, I'm murmuring inside. *Thank you, please let me make it.* When I get across Allston I turn my head and howl, "I'm returning your stupid bike!"

He shouts back something I can't hear, throws up his hands, and stands in the middle of the street waving his arms, balling both hands into fists and thrusting them into the air.

I keep pedaling east toward Cedar Crest.

Once I dump the bike, propping it up by the side of Tyrone's garage, I power walk as fast as I can without actually running, circling all the way around East Hill and across Redwood to avoid Tyrone or anyone else, until I can slip onto the commuter bus. I'm drained, but I walk with my head high, as if it's the most normal thing in the world for me to be half jogging on a Thursday morning, pulling my green luggage, headed in the opposite direction from Canyon Valley High.

After the bus drops me off at the BART station, I slide four crumpled dollar bills into the ticket machine, press Yes for my ticket, hop off the escalator onto the platform as the San Francisco train is pulling in, and pile into the half-empty train. Wiping perspiration from my face, I slouch into a seat, lean back, and rip open my backpack for the Miss Sarah Armstrong folder. *Let me get lost in her world for a while and be inspired by her courage. I'm going to need it.*

The Bird Man

In the farthest high meadow, field hands sweated. Absorbed in cutting the big tobacco leaves to dry, most didn't notice the peculiar, squat man who waddled toward them. But Sarah saw him.

She instinctively moved away, aware that no unfamiliar white man had been out here before. She shifted position, moving slowly, trying—as Mama had taught her—not to call attention to herself. But the short, seemingly muddled man waved at her, lurched forward, and called out, "I'm from Ontario."

What's that? she wondered. And why was he talking to her?

"I'm a professor," he continued, stumbling in her direction. "A teacher. In a big school. A university. I have free rein to walk all over here. Permission." He stopped and waved his hands around. He had an accent, and a different way of talking. "To collect bird observations." The pudgy man inched closer, until he almost touched her.

She avoided his eyes, kept her hands busy and her head down while she continued to move away slowly. She had no idea what he was talking about.

"I've been welcomed by all of Virginia's planters as an eminent scientist," he said. His hands, continually in motion, waved to the sky as his blue eyes bored into her. "I'm an ornithologist."

Sarah turned her head away and kept working. Her fingers stuck together from the tobacco gum.

"A bird-watcher. That's what I do." He pointed to a circling broad-winged hawk. "I study birds like that." Next he gestured toward a goldfinch. "And that. I write books about them. Birds in flight. Flying free." He turned to give her a penetrating stare.

Why are you here? Sarah wondered. She thought he must be truly mad, and edged farther away while trying to brush tobacco gum off her fingers.

"Have you seen any nests?" He kept following her, chattering. The driver seemed curiously unconcerned. As if the lunatic scientist could read her mind, he said, "All the planters know me here. They've given instructions ..." He waved vaguely. "I can go anywhere and talk to anyone." He paused. "Don't you know of any nests I could look at?"

Sarah didn't know whether to answer.

"I won't hurt you," he said quietly. "A big, strong girl like you ..."

She was tempted to lie and say no. But she remembered Papa saying, "Don't tell a lie for credit when you can tell the truth for cash."

"An eagle," she mumbled. "Over by the side of the field." She lifted her chin to point the way, but kept working. She noticed she was taller than he.

"Can you show me?" He looked so awkward standing there in his suit, perspiration rolling down his red face. He kept mopping his fat cheeks and neck with the handkerchief crumpled in his hand.

Sarah looked at him and shook her head. "I can't leave!" she said. *And I don't want to,* she thought. *Not with you.*

"I'll ask the foreman. I am sure it is all right." At least that was what Sarah guessed he'd said. It was hard to understand him, with his accent.

In minutes he was back, tugging on her arm. "Show me the nest."

Sarah turned to look at the foreman, Ol' Sam. He nodded, pointing his leather riding whip. "Go on!" he said, then called out after her back, "Five minutes!"

The two walked a hundred yards—Sarah striding, the man hopping to catch up—to a gnarled old tree by the edge of the field. Looking back, Sarah saw how small the field workers looked. She was hardly ever off this way alone. But she wanted to remain within sight and sound.

Suddenly, Sarah heard her mother's sweet, rich voice. "You have to make your own way." The tone was so clear she turned her head, startled. Then her mother's song pierced the air. "Steal away, steal away, steal away home." Was she going mad?

"Quick," the bird man whispered, "listen to me. I've come here to help you run away. To the North. Or Canada."

"What?" Fear scoured Sarah's body and closed down every vein. She couldn't breathe. Even the sounds of the warbling birds stopped. Silence filled the world.

"I'm an abolitionist," he said in that funny way of speaking. He kept wiping his forehead and neck. "Dr. Ross."

Sarah's mouth hung open.

"I'm here to pass out compasses. And directions north."

Still she couldn't speak. Was this a dream? Her stomach lurched; she was afraid she might slip to the ground. She tried to wake up, but he kept talking.

"Make for the closest free land." The man's voice pressed in on her. "Washington, D.C. We have people to help you once you reach the city. Washington has a long bridge." His words pummeled her ears, and she tried to remember what he said. As she did so another part of her brain wondered, *Is this some kind of trick?*

The bird man advised her quickly, giving details. "If you can only get to that bridge, once you step onto the other side, there will be free black people and abolitionists and churches to help you."

"How will I get there?" she dared ask, hoping she wasn't falling into a plot that would be yanked out from under her as soon as she let her heart hope.

"On your way, look for lanterns in a window late at night," he said, and bending awkwardly, the pudgy man sketched a map in the dirt with his cane. "Here's the river. When you go to the woods behind the cabins, go upstream. Follow the North Star. Stay near the river. After three or four days you'll see a lantern and a quilt hanging on the line, one that looks like this." He drew the outline of a house that seemed to have a smoking chimney. "Just tell them you're a friend of a friend."

Sarah felt the warmth of the sun on her neck, and heard the birds again. She felt pebbles and dry dirt under her bare feet.

"The woman in the house with the lantern will tell you where to go next. Knock on her back door."

Before Sarah could absorb the news—and the fact that she was talking to an abolitionist—the man slipped her a tiny compass and hurriedly showed her how it worked.

Suddenly, he said, "Point to the eagle nest."

Startled, she turned and stretched her arm out, her sticky fingers pointing to the nest high in the tree.

He nodded, muttered, "I've got to go," and seemed to vanish.

She felt the hard metal in the center of her palm. If she hadn't had this shiny new circle in her hand, with its needle pointing to the N, Sarah would have thought she'd dreamt it all. She slipped it into her pocket and staggered back to the field.

Late that evening, Sarah told Amely and Ruth of the visitation. By morning she heard that Dr. Ross had also appeared to Stinson, a gaunt man working near the house, who'd received the same directions and two coins. And to Big Bertha, in the kitchen, he'd given a compass like hers.

Feeling freshly awake, Sarah heard with new ears the song: "Follow the drinking gourd! The riverbank makes a very good road, the dead trees will show you the way. When the great big river meets the little river, follow the drinking gourd."

As she drank her evening tea a kind of grace began to settle, flowing like a healing balm into her bruised heart. Strengthened and inspired, she understood that if she focused all her energies on one point—freedom—a path would open. It was already appearing. Her numbed body tingled as blood flowed again. She felt she was coming back to life.

Now she knew that when she had a chance, she'd be following the North Star and the heavenly gourd to freedom. To the Sweet Land she'd heard about, where she could walk wherever she wanted to, and where she might find her brother and sister. Snatched from the jaws of evil, she'd be doing God's good works, like Mama said. He had, after all, sent another miracle.

She learned more about Washington, D.C., from Preacher Thomas, who'd been recaptured years ago after living free for six months. He told her about whole communities of free black people and thousands of fugitives. She heard about churches that helped runaways and buildings that belonged to black people. This inconceivable city tantalized her.

Could Albert and Esther be there, living free? But who would be taking care of them? Thoughts of her brother and sister—worry, and an ache—flooded her. As she daydreamed, she rejoined day-to-day life, catching fish and poaching rabbits. People in the quarters feasted, adding potatoes roasted in ashes, hot cornbread, fried eggs, milk, and whiskey. Sarah was reminded of the joyful feasts her mother used to oversee, of the Sunday dinners with her father, and those thoughts made her long for her parents, both so far from the promise of river paths and lantern guides. Sarah tried to make the food inside fill the empty place that was always there. But no matter how much she ate—even until her belly bloated—she couldn't fill herself up.

When Sarah watched others with their mamas and papas and brothers and sisters—the few who still had them—a lump rose up into her throat and she imagined herself in their places. When she saw beads of red glass on a charm string, like the one around Amely's neck, jealousy burned her chest. A pretty necklace like that might make the lump go away, even for a while. One day, she did steal something: a small orange bowl carved from a gourd that Jeremiah's sister had given him, which he'd whittled designs onto. He used it in his crowded cabin to hold pine nuts, or other days it sat empty. Sarah went into his room and picked it up, cupping it in her hands, feeling the smooth sides. Maybe if she took this totem of family love, her family, or at least her sister, might magically appear. When she heard someone walking near his door she thrust the bowl under her dress; later all she'd been able to think to do was bury it, so no one would see it. But instead of the lump dissolving, the pain in her throat got bigger.

When the old man came after her the next Sunday, asking if she'd seen his bowl, she couldn't hold back.

"Yes," she admitted, staring at the ground.

He stretched out a reedy arm and tilted her head up. When he saw the tears pooling in her eyes, he said, "You keep it, little sister."

"No." Sarah leaned against the bony old man for a moment, then ran to the woods to find the bowl. She dug with a stick in the place she was sure she'd buried it, where she'd put two rocks to mark the spot. Nothing was there. Had someone else watched her, followed her into the woods, dug it up, and taken it away? Desperate to find the bowl, she'd dug holes all around the small clearing, moving farther and farther from the spot where she was sure she'd dug. Suddenly, she saw the two rocks, placed exactly as she remembered. Frantically, she dug until her stick hit something hard. She tapped it, poking the hard, dry dirt with her stick until she could scoop out handful after handful and finally reach in and pull out the gourd. Scraping it as clean as she could, she carried it back to the quarters, walked triumphantly into the little cabin Jeremiah shared with eight others, and placed it into his welcoming hands.

Later, she thought miserably, having the bowl didn't help, didn't bring her family any closer. What would?

"When that old chariot comes, I'm going to leave you. I'm bound for the promised land, friends, I'm going to leave you." The old words pounded in her head. But now the promised land meant Washington, D.C.

At night she joined with others singing, and knew that now, when she had a chance, she'd be following the North Star and that old gourd to freedom. The words rang in her mind: "Daughter, you work with what you got." What she had was two strong legs that could carry her north. Her mother and father had not been able to save themselves; she wasn't going to let herself get sold the way they had. Her spirits rose. Though restrictions tightened every day, her heart began to beat in a new way. She had a spring in her steps.

Weeks passed. She looked for opportunities. *Will this be the day?* she asked herself when she set out to shuck corn. *Or tonight,* she wondered when she joined others stuffing a mattress with the corn shucks.

Soon, she thought, while she and Ruth hoed a small garden of cabbages, collards, and turnips, next to the shingled cabins. When? she tried to guess, but she did not yet know. Although about to join a mass exodus, she did not yet see the path.

On Christmas Day Sarah joined the children, laughing, as they pulled syrup candy. During the week of feasting, she lay under her quilt of bright-blue squares in the afternoons, and though icy wind blew through cracks in the cabin walls, she was at peace.

Her world looked the same, but her soul had shifted. She would be going north. And it would be soon. The joy of freedom filled her soul.

She still dashed off hungry in the morning to the faraway fields, rushing to get there before the bullwhip began to fall. When the lower field flooded again, Sarah, with a gang of others, did the heavy, messy work of draining and clearing it.

She sped through the days; her muscles ached and spasmed, her back pulled, and by night she couldn't lift her arms to carry water from the spring or build a pitch-pine fire. But inside, slavery fell away.

As it shredded, she began to hear news that pointed a way. Of a specific cook on a plantation five or six nights' walk north, who hid refugees under the kitchen floor. Of lanterns and bells that signaled safe houses. And rumblings of northerners planning to end slavery altogether.

It wouldn't be long. She had to wait. And now she knew that when the right time came, she would recognize it. She didn't know how, but she felt sure something would push her and pull her, and it would simply feel right. Her ship could ride to glory over calm seas. Sarah Armstrong understood that she was getting the call; her soul was settling. She would make it all the way to Washington—without a doubt.

CHAPTER 11

Something would push her and pull her, and it would simply feel right. How long it's been since I've felt that way. Where's my miracle, my message from God? Why have I been left to do everything on my own?

At Montgomery Station in San Francisco I bump my suitcase up the stairs to the street and try to appear normal, like I know exactly where I'm going, even though I've never been to the Transbay Terminal before. Inside, it's dark and dirty. People race by; stained concrete barriers block off whole sections. Since I don't see the ticket window, I ask a tall, smelly old man stretched out on a bench, "Where do I buy a bus ticket?"

He gives me a slow look, then props himself up on one elbow. "Wanna me ... me want ... to show you, baby?" His words slur, and when he reaches toward me, he rolls off the bench and tumbles at my feet, giving me more than enough of a whiff. I hold my breath and back up, until I bump into a woman with a head wrap sitting on an ancient black suitcase. "Sorry," I say. Bundles spill around her while three small children play nearby. She seems safe.

"The office is over there, in the corner." She lifts a skinny finger and points to a Greyhound window, where a light shows that it's open. I thank her and walk away, checking behind me to make sure the old man stays put. "Where to?" the clerk asks sourly.

"San Luis Obispo," I say confidently, knowing I have time to spare. "The ten thirty bus." It's a seven hour and ten minute ride, according to the schedule, plus Fran told me I'll have to take a half-hour taxi ride to her place, so I'll arrive tonight. And I'll be far away from all my problems.

"That line's not running today." He looks up and narrows his eyes. "It's the strike."

"The strike?" I repeat numbly.

"Yeah, the drivers' union shut down all California trips today."

"What? When will the strike stop? When will the bus go to San Luis Obispo?" I try to keep breathing.

"Tomorrow morning, same time, best we know." He's still squinting at me. I hope I appear older, tall as I am. I smeared on some lipstick and eye shadow while I was on BART as a precaution.

The clerk presses a buzzer and lifts an arm, signaling, it looks like, to someone back in the shadows of the room. "Next," he says, turning to the man behind me.

I walk to the center of the station, shaking, while people rush past. Where can I go until tomorrow? One girl in a long skirt keeps stretching out her arms to catch a baby who's running, shrieking. The girl, who doesn't look any older than me, practically trips on her long hem. I'm watching them when a small woman strolls up to me. She glides like a dancer. "Lost?" Her skin is dark, a purple-black, and she stands completely straight with her shoulders way back. Her eyes are dark and shining, beaming up at me while she waits for me to answer.

"No," I finally say.

"Where are you off to?"

I tighten my mouth, the way I've seen Mom do when she doesn't want to talk.

"That's all right," she says smoothly.

I pull back and hear Mom: *Nina, don't talk to her*. The voice sounds so real I turn around. Even though Mom treats me like a child, at this second I wish she were here, just for a minute, to get rid of this creepy little woman.

"Don't be frightened. My name is Imani." She extends her tiny hand. "I'm a social worker."

I pull back.

"Imani Hairston. I help runaway kids." She drops her arm, smiling, then sweeps her arm around the room. "Doin' my job, looking for runaways before they get in real trouble."

"I'm not a runaway. I'm on my way to a friend's." Tears cloud my eyes.

Her face stays calm and kind. "Right. A 'friend's' " she starts. "I'm here to help out. Especially young sisters."

"I'm not your sister!" Even here I can't get out of my black-and-white world.

"Really?" She looks amused. "All right," she says soothingly. "You know you've got to go home. Even-tu-ally." She draws out the word and looks at me expectantly.

I shake my head. Not with Dad ready to murder me, and no friends, anyway. "I'm going to San Luis Obispo." I jiggle my suitcase for emphasis.

"Do your parents know where you are?"

I'm struck mute; I don't want to lie, but I don't want to tell her the truth either.

"You're going home, young lady. Soul sister or not."

Who does she think she is? She can't boss me around. And

why is she pestering me about running away? I *am* planning to visit Fran, so she has no reason to grill me.

"You can't run away, you know, blaming everybody else for your story. Trust me, sister, I can tell these things."

What is she talking about? I smile in a fake way, like she's a crazy woman I'm trying to humor, and take a step back.

"Oh, you think you have it tough with your sorry little story," she says, leaning toward me. "Whatever it is. You haven't seen anything, sister, until you are out on these streets. Now *that's* tough."

I start to walk away, pulling my case. Don't I have any rights? I have money, I have a safe destination, I'm just waiting to take the bus, is all. She can't keep me.

"Young lady," she says loudly. "If you need help at home, we have services. Tell me— "

I keep scrambling through the crowd, even though I hear her calling, "Wait!" Soon she's behind me, talking to the back of my head. "Young lady, you are going directly, as in *right now*, back to your life, wherever that is. You are not going to land on these mean streets, not on my watch. And they are mean."

She's giving me the creeps. "You are going back the way you came," I hear her say while I'm moving fast. I weave between people, knocking over luggage and crashing against a stroller, until I turn the corner that leads to the bathroom. In case she's still behind me, I rush into the women's room, hide in a stall, and climb on the toilet, like in a movie. Then I wait, panting. One person flushes a toilet. Afterward I hear water running in the sink and heavy footsteps plodding out of the restroom. Still, I stay up on the toilet, crouched down. *I got away*, I think proudly, forgetting all about my telltale green suitcase on the floor until it's too late. But it doesn't matter. When I finally peek out from the stall, the bathroom is empty.

For an hour I hang out in the bathroom. Whenever anyone

comes in, I pretend I'm going into a stall or about to wash up. Finally, after my hands are so clean they're puckering, I tuck my chin into my chest and run to the nearest exit.

With twenty-four hours to kill until the bus tomorrow morning, I'm not sure which way to go once I leave the terminal. I turn from side to side, hoping a refuge will catch my eye. Instead I see a pack of men in black leather jackets milling around by motorcycles parked at a bike rack at the curb. A couple of them, sitting on their bikes, gun the motors. "Where you going with that bright-green suitcase, pretty lady?" one calls out. "Hey, wanta take me along on the trip? Hop on."

I try to get away from them and head up Market Street, but a biker follows me, whistling, and soon I hear another man join him. "We want to go too," I hear behind me. Both of them are half walking their bikes, with their legs on the ground. "Take us with you. We'll have a good time!" Snickers follow the statement.

Now they're on either side, hemming me in. I stare straight ahead, walking faster, but I can smell them: greasy leather and sour wine. "We'll take you anyplace you want to go," the one on the left says. His stench drifts over me. Out of the corner of my eye I see him: the guy's so skinny he hardly fills half his black leather jacket.

I keep walking up Market toward Civic Center, trying to ignore them; maybe I can make it to the Main Library and hide inside until tomorrow, or if the strike isn't over then, until the next day.

"Come on," one pleads. "You're too good-looking to be walking around alone."

"Don't you have a boyfriend? I could fill in," the one on the right says, and laughs. He's older, with tattoos on his neck and even his wrists, which poke out from his jacket.

His hand brushes my back.

"I'll be your boyfriend today," he whispers, and I try not to shudder.

The hand moves to my leg, and I feel his hot, boozy breath on the side of my neck. "Now." He leans around to my face and leers, swaying.

I gag.

"Come with us." He growls. "Tiger, scratch me."

I look around, trapped between the motorcycles. Won't someone help? Their noisy motors sputter, spewing fumes. The man on the right keeps reaching his hand out to touch me. Each time I barely duck away from him, and I can't take any air into my lungs.

"You're my tiger cub," I hear him growl again, and then the roar of both motorcycles as they rev up the motors.

Suddenly, I act fast, like Sarah would. "Stop it!" I yell, whirl, and run back the way I came, bumping my suitcase.

"Oh, chases, I like chasing girls," the skinny one howls.

I spin, ram my luggage in front of his wheel—which stops him short—then tug and flee into an open Nordstrom's door. I stagger into the bathroom on the fourth floor and slump inside a stall, not bothering to lift my feet. What am I going to do, spend the day and the night in bathrooms? It's only ten in the morning. I sit on the closed toilet seat, trembling, wishing I'd never come to San Francisco. Where can I hide for twenty-four hours? I pull out my phone to text Fran about the strike—but no, it's dead. Darn! I left my charger at home.

Finally, I gather my courage. Venturing out, I scoot up Market Street toward Civic Center, and when I don't see any motorcycle guys I let myself wander, checking out store windows, dodging a couple of guys drinking out of paper bags. But they're harmless, like the men who sit on crates, nodding, holding up cardboard signs asking for change. I turn and wave to one old guy. "God bless you," he calls out as I pass him.

If it were only that easy.

A concrete ledge by a bank looks like a good resting spot while I try to come up with an idea about where to spend the rest of the day and, more significantly, the night; I climb up and sit on the ledge, swinging my legs, listening to a saxophone hit the high notes and watching people drop money—coins and a couple of fluttering dollar bills—into a soft blue-velvet case. Pigeons peck on the ground below me, jerking their heads up and down. When I tear off a piece of bread from a sandwich I packed and throw it to them, they peck, peck, peck before they flap away. It's peaceful here on the ledge, and for the moment I calm down, with the pigeons pecking and jazz notes wafting into the air. The music reminds me of Mom, with her jazz or soul playing constantly.

Soon four girls who look about sixteen or seventeen saunter by, laughing. I wonder where they're going and why they aren't in school. Two are white, I'm pretty sure, and two are definitely black, with long, dark dreads shot through with red highlights. They all have their arms around each other and look like they're having a good time. Was Mom right, that after ninth grade things get better? "Social life is more fluid," she said. "Not as exclusive."

I won't last till then.

After I finish the first of my three cheese sandwiches, I stroll toward Civic Center. The plaza there is a nice open space where people hang out. But when I get to the corner of Taylor Street, something tugs me across and off to the right, and soon I'm headed up Taylor. After meandering up the hill for a few blocks, I notice Glide Memorial Church over to my left, on Ellis Street. Should I head over there? The church, where I went to services a few times last year with my dad, is known for welcoming everybody, from homeless people with AIDS to politicians who live on Nob Hill. The congregation looks like the UN, and they have a great choir too. The service was jammed every Sunday we went, back before my parents split up. I might even score a meal there.

No, for some reason I want to keep heading uphill. Stretching my legs feels good. Is that what's drawing me up the steep slope?

After twenty minutes my calf muscles are feeling the climb

and my left shoulder throbs from the effort of dragging my suitcase up the hill. I'm about to turn back when that "something" nudges me to turn my head left. I instantly see what drew me here: Grace Cathedral, thrusting its spires into the sky. That awesome Gothic cathedral is why I've come. My parents brought Jimi and me here a couple years ago, once for an organ concert and once for Linda Tillery's Cultural Heritage Choir, where five women sang Negro spirituals—that's what they called them—and other old songs. The drums reverberated off the incredibly high stone arches, which my parents said are built like Notre Dame, and I remember how peaceful the whole vast sanctuary felt, even with the energy of the music bouncing around.

I bump my suitcase up a few flights of stone steps and face a glowing bronze door, double paneled, gigantic like everything about this place. It's covered with raised figures—biblical scenes, maybe. *The Gates of Paradise*, a small sign says. As I step inside, light floods the stained glass windows that fill every arch, sprinkling intricate designs—blue, red, gold—over the yellow stone floor. There's a hush, even with a couple of tour groups tiptoeing around the huge stone labyrinth in the lobby, which is paved with white and gray stones. Dragging my suitcase behind me, I walk down that amazing center aisle toward the yellow stone altar and fall into a pew. The silence in this huge space relaxes me in a way I haven't felt since Mom rubbed my forehead that night, before she got all freaky. I look around to see if anyone notices me, if they're glaring at my squeaky suitcase. No. I draw in a deep breath.

Half an hour later, I'm aware of someone by my side and look up. "May I join you?" the young man says quietly, flashing me a broad smile. Even with his cassock, or whatever it's called, he looks like he's hardly more than a teenager himself. The white collar digs into his brown skin. It's darker than mine, with a yellowish tint, and his eyes and straight black hair look Asian, maybe. Or Hispanic. Or mixed. I can't tell, but I'd never ask "What are you?" the way people always quiz me. *Anyway, what does it matter*, I scold myself.

"Uh-huh. Sit wherever you'd like."

"I'm Father Jorge," he says, extending his hand.

"I'm Nina." My name is out before I can pull it back. But at least he doesn't know my last name. I definitely won't tell him that.

"No school today?"

Oh no, another grilling, like the woman at the bus station. Do I really look that young? I thought I'd lost the baby fat in my cheeks.

"Uh-uh." I shake my head.

"And you have a suitcase," he observes.

"Hmm," I say noncommittally.

He looks intently at the round stained glass window above us. "Stunning, isn't it? I never tire of God's magnificence."

I nod, wondering what he wants.

"How can I help you, my child?"

Child! "I'm okay."

"Anything you'd like to share with me? In confidence. Maybe some trouble with your parents? Or your friends?" His face beams as he leans toward me. "This is a safe space."

How did he know? He's so kind I'm tempted to talk, but can I count on him not to tell? Isn't there some law that grown-ups have to let the authorities know if they find a runaway kid ? Even Sarah didn't dare tell anybody she was leaving. If she could keep that all in, so can I. I grit my teeth. "Everything's fine."

"Why are you here?" he probes gently. "What solace do you hope to find?"

"I don't know," I shrug. "It was just so ..." I stumble. "So beautiful. I wanted to come in."

"Into the house of God." When I don't answer, there's a long silence, until he says, "Let's pray, shall we?"

I nod.

He closes his eyes, I shut mine, and I hear him murmuring softly. I'm lulled by his soothing voice. When I tune in again he's whispering, "We pray for divine guidance for Nina, for her to choose the right path, for her safety wherever her journey may lead, and we pray for Nina to find her way home. Pray for guidance ..."

He continues but I'm stopped by that phrase. Those are exactly the same words Yasmine said to Sarah when she was forced into the wagon, sold south. Is this what Dad is telling me to do, pray for guidance? Or is Yasmine telling me? Or Father Jorge? Or even God? I'm hearing the words from all these voices overlaying each other, coming from every direction. But I don't hear my own inner voice calling me.

"Pray for guidance," I mouth the words softly, adding to the river of sound.

"... the highest and best for Nina. I give thanks and release my prayer, knowing it cannot return to me void. Amen." After Father Jorge finishes he sits quietly for another five or ten minutes.

"Is there anything else I can offer you?" he finally asks.

"No." I shake my head, but my heart feels a little lighter.

"You might want to walk the labyrinth," he says with the sweetest, deep voice. "There's one in back. And another outside by the Interfaith Meditation Garden." He pauses and stares at me. Is he's wondering what religion I am? "It's a divine imprint, very ancient, found in spiritual traditions all over the world, from Crete to Rome to India. The labyrinths here are replicas of the one at Chartres."

I must have raised my eyebrows, because he adds, "The medieval cathedral in France. You should try walking one here. It's quite an experience. The labyrinth has only one path. It winds around, and as we take each step we feel different. The path becomes a mirror for where we are in our lives." He's speaking gently, almost in a trance. "Walk it with an open mind and an open heart. And see what happens. See if it doesn't give you guidance. Stay in the center as long as you like. That's the point of illumination, of prayer. Receive whatever is there for you to receive."

"Thank you." I smile back at him. "Thank you so much."

"And on the way out, release whatever you need to release. May the hand of God be upon you." He touches my head lightly, and then with another smile and a slight bow of the head he's gone, gliding up to the redwood gates below the altar where he joins a knot of women in wheelchairs.

I leave my suitcase outside the labyrinth and take a few tentative steps at the beginning of the path, marveling at the fine stonework. How did people know to create this same intricate design all over the world, for thousands of years? Is there really only one mind, the eternal mind of God? As I walk slowly, twisting round and round, I will my mind to quiet. "Pray for guidance ..."

Becoming less conscious of my surroundings, I move more and more slowly, hardly aware of my thoughts until a heavyset man brushes past. He's rewinding his own path, going in the opposite direction, but he startles me from my reflection. Once my reverie is broken, I notice my rumbling stomach. How long have I been here? What time is it? I force myself to focus again on the path until I reach the center petals and stand in the circle, waiting for inspiration. How can I bridge the gap between my black and white friends—or should I say my former friends? Slowly, I present my problems one at a time, "surrendering" them in the way a small placard next to the labyrinth advises. And I wait, seeking to recover the peace I felt with Father Jorge. I begin to feel a calmness, but the divine message I'd hoped for doesn't come.

After several people step around me, I begin to feel silly rooted to the center spot, and, feeling as unenlightened as when I began, slowly retrace my footsteps back to the beginning. Disappointed, I take hold of my green suitcase's handle, push out through the

Gates of Paradise, and bump down the stone steps. As I head off across the plaza, the outdoor labyrinth catches my eye. Like the one inside, gray and white paving stones mark a winding path to the center. A long, gray stone bench surrounds three sides of the gigantic labyrinth, with a flowering border on the other side, and a few trees. This must be the interfaith garden.

Wearily, I nestle into one corner of the bench; only one other person, a woman pushing a baby carriage, is strolling across the plaza. I close my eyes. What just happened inside the cathedral? Why didn't I get any answers from walking the labyrinth? Is it because I'm not good enough? Because I acted out to my parents, because I doubted God? Father Jorge's gentle face appears in my mind. He was so kind; he prayed with me, he didn't turn me in. If he only knew how bad I was, running away, he might not have been so nice. Confused, with too many questions swirling through me, I shake my head so hard my hair flies into my teeth. I'm starving too, but I don't feel right eating in the meditation garden.

Stumbling back downhill to Market Street, I find myself once again perched on the ledge in front of a bank. Ravenous, I unwrap my second cheese sandwich and gobble it up, wishing I had a quart of milk to wash it down. And a chocolate bar.

Somewhat calmed after I eat, I pull out my ace in the hole: Dad's folder. I'll read another chapter of **MISS SARAH ARMSTRONG** here on the ledge, if it's not too windy. That way I won't have to notice where I am for another half hour, I won't have to think about whether I'm bad or good, or where to hang out until the bus leaves tomorrow morning. I won't have to care about not having any friends or think about Dad and Mom being mad. Or worry about Jimi. How is he going to stay safe without me: from burning down the house by cooking alone, or from Tyrone Jackson and who knows what else?

I escape into the pages. *Sarah, Sarah, tell me what to do.*

A Taste of Freedom

After Sarah resolved to use what the bird man had given her as soon as she had a chance, fortune smiled upon her. As she left her cabin, expecting another painful, hot day in the fields, she spotted ol' miss walking toward the slave cabins. But instead of the expected lashings or cruel insults, the woman approached and said in a curt tone she'd come looking for "girls to help me in the spinning house." Sarah's mind flashed back to the hours Aunt Suzy had spent teaching her young hands to master needle and thread. Her apprenticeship would now be her reward. Soon she and Ruth started working with two other women to make the clothes for everyone on the plantation.

Within a week, it seemed as though the heavens opened and God's big black hand poured her out a blessing. A small factory in town had a rush order and needed extra seamstresses. The factory manager sent word by messenger to every plantation in his side of the county saying he was willing to hire slave help—with the cut-rate pay going directly to the owners.

Old Armstrong, eager for cash, called Sarah and Ruth onto the broad porch where Sarah's parents had married, jumping the broom fifteen years before. "I'm sending you into town to do needlework. Be on the job by the time the first cock crows." Sarah and Ruth, he explained, were to walk into town with seven Armstrong tobacco workers—who tied the tobacco into bundles at the manufactory—and two woodworkers he'd also leased out.

Sarah's first trip into the world seemed unreal. Lagging behind the others as she walked the three miles to the brick factory, with only her slave pass for company, reminded her of the feeling she'd had in her dream. Except then she didn't carry a pass that said, "This is an Armstrong slave. Anybody that bothers her got to answer to Mister Jake Armstrong." Sarah moved down the dirt road, her eyes big. *Am I under a spell?* she wondered.

At the small plant, she worked as if in a trance, rarely turning to talk to others, racing through her needlework tasks. Soon she became the quickest sewer. "I'm going to ask if you can work Sundays too," the redheaded manager told her one Saturday afternoon.

Armstrong agreed, and Sarah had to suppress her joy. Master Armstrong pocketed all Sarah's wages, except for occasional evening pay: the "overwork" money. Sundays, however, would be different. In this part of Virginia, captives had won the right to be "Sunday Freemen"; Sarah would be able to keep half her Sunday wages.

Going to town alone for the first time, Sarah had the chance to rub elbows with those outside her circumscribed world. She asked questions of everyone, trying to find out about their lives: how they lived on other plantations, what they ate, who'd been sold, and how strict their masters and mistresses were.

Evenings, Sarah got to spend a few minutes outside the tobacco factory, where she met up with the hired-out Armstrong people before they all plodded back to quarters. One evening, Sarah struck up a conversation with Henry Brown, a hired-out man who wasn't from the Armstrong place. He worked up tobacco full-time. But, he told her, he'd negotiated an unusual arrangement with his master. "With overtime pay I saved, I hired my wife, Betsy, from her owner and set up house in town."

Sarah's eyes grew wide. She had never known a black person living off in a house on his own. And in town.

"Yes, I live with her and our children." Henry Brown patted his stomach. He looked like a satisfied man. Betsy, he explained, was a laundress; she supported them. "My main wages," he said, "go directly to my owner ..." Here he twisted up his small, dark face. "And I have to give my overtime pay to Betsy's owner for her 'work' for me." The wiry little man gave a bitter laugh. Maybe he wasn't so satisfied after all.

Sarah, fascinated, nevertheless had to rush back home. But on many evenings after that she spoke to Henry Brown, always inquiring after Betsy and the children.

One Saturday that spring, only weeks after Sarah began her needlepoint work, news flew among the small group trudging back to the plantation. "Betsy Brown's been sold south. Heard someone say she's already gone."

"No!" Sarah screamed. Memories of her own family's sales flooded her, and the ground underneath rocked and swayed.

"We don't know where she is," the man walking next to her said furiously. "Not even what state she's going to."

"No, no, no ..." Sarah said. Ruth, who was walking on her other side, held her up when her body started to sag. "Where's Henry?" Sarah managed to ask.

"He was at the factory today. He says he's going to die. Or kill her master. And his too."

Sarah gripped Ruth's arm so tightly that the next day she saw dark bruises there in the shape of her fingers.

The following Monday evening, Sarah found Henry outside the factory after work. She approached him and put her hand on his elbow.

"I can't live without them," he said, his voice trembling.

"I know." She thought how often she'd felt the same way. "You can escape and find your family," Sarah said. "Or go north. Run, earn money, and buy their freedom."

"I can't live ..." Henry repeated, staring vacantly.

"You have to," Sarah urged.

"Yes," Ruth, who'd appeared at Sarah's elbow, agreed. "You have to. Otherwise, who will save them?"

By the end of the week Henry shared the news that he'd begun to plan an escape. After talking to friends, and coming up with one desperate plan after another, he'd spoken to Samuel, a wizened white shoemaker who'd rented Henry and his wife their cramped dwelling. Samuel agreed to help, for a fee. Henry had to pay the man his entire meager savings, but Henry was so distraught, he was willing to do anything. He'd also enlisted Bacchus, a young black carpenter outraged by the abrupt sale of the family. In fact, the bizarre idea the three finally settled on was Bacchus's idea.

"They're going to mail me to Philadelphia," Henry told Sarah, a wild look in his eyes.

"What?" Sarah froze.

"In a wooden box. Bacchus will build it. He can take wood from the factory, and Samuel will mail it." Henry's small face contorted with an odd glee, while he scuffed the dirt outside the factory with his foot. He waved his arms with a grand gesture. "Samuel knows an abolitionist in Philadelphia he'll mail me to."

"In a box?" Sarah then noticed her friend's frayed shoes under his dirty pants. Listening to Henry rant, she understood that the loss of his family had driven him mad.

"Yes, and I need your help." Tears brimmed in his eyes.

She agreed to do whatever she could, though the plot was insane. There was no way he could be mailed, let alone make it alive, to Philadelphia. Surely a station master would discover the man inside the box and turn him over to pattyrollers or, at best, have him jailed.

Yet Sarah knew that Bacchus crept over to the shoemaker's house each evening and, using stolen wood, worked for a scant half hour before racing back to the Armstrong plantation. During that brief time he frantically constructed a two-and-a-half-by-three-foot box, the largest allowed on railroad cars.

"Hurry, man, hurry," Henry pushed Bacchus. "I've got to go. Before I kill somebody. Or myself."

In eight days Bacchus finished the box. Sarah lined it with soft baize and Bacchus drilled three holes for air.

On an overcast morning while Sarah was confined at work,

Henry squeezed into the tiny space. Sarah heard later it was barely big enough for him to crouch, and he'd taken only a pig's bladder filled with water and a few hard biscuits.

She also learned from some of the hired men that Samuel and an accomplice tied the box with hickory hoops and carefully labeled it "This Side Up With Care" so Henry could stay on his feet. Together they carried the heavy parcel to the post office, where Samuel signed the slip and mailed Henry to Philadelphia.

From the moment Henry's box left the station, everyone who was in on the plot waited.

One day passed, with no word.

Another.

Each evening Sarah lingered as long as she could after work, desperate to hear what had happened. Samuel promised he'd send a runner to the tobacco workers with news.

Finally, after two weeks, a detailed letter arrived.

The box had traveled to Philadelphia. On the way, most baggage handlers hadn't bothered to read the instructions on the label. At Richmond station the handlers had turned the crate upside down, leaving Henry on his head. Since he was so cramped, he couldn't turn over. The pressure was unbearable. His eyeballs popped out of his head and he thought he was dying, until another baggage handler, looking for a place to sit, turned the box right side up; that way it made a better seat.

Later, while baggage people switched Henry from one train to another, they threw the crate so roughly that when it landed—again upside down—Henry heard a cracking noise in his neck and passed out. When he came to, he was on his side.

But after twenty-six agonizing hours, the postal service delivered the large box to the home of an Underground Railroad agent, where the man waited with friends.

"Hold on! You're here," they hollered to Henry.

According to the letter, since he couldn't see who was speaking, he didn't answer, wanting to make sure he was safe before he acknowledged himself as human cargo.

They rapped their knuckles against the wood. "Is all right within? You're among friends."

Silence again.

They tapped frantically.

"Yes." He croaked out the answer. "I'm alive."

As fast as they could, the small group cut the hickory hoops and pried open the lid. Henry untwisted himself and climbed out, hobbling around the room, weeping and shouting, "Praise the Lord!" He smelled, he hurt, he was hungry. Before he fainted, though, he screamed, "I'm free!"

Through the mutterings around town, it became clear to Sarah that news of the daring escape had traveled the country like fire. According to Samuel, "Box" Brown, as people began to call him, had even become a cause célèbre in the North. He went on tour, mesmerizing audiences with the horrors of slavery and his own reckless flight, and raising money to track down and buy his family.

But six months later, police entered town, asking after Samuel. Sarah later discovered they'd traced the box through the post office in Richmond, where it was mailed, to the old shoemaker. Though he'd listed a false name, officials identified Samuel as the sender. At his lengthy trial, the prosecutor urged the judge to "make an example of this man, lest we have abolitionists mailing valuable contraband to every northern port in the country!"

Samuel got word to the Armstrong place through a janitor who swept up at the penitentiary. "Tell them to run," his message said. "Right away. I can't hold out any longer. Go now."

Aiding an escape, especially a successful one, was sedition. Sarah had heard the word whispered and seen it in newspapers. She'd read that the Fugitive Slave Law of 1850, passed three years before, meant runaways could be captured in any state. The law affirmed that enslaved people were not citizens, no matter where they were.

When Sarah heard that Samuel was going to confess, she knew she had to go. Immediately. Her first thought was that she and Bacchus could escape together.

"No, I'm going to hide in that shack by the marsh. My wife and children are here. I'll hide out for a few months" was all he would say. "They'll bring me food." Then he was gone.

Sarah would have to run alone.

Of all her childhood friends, only Ruth remained. Few uncles and aunties still lived on the plantation. In fact, Ruth, Old Hannah, Jeremiah, and Aunt Suzy were the only people she could confide in. Yet she didn't want to burden them with the secret, for knowledge about a runaway could bring any punishment, from whipping to death. Still, she had to say good-bye. At least to Ruth.

Sarah walked over to her friend's cabin. Her hand stretched out to push open the flimsy door, but something inside, insistent and strong, said, *No. Don't tell her. She'll understand. Go. Now.*

Sarah turned away, wiped her eyes, and hurried back to the cabin she now shared with Hannah, Aunt Suzy, and several others. She'd have to be quiet, and she'd have to be quick.

Soundlessly, she tucked her mother's worn, miniature Bible and three bone buttons into the pocket of her shirt. It was a coarse woolen one she'd saved for this moment. She quickly rolled her old green blanket, slid the tiny compass from the bird man into her pocket, and wrapped a brown scarf around her head. Stowing a piece of salt herring and two ash cakes into a scrap of cloth, Sarah stepped out of the cabin. As she took her first steps away, heading directly into the woods behind the cabins, Sarah still longed to go and hold her friend one more time. Ruth would understand why she'd had to go. Still, Sarah hated to imagine Ruth's face, twisted with grief and worry, in the morning. She'd know first thing that Sarah had run. Silently, Sarah wished her friend her own successful escape — though Ruth always maintained she would never have the courage — and bid her a mental farewell.

Sarah had to focus on her own survival. She reached out and touched trees as she walked. The North Star gleamed behind moving clouds while her compass confirmed moss she could feel growing on the north side of trees. She was headed in the right direction.

Memories flooded her until Sarah felt faint. "That was then. This is now," she had to tell herself. "Keep moving. I can't get caught." Her throat was so sore she had to gasp to keep from hacking. Every inch of skin was covered with scratches, some of them deep, while her arms and legs burned with mosquito and chigger bites. Her bare feet bled and the hair on her arms stood up each time she heard the blood-curdling cry of a wild animal. Still, in spite of the danger, and understanding the risk that she might never make it to freedom alive, she knew she had no choice but to keep moving north. It was too late to turn back.

The more she walked away from the Armstrong plantation, the sharper and clearer her childhood memories were. But Sarah lurched on, pulled forward by the hope that Esther and little Albert were somewhere up ahead. She'd been gone from home for five endless days. Her stomach growled. She'd never been so tired. Or lonely.

In truth, she'd never been alone in her life before. Every night she'd slept in a room with her mother and brother and sister; every day she'd scampered among dozens of people, all moving to the rhythm of their work. Now she spoke only to the owls, who answered back, and the wood rats and raccoons and foxes she heard running nearby.

Sarah was so hungry she scratched with her bare hands to rip out bits of pine roots until blood seeped from under her fingernails. She found sassafras buds to gnaw on. And, grateful for the moonlight, she saw clearly enough to pick blackberries. The sound of crickets chirping kept her company, though walking without any people nearby felt stranger and stranger. She wondered if this running away were a dream. Maybe it was, and she was simply back on her pallet on the floor in the quarters? Then a sharp jab in her foot reminded her of the reality she faced.

Sarah kept to small paths, some no more than deer trails, always staying near the river. She waded back and forth across the water, and once floated on a pine log so any bloodhounds set out after her would not be able to detect her scent.

In a driving rain she shivered, and her throat seared so badly she wanted to scream, to cry out, to have Mama or Papa appear. She wished someone could hold her, even for a moment. She knew the pain in her throat would get better if only she could have a bowl of warm soup and a friendly arm around her, or a hot compress on her chest. But instead she was alone in a terrifying and thick forest, freezing, while she followed a jumble of paths that might, for all she knew, be leading her right back home. Uncle Jeremiah's voice rang in her ears: better the devil you know than the devil you don't.

Had it been a terrible mistake to leave after all?

CHAPTER 12

By the time I finish the chapter — catching pages that blow all over — and devour my last sandwich, it's late afternoon. I try not to think of the last line of the chapter, of Sarah alone and without food.

I still don't have a plan for the night, so I mosey farther along Market up to Civic Center, waiting for inspiration. Nothing seems scary. That social worker didn't know what she was talking about. If she *was* one. I wonder what Miss Sarah would think about me now, running away. It's different from what she faced, but still, she might be proud of me, taking my fate into my own hands. Why should I stay back in Canyon Valley without any friends, waiting for my dad to double-kill me — once for sass, twice for stealing his manuscript — and then let my mom punish me too, like she promised? A tear dangles off my nose.

A few times I stop to listen to a harmonica, then a guitar, until before I know it long shadows fall across the sidewalk. I'm shivering. When I get to Civic Center Plaza, homeless people — men, mostly—are sitting all over the place with bulging shopping carts, and a few men lie on the pavement. Or pace. One young woman sits cross-legged with a huge German shepherd sprawling next to her. The girl's head falls over her knees toward the sidewalk. All I can see is a mass of hair bleached like straw, tangled, dangling over her face like a tent, until a gust of wind blows it back. I catch sight of her sunburnt face and hollow green eyes that stare out at nothing.

After I stroll around the plaza a couple of times, wondering whether I should keep heading up Market to the Castro, a scruffy young guy approaches. "Help me get a hot dinner," he begs. When I shake my head no, he mutters, "Cheap," and shoots a mean look. "I'm starving to death out here, sister," he says, changing his tune, while he keeps his palm out.

I don't want to pull out my money, which is wadded in my back pocket, while he's watching. But I feel sorry for him since he sounds desperate, and I know how much I hate to be hungry, so I reach in, unpeel the roll as fast as I can, and hand over a five.

"Thank you, sister. Sonny's gonna eat tonight. God bless you." He's beaming.

Still, I've got to find supper myself, and a place to sleep. The San Francisco fog is billowing in, a wind is whipping up, and it's freezing, with that penetrating damp chill. I know better than to linger here on the plaza after dark, but with no idea where to go, I stand still and look around. Maybe I should head back to Glide? When I was there last year I think they said something about a shelter where you could wait in line for a place to sleep. But that sounds too scary. Sonny must sense my uncertainty, because he points down Larkin Street, his arm pulling him forward until he lurches in the direction he's aiming. "Over at Burger King, I could buy you dinner," he says with a strange laugh, a cackle that ends in a moan.

"No, thanks," I say, eager to escape.

As the shadows lengthen I haul my luggage back down Market Street, warming up, until I find a sandwich shop with a sign in the window—*Cheap Eats, 24 Hours*—that calls to me, and duck in. The smell of old grease frying hits me hard, making me nauseous. Still, I'm hungry. And numb with cold.

"Welcome," the waitress at the counter says with a huge smile, and in ten minutes I'm wolfing down a tofu burger and a plate of fries. With food in my belly my brain starts spinning again, until Sarah's world and my world are all mixed up. It's so strange and surreal being here; *I could hide in some bushes*, I think groggily, *like she did*. But where? Golden Gate Park is too far, and so vast it frightens me. I start imagining a small, cozy park with only a few shrubs, enough to shelter me but not so many that lots of other people would sleep there. Certainly I can stay out for just one night—lots of people do it—and in the morning I'll return to the safety of the terminal and catch the bus to Fran's. I curl my frigid toes into my shoes.

Once I've decided to sleep out tonight, I linger in the sandwich shop as long as I can, drinking water ("Yes, more, please") and using the restroom until, by the time I push open the door of Cheap Eats, the moon is out, casting its silvery light and shadows. As I stumble, exhausted, back down Market Street toward the Embarcadero, I see the forms of people lying in doorways under blankets. I never thought to bring one, and I can't imagine how they spend the entire night on cold cement. I'm trembling uncontrollably; I've never walked along Market at night alone, or been anywhere by myself after dark in the city. The street is deserted, with closed shops and boarded-up storefronts, until I get to Powell Street and turn left, trudging up the familiar street, where I see cable cars. I hope I can find a patch of ground with bushes somewhere up the hill. It would be less creepy tucked under some vegetation than out in the open, and I'll have to be on dirt; the cement is way too hard.

People jam the sidewalks on Powell — tourists staring into store windows or hurrying by, and locals loitering in small groups, pestering, "Spare some change?" I tug the suitcase uphill again, huffing, catching glimpses of people rolled up in sleeping bags and sprawled across every shuttered doorway. But I can't find any kind of space that looks comfortable, so with my eyelids closing, I turn back down the hill and drift to the other side of Market Street, the seedier side. I rush along, hurrying past strip clubs advertising *Adults Only.* In front of one, a brightly lit marquee startles me: *New Shows, Auditions Daily.* I stop short. For a horrified moment I wonder how disgusting that would be, to stand naked in front of people. I scurry past the sign, head down. No, I'll never be that desperate.

A block later I spot a small park ahead, surrounded by a low fence. As I get closer I see the wall is purple concrete, full of handmade mosaics. Circling all the way around the edge I find two gates, both locked, but it's easy to clamber over and I haul my green suitcase up behind me. Once inside I crouch by a series of blue benches shaped like train cars, next to two tire swings hanging over orange rubber matting, and an orange-and-blue jungle gym with a short slide. It's a kiddie park. I scoot over to an area of low bushes, hard up against the wall. Pulling my suitcase in next to me, I crawl under a bush that smells like pee. The ground is unbelievably hard and the leaves drip incessantly from the heavy fog blanketing the city. In five minutes I'm wet, hungry again, and I have to go to the bathroom.

A police siren screeches by, then another. Cars honk. A fire engine roars past. People on the sidewalk, right on the other side of the wall, talk and laugh. One woman screams "Help!" No one comes, even when she screeches "Help!" once again. Then there's no sound until someone vomits, gagging on and on while I squirm on the cold ground. Every time I roll over, carefully, quietly, another stick prods me. I can't get comfortable and I can't stop sniffling. Two or three men start to yell from somewhere on the next block, until a woman shouts "Shut up!" and they do. Apparently those are the magic words out here.

After a restless hour I see a flashlight swing into the playground, swaying back and forth. In the moonlight I catch sight of a man circling the jungle gym, shining his flashlight into an orange cubbyhole at the base. My heart pounds. The light swings closer, moving toward me; I hear footsteps pound the rubber matting, then the cement bordering it, and finally the solid ground close to the bushes. I go rigid and cover my mouth with one hand to smother the sound of my breath.

The light shines near me; I can see his scuffed, black lace-up shoes. But in a minute the beam moves away, swinging rhythmically until, unlocking the gate and then clanging it shut, the guard leaves the park. After he's gone I curl up and cry, muffling the sound with my arm. Why did leaving home ever seem like a good idea? But I know I'm way too proud—and scared—to go back. I've never felt so forlorn, so alone, without a friend or confidant in the world. Only the image of Fran's smiling face under her curly black hair keeps me going. I hope Jessica didn't tell her too many lies about me. A prayer comes unbidden while I drift off to sleep. *Please, let me get through this night alive, keep me safe, show me the way. Yea, though I walk through the valley of the shadow of death, I will fear no evil … thy rod and thy staff they comfort me …* Even half asleep, I argue, though: Is it true? If God is love, I don't see how such terrible things as slavery could happen. Or friends splitting by race. Or lying about each other. God isn't supposed to let stuff like that happen. But a part of me argues back, telling me that just because things aren't perfect or easy or right, it doesn't mean God's not here. That the world is totally broken. I remember the peace I felt in the church, the comfort Father Jorge's words gave me, but my mind still wants to fight back. My sore heart hurts even more as I wake and sleep in fitful bits, reaching for the comfort of the psalm while my mind rejects it. "Pray for guidance" becomes my mantra as I toss through the night.

When I wake at dawn, I'm soaked, drenched to my underwear. Every inch of me is sore, and I'm shaking so hard I can't stop. But while my eyes are still closed, the memory of a vivid dream rushes in, full force: Sarah and I were flying, holding hands, floating over houses. Canyon Valley and even San Francisco looked like toy villages, with patches of round, green trees, like a Faith Ringgold quilt. Cars were colorful bugs crawling along the streets. We steered by leaning one shoulder down, gliding, floating. She was a girl my age, my friend, and we were wonderfully free.

Then she was old, with white, wild hair. "Great-great-granddaughter," she told me sternly, in quick bursts. "You've no business wandering all over San Francisco during the night. Get on home!" She glared. "This is nonsense. You're no slave. Get out of your own way, daughter. You have two parents who love you. They're mad with worry." She stared so hard I got chills. Her voice was a low rumble, like thunder. "Many have much worse troubles, Nina Armstrong." Bent over, she peered up at me. "Ask me how I know."

When I started to say, "But— " she clutched my shoulders with both hands and squeezed me hard, until I woke, struggling to get her arms off my shoulders. Still she spoke: "Take charge. Listen to your heart, what guides you. Only you can."

Rubbing my eyes, I shake my head to clear away her voice, concentrating on dismissing the words that echo—"Take charge, listen to your heart, only you can"—and, eyes wide open, I stare around the park, determined to put my attention on my surroundings instead of a bizarre dream.

Above, the sky is gray, flat. Under my back I see filthy dirt, littered with dry leaves and cigarette butts. Broken bottles—green and brown — are scattered nearby. Sharp sticks and pebbles are strewn all over the ground too, sprinkled between dozens of hard, large roots. Those were the spikes I felt all night.

Trembling with cold, I crawl out, stand up stiffly, and brush off my pants, trying to wring them out on my legs. I snatch my suitcase, soggy from the heavy fog, clamber back over the wall, and head toward Market. There's hardly any traffic. It must be early. I wonder where to get hot food without spending much of the money I have left; I'll need it for the bus and taxi and food along the way. My teeth are chattering and I can't stop shaking, but the image of old Miss Sarah Armstrong lingers, in spite of my effort to ignore it. With her unruly hair flying around her head like a halo, she accompanies me, and I have to admit she makes me feel protected.

When I'm back on Market Street, standing on the corner waiting for the light to change, a black cat streaks in front of me. Some people say they're unlucky, but I've heard Mom and Dad say different. Mom said that in Ireland, a black cat crossing your path means good luck, and Dad laughed, because, he told her, in African American tradition black cats also brought good fortune. Especially one with its tail up, which this one has. Maybe my luck is changing. I'll wake up and discover that this last month was all a dream. Dad and Jimi still live with us, Jessica is my best friend, Claudette never moved to Canyon Valley, Jimi didn't steal a bike, and I never heard of a boy named Tyrone. Dad still calls me Lilla Bit and Mom's eyes go soft with love every time she looks at me. Maybe Dwight even likes me. I press my fingernail into my wrist as a test, but it hurts like the devil, so I know I'm awake and really standing alone, shivering at dawn on Market Street in San Francisco. The cat waves its tail gracefully, then lowers it and slinks back to the corner. It crouches, stalking a small rat frozen at the curb. Still, this cat *is* a good sign. I watch the cat sink down, getting ready to pounce, while the light turns green and red again and I try to come up with the right name. In a flash I realize cats have nine lives, so I bend to whisper, "I'm going to name you Number Nine. From now on, that's my *lucky* number." I start a rap, "Nine be fine," and click my tongue. "Nine be mine."

Number Nine bolts across the curb and hides under a car. I drop on my knees to look underneath, but no cat. When I unbend myself, stand, and wipe the street grit off my palms, I'm shaking with cold, worse than before. My teeth are chattering so hard their clacking sounds as if it could wake people sleeping in apartments over the stores. I rub my hands together, wishing for gloves, which normally I never wear. While I'm waving one arm at a time, trying to warm up, I cross the street and, first thing, see a scruffy woman watching me. She hardly has any teeth — a couple molars left on the sides — and her clothes are stained and torn.

"Come 'ere, luvie," she motions me to an alley, "if you're hungry. You look starved. New to this life?"

The grungy alleyway sits between a boarded-up storefront and a souvenir store window full of tiny cable cars. I edge in behind her, picking my way slowly, ready to run. A rat darts in front of me. I flinch, but hunger pangs in my stomach keep me moving. This must be where the garbage cans are kept, because I haven't seen any on the street. We walk farther into the alley. Yes, there they are, a jumble of battered green and gray cans spilling over with trash.

Nobody else is around this early, and the old woman, without another word, pries open one of the largest cans, a gray one with a dented lid, full of white bags tied with green twisties. She pries open one bag, but when the stink of old chicken hits us, she slams the cover down. Mesmerized, I watch her open another can: it overflows with rotting fish scraps and smells even worse. "Phew," I say, holding my nose.

The third can has a partially opened lid already, and half-chewed pastries strewn around it on the ground. This must be trash from a bakery. Inside the can a loaf of bread is ripped in pieces, as if raccoons were here last night. The woman reaches in, snatches two hunks of bread, and stuffs one in her mouth while handing me the other piece. It's rye, leathery in texture, with sesame seeds, and I'm so famished it smells delicious. But I can't put it into my mouth. The idea that raccoons might have drooled on it, or that it could be a leftover from somebody's plate, makes my stomach clench. I hand it back. She doesn't say anything but pops it directly into her mouth all in one bite so her cheeks are puffed like a chipmunk's. I watch while she pokes around in the can until she pulls out two broken muffins and a bag of biscuits. Again she reaches over to me, holding out one of the muffins, but I shake my head. "No, thanks." I inch away and glide toward the alley. When I look back from the street, I see her squatting silently next to the row of garbage cans. "Thanks anyway," I call out, but she doesn't reply.

With my stomach grumbling, I duck into a coffee shop and order a bagel ("cut in two halves, please, wrapped separately") with cream cheese and one hot chocolate to go. I hate to spend the money, but I can't eat from a garbage can.

Walking out of the shop munching, I stuff the other half bagel, wrapped in paper, into my jacket. Jamming it in reminds me of Jimi, who always stuffs his pockets with treasures. He copies everything I do, yet I don't want him to run away too, looking for me. I wish I'd brought him. I could've sworn him to secrecy about where we were going. What's he going to do without me when he comes to Mom's after school? Or at Dad's? He could hurt himself while home alone. Or get caught by Tyrone, who might not be in a forgiving mood—he doesn't look like that kind of kid—even though I took his stupid bike back.

My throat aches with worry. But I shake my head, *No, I can't worry about Jimi now, I have to think about myself,* and retrace my route, making my way up Powell Street along the same blocks I hobbled down last night.

I have to get back to the bus terminal, but I know it's way too early. The terminal's probably not even open. Still, it's too cold and windy to sit down, especially in my wet clothes. I have to keep moving.

Two empty wooden benches up ahead in Union Square look inviting. I'd like to settle there for a while, but the fog has soaked even my hair. If I'm not on the move I might freeze to death. I abandon any thought of stopping until I'm next to the square and spot a navy blue blanket crumpled on the end of a bench.

I spin around. The entire park is vacant. Has the blanket been abandoned? Did someone lose it? I smile; my luck *is* changing! I could lie down, wrap up, munch my bagel and sip my hot chocolate and pretend I'm home eating breakfast, with Dad cooking me a big, yummy pancake. I can almost smell it.

But as I actually get close to the blanket and imagine the people who might have wrapped themselves in it—street people who hadn't had a shower in weeks, or might be sick or have lice—I can't do it. I'll just have to count on the hot chocolate to warm my insides, and let my outside freeze. I try sitting there, but my butt's way too cold on the bench to read, no matter how much I want the distraction of another chapter while I wait for the terminal to open. Instead, once I drain my drink and munch the last of my bagel, I stagger over to the warmth of a McDonald's on the corner, slouch into the bathroom, and sit on the closed toilet seat to read one more chapter before I try to brave the bus station again.

On the Run

"Look for the lantern!" "Listen for the bell." These phrases, whispered about the plantation, had become her watchwords, her hope of survival. But she should have seen the lantern by now, noticed its beacon in a house with a special quilt hanging on the line at night. The bird man had told her it would be three or four nights of walking. She'd missed it. Or could it all be a story? Perhaps he'd been sent as a cruel trick, tempting people to run away into thickets from which they never emerged. Maybe there never were any lanterns or bells, and no people who helped runaways. She might die in these woods after all.

Still, she stared through the night at anything that might be a flicker of light. But as much as she squinted through wet eyelashes she saw no lanterns, and as much as she strained her soaking ears she heard no bells. As the night wore on toward morning, the rain stopped but fog rolled in, shrouding every tree and bush. It cloaked even the ferocious cries she'd heard earlier in the night.

Stillness descended.

Now fog blocked out the stars so she couldn't read them for direction. Her compass confirmed that she was still heading the right way, but she began to stumble, and her sense of being absolutely alone, without any help, grew so acute she trembled. The shuddering took hold of her body until she wobbled on her feet.

I should turn back now, she let herself doubt again. *Before the hounds get me. Or pattyrollers. Or a wild animal.* She shivered even more violently, remembering some of the sounds she'd heard in the night.

Go back, the voice in her head murmured, growing louder. *Let them whip you. So what? Later you can wrap yourself in a blanket and lie down and be warm.*

Her heart argued, *Keep going. You can make it. You have to find Albert and Esther.*

But the nagging voice in her mind talked back, sounding wiser and wiser. *This is foolishness! You're only a girl,* it said. *You can't go all this way alone. You'll never make it. You'll die of hunger or be eaten by a bear or a wildcat. No one will even find your bones.*

Tears trickled down her filthy face. Her throat was raw. She was so thirsty she thought she would faint. Finally, when she wanted to throw herself down on the path and give up, Sarah thought she saw a lantern. Could it be, this late? The fog, along with her fear and hunger, might be playing tricks on her eyes.

As she moved closer, she saw the faint outlines of a house. She circled it at a distance. Yes, there was a light in the window. Her sense of time had grown vague, but she knew no farmer would be up this late. Or this early in the morning.

Pray for guidance ...

Sarah crept closer until she stood just outside the lantern's glow. Something large flapped in the night breeze, right next to the house. She put out her hand and felt damp material.

Why was a quilt hanging on the line at night?

Suddenly, through her terror, she remembered what she'd heard from the stranger on that miracle day up in the field. Sarah grabbed the soggy cloth and tried, in the dim light, to make out the pattern. There it was: a house with a smoking chimney design.

The pattern that signified a haven.

Sarah walked as quietly as she could around to the back door. She knocked softly three times, with her heart thumping as loudly as her knuckles on the wooden door.

"Who's there?" a low voice asked through the closed door.

"A friend of a friend," Sarah responded, just as the bird man had told her.

Silence.

Had she given the wrong answer?

When the stillness continued, Sarah started to move away from the door, ready to run. But a firm arm cracked the door open a few inches and pulled her in.

When Sarah saw a white-skinned woman holding on to her,

and felt her big arms wrapped tightly, she shook so hard she thought her bones would break.

Oh no, Sarah thought. *She's going to squeeze me to death. She's a relative of Master Armstrong and the bird man sent me here to murder me. She kills runaways.* Sarah's terrified mind imagined this was her last moment alive, her final minutes on earth. She slumped in the woman's grip.

Then a hoarse voice said, "You're freezing, child," and the big arms rubbed against her thin ones, trying to warm her.

Sarah felt faint. The last things she saw were black curls escaping from a bonnet and a round face with brown eyes staring worriedly at her. She felt the big arms catch her and she let herself slip away. As she drifted, she felt as if she were plunged into a pool of soothing, warm water. After days of vigilance, letting go was a relief.

When Sarah came to she was lying on a small wooden bed, wrapped in two thick, brightly colored quilts. She looked around the small, sunny room. A loom stood near the doorway. Soft white curtains hanging over an open window blew lightly. In a moment the heavy face, joined by another older, darker version, hung over her.

"You have to eat," the first one said, while she propped Sarah up and forced hot soup through her chattering teeth. "I'm Miz Jackson."

Sarah, dazed, said nothing. But she guzzled the soup and felt the steam work its way down into every sore place inside. Her flaming throat relaxed and felt soothed the way it used to when Mama made soup; often short of salt, Mama would pull up a board from the smokehouse, where hams hung in the rafters. The board was soft, soaked with salt and grease that dripped from the hams. She'd drop a piece in the bean soup, cooking the salt and fat right out of that board. Tears smarted Sarah's eyes when she remembered.

"You lay down," a second husky voice said. "Rest until we have to send you on your way."

Sarah slept and slept. When she woke it was night once more. The ache in her throat was hardly there.

More soup, some chicken, hot milk, and corn bread slathered with lard and molasses. "It's time for you to go," she heard two quiet voices say. "We'll tell you the way. When you come to the first fork, go left ..." The first Miss Jackson squeezed her left arm, and held on for a minute. "That's for the first fork ..."

Can't I stay? Sarah thought. She lingered as long as she could over her meal, but then let herself be hustled gently into the dark. This time Sarah carried a bundle of biscuits, strips of smoked chicken, and a large piece of dried pork wrapped in her faded cloth. If she didn't have the food to show for it, she would have thought this past night and day had been another in her series of bizarre dreams, so strange had it been. Hardly having a way to think about the extraordinary encounter, she put it away for future study. Later, she would try to understand who those women were, living in a house off by themselves, and why they did what they did. Now, she would put one foot in front of the other. Now, she would keep moving toward Esther and Albert.

Sarah walked again through the night—this one clear and bright with stars—as each footstep continued to carry her farther away from all she knew.

The moon that had shone so brightly her first night out was now half the size. She saw it glide low to the horizon, which meant she'd soon have to stop for the day, although she needed to cover a little more ground this night. She must be getting close to the refuge the women had told her about; it was supposed to be right after the circle of homes she was to avoid. But Sarah saw nothing. Had she taken a wrong turn?

She had to be almost there. A low sun, near the horizon, peeped out behind dark clouds, and she lay down to rest.

All day Sarah lay on moss near the river bank, waiting for the sun to slowly cross the sky, occasionally reading snatches from her mother's small Bible. Finally she watched the ball of fire melt below the trees, listened to a racket of blue jays screeching, and prepared to resume her weary trek.

Hearing no one about, Sarah let herself creep over to the still pool in the little inlet near her hiding place. As she bent over to scoop water onto her head and into her mouth, she stopped. A rippled reflection stared back at her: the face of her mother. Could she have grown so old since she'd last seen herself in a cracked piece of tin? She looked intently, while equal parts grief, longing, and delight warred inside her. She gazed solemnly at her mother's features: the familiar high cheekbones, wide mouth, heavy brow. When she could stare no more, she drew a deep breath and splashed the cool river water all over her neck and shoulders.

As twilight deepened and she began to move, Sarah felt her first peace in many months. Her mother was with her, after all. And tonight, with the clouds scattering, it should be clear; the North Star would confirm the shaky little needle in her compass.

CHAPTER 13

My stomach is gurgling in spite of the bagel — or maybe because of it — and both knees are stiff. When I look in the mirror I see that I'm crusted with leaves, the red, yellow, and brown bits sticking to me, covering my jacket and pants. No wonder the woman who took me into the alley knew in a flash that I'd slept on the street.

While I'm brushing the dirt off and wiggling to fire up some body heat, I try to imagine what it must have been like to be Sarah stumbling through the woods, and I tremble, cold and fear coursing through me. After I slip outside, a shaft of sunlight breaks through the fog, warming my shoulders, so I stand at the corner of Market Street, basking, before I head up to Union Square to trot once around it before I go back down to the bus station. It's early light, shining at an angle. Crumbs of dust float in the rays. The whole street looks like a stage that's backlit. Even the rust-colored branches of the trees overhead on the square seem brighter. It's the morning sunbeam, I guess. The edges of everything have a tiny shadow, and shafts of light are dancing in the wind. It's a magical morning.

At that moment, standing on the edge of the square, I have a divine insight. I take a deep breath, exhale, and suddenly know, in every cell, every joint of my body: Sarah was running *to* something—to freedom. She was brave. But I'm running *away* from my problems. Not solving a thing, as Mom would say. I might even be making things worse. Yeah, I guess she could've told me that a while ago, but I had to come to it in my own time, like she says too. "Every flower opens when it's ready, not before." Funny how Mom feels close to me now, even though I've been so angry with her.

I see all this, clear, like the light, and it's equally clear that I need to run *home,* not to San Luis Obispo. Then my other mind, the everyday one, jumps in arguing: *If I go home, what would be different? Isn't Dad going to be furious, and Mom too?* Plus, I'd still have to choose between Jessica and Lavonn, if either of them even wants to be friends with me.

For a second, the divine spirit returns: I can see they each have qualities I like, ways they act and talk and think that make me feel comfortable, like I used to feel at home. Is that what Saundra meant by a "big life": being friends with everybody? Like those older girls I saw yesterday. Was that my future strolling by? Like one of the miracles in Sarah's tale?

Yet my mind argues persuasively: *that's impossible.* Jessica and Lavonn can't stand each other, and they've both made comments that show they'll never get along. If I'm with Lavonn, Jessica and Claudette are going to harass me as "ghetto." And if I even could hang with them, the black kids will diss me as "too white" and hate me. There's no way to take charge, like Sarah told me to do in the dream. She doesn't know anything about life today. It's hopeless. I feel an urge to heave my suitcase, smash it. I want to break something, and as quick as it came, the clear moment slides away again and I'm only me: scared, shivering, confused, and angry.

But there's a spark of light left inside. I do get that there are different kinds of running away—one kind solves problems and the other makes them. That spark of light reminds me of Sarah just "knowing," in Dad's book. I've heard him call that the Divine Intelligence at work when he speaks about it. This must be how God speaks. I was asking for guidance, and now I got it—through Sarah, through the voice in my heart, and through the clearness in my mind. Even though I don't completely want to listen. Going home still feels too tough. Yet traveling to Fran's all day on the bus doesn't feel so easy anymore either, and what would I do there when she goes to school on Monday morning? I hunch my shoulders and stand with my face turned up to the sun.

"Jimmy!" I hear a woman's voice behind me scream across the square. "Jimmy, wait up."

When I turn around to look, she's running to catch a bent man hurrying ahead of her.

"Jim!" she calls again. "Don't leave me here alone."

But he steps quickly, and in her high heels and pencil skirt she can't catch up. She's tottering, carrying a giant black leather tote bag.

"I'm sorry!" she screams, falling farther behind. "I won't do it again. I promise!"

He turns for an instant, shakes his head, and keeps on moving, never breaking his stride.

"Please!" she bawls.

He doesn't stop.

The woman, who I now realize is young, halts and stares across the square, calling out frantically, "Jimmy, don't leave me here!"

He doesn't turn again, and soon disappears into a side street. She stands watching him go, still calling. Finally, after he's out of sight, she throws up her hands and staggers toward the corner where he vanished, but I know she won't catch him.

I stand, paralyzed, as if I've watched a play on a set, acted only for me. What terrible thing had the woman done, and why was she so afraid to be left alone? The image of her wobbling off, whimpering, stays with me long after she's out of sight.

A picture of my Jimi flashes. I can't imagine leaving him alone forever. He needs me to protect him. And even though he has friends now, in a couple of years he'll be in high school, coming up against the same pressures I'm facing.

Jimi, wait for me too, I want to call out. *Wait. I'm coming home.* Suddenly there's no more question, no arguments from my mind throwing up reasons to stay away. I tighten my grip on my suitcase and take off, running downhill toward the BART station. But as I race I trip on a crack on the sidewalk and roll down the hill, crashing smack up against a trash can with my suitcase on top of me. Two men in suits stop. "Ouch," I say, wincing when one puts his hand gently on my shin.

"I don't think anything's broken." He looks down kindly. "You seem able to move. Can I give you a hand getting up? Let's make sure you're okay." He offers me a dollar, but I don't take it. He must think I'm homeless, with my hair matted and covered with debris.

I don't know what will be different at home—except maybe me—but I know I have to get there. Jimi might be hurt already. Gasping, I stumble into the station and shamble downstairs as fast as I can for the train. It's waiting. By the time I'm about to step in the doors start to close, but I slide my hand in the opening, push them apart, and squeeze in, yanking my suitcase behind me.

Even this early in the morning people fill up the train, carrying backpacks or briefcases, and one wrinkled older man in my car has a bike. I take a deep breath before I stumble to a seat and wedge myself in. I have one more chapter of **MISS SARAH**

ARMSTRONG, so I could finish the whole manuscript before I go home. But I can't read here, not now. Not with tears glazing my eyes.

While I'm limping up Redwood Road to Calusa, getting near my house, I start thinking about home. Mom must have found me missing when she came home from work. I'm sure she called the school, and they told her I never got there. What did she do? I'm shivering, and I try to duck behind the live oak trees lining the sidewalk every time a car drives by. I'm not ready to deal with anyone I know yet. When I pass the real estate office at the corner, I catch sight of myself in the window. My hair is wild like Mom's but more tangled. I run my fingers through the snarls and walk slowly, scraping my feet along the pavement, listening to Sarah's voice in my head. "Were you running *away* or *to* something?" There's only one answer.

If I stay outside any longer, somebody I know is sure to see me and call my parents before I'm ready to talk. A few people are out walking their dogs, two runners jog on the other side of the street, and cars whiz by. The doors at Café Suzette, my favorite coffee shop, are opening, so I go in to use the bathroom. But once I'm inside, smelling the fresh coffee and croissants and feeling the warmth, I can't leave. I decide to curl up in the back corner on a wooden bench, spend the money for another cup of hot cocoa, and read the last chapter before I go home.

The Dark River

Sarah trudged through the dark, keeping alert for sounds of people and animals, while she thought about the terrible night she'd left the Armstrong plantation. It seemed a lifetime ago. She'd lost count of the days but vividly remembered the tangle of feelings when she set out: relief that she was finally going, mixed with terror of an unknown future.

That night, like this one, there was enough moonlight to illuminate the path, yet not so much to make her an easy target. But the moon was getting thinner each night; in another few days there wouldn't be any light at all.

As she followed the river, Sarah searched for signs she was getting close to the next checkpoint. Owls hooted as if urging her on. There it was! Sarah spotted the signal Miss Jackson had described: a yellow light shining just below blue.

Cautiously moving along a path on the bank, Sarah approached a small boat and called out, ready to run. "A friend of a friend sent me."

"Jump in," she heard the quiet answer. A young man moved quickly, taking her hand and pulling her into the boat. To Sarah's surprise, his skin was the same brown hue as her own. "I'm Jason," he said, his eyes scanning the horizon. "You'll need to get under there."

She crept in the direction he pointed. As day began to light the sky, he rowed her upriver, hidden under nets and fishing gear. Her heels itched from the cracks that split them and the earwigs that crawled on her legs, but she didn't dare scratch. Whenever she moved, Jason hushed her: "Stay still."

All day she heard the slap of the oars, felt drops of water from their spray, and heard him talk softly to her from time to time.

"I'm free," he whispered. "Soon you gonna be too. You're real close now. I'm gonna tell you where to go. You do like I say and you'll be all right."

Papa used to sing a song like that: "It's all right, it's all right, my soul's got a seat ..." Sarah fell asleep, rocked by the boat and the memory of her father's sweet song. At twilight Jason let her out, handed her another bundle of food, and gave final instructions. "Stay to this side"—he touched her left arm—"at the fork. You don't ever want to go over to that side." He grazed her right hand to reinforce his message.

"Thank you," she said, squeezing his hand, and took off at a run.

That night she kept moving in the direction he'd pointed. And exactly as he'd predicted, she came to a fork in the road. Weary but energized by anticipation, she took the path on the left and trudged on, around one curve, and then another.

Had she remembered the correct instruction? She had her answer when she reached an abandoned cabin, where a tired man waited. "Free," he grumbled as he shoved her under burlap, into a wagon brimming with onions. "Free. But I don't feel free. Drivin' all these runaways ..." He moaned and complained all day, until he let her out "one night's walk, if God's willin'," from the city of Washington.

While it was still night, Sarah saw the dark waters of the Potomac River. It looked exactly as everyone had said it would: wide and muddy and marshy, with narrow spots where brush grew into the water.

She crept toward its banks crouching low, for the waning moon still was bright enough to cast a dim shadow. Thirsty, she scooped up water in her hands and drank. She dunked her arms and splashed chilly water all over her head.

Shivering, she looked up and saw the Long Bridge.

After all these years of wanting and wishing, and now these cold nights and hungry, terrifying days of running, was she really going to be free? And would she find her brother and sister?

Sarah took a deep breath and looked carefully around. No one was in sight. She couldn't get caught now, not when she was so close. But was it safe to be out in the open the way she'd have to be? She stood, indecisive, and then stole toward the bridge, bending as low as she could. Reaching its entrance, she stood resolutely and began to walk, still stooping, afraid to run in case anyone noticed her at this early hour.

For ten agonizing minutes she walked as fast as she dared,

her heart thumping with fear and exertion. As a brilliant pink rippled the sky, her feet touched land.

She walked for a few minutes, following the muddy road that led her off the bridge. When she passed two young men, they strode by her with an air of confidence she'd never seen in other Negroes. For a second Sarah stared. They gawked back, then smiled and waved; tempted to speak, she nevertheless ducked her head and darted away as quickly as possible. *Don't trust anyone*, she scolded herself.

Soon, spotting the entrance to an alley, she stepped off the road. Once again, Sarah felt as if she were in a dream. Could she be walking, for the first time in her life, on free soil?

She straightened her shoulders. *"Keep your head up, daughter."*

Yes, Mama, yes, Papa, I am.

She paused for a moment, but knew that, even now, she had to keep moving. Slave catchers might be about at this early hour, on the lookout for people like her. The bird man had warned her, and so had everyone she'd met on her journey. "There are auctions in the capital," people advised. "Stay away from them; the traders might snatch you up." She'd heard of bounty hunters who searched the city streets, knowing that runaways mingled with the city of Washington's free blacks — or with slaves who worked on gangs in the city digging ditches, building roads or government buildings. She still had to be alert, ready to flee at the slightest suspicion.

Sarah walked farther into the alley, turning her head from side to side to look around. Small two-story wooden houses jammed up against each other. *These places could belong to slave catchers*, she thought, trembling. *White people must live here. No colored person lives in a two-story house, even an undersized one like this. I should get off the street*, she worried. *But where to go?*

Walking to a house with a small, pink flower breaking the monotony of gray cobblestone and dirty gray clapboard, she crouched close by its short brick steps. A door inside slammed. Startled, Sarah threw herself flat on the ground next to the house and lay still. Who was inside? The woods, even with the cries of wild animals and the possibility of snarling bloodhounds, seemed suddenly preferable to this strange city where she didn't know who to trust or where to go. In the woods she knew how to interpret the sounds; she knew how to find enough food to keep from starving, even if her stomach constantly growled.

Here, among all these houses, what were her clues? She needed shelter and safety and food, but didn't know how to find them. All her benefactors had focused on getting her here, instructing her about forks in the river and lanterns and bells. When they talked of Washington, they mentioned "free black churches that help runaways" and "a vault in a burying ground that's a safe haven," but they'd been vague on details.

Sarah remained flat against the steps, heart pounding, trying to fade into the small brick stairway. *Wasn't I better off back on the Armstrong place? There, at least I had regular meals. And people I knew,* Sarah thought, feeling sick to her stomach.

She heard a creaky wheel and the click-clack of hooves on cobblestones—a wagon pulled by horses, with a driver calling out, "Whoa ..." She burrowed deeper into her hiding place. Somewhere a cat meowed. The beseeching high pitch of the cat voiced the sadness rising up in her, a lonesome, weary grief. The insistent whine mirrored her misery exactly; she felt a kinship with this stray that also had no warm, safe place to turn. Suddenly a touch on her arm startled her, and she jumped. It was only the cat brushing by; soon it rubbed in earnest. As she felt the warmth of another creature, tears gathered in Sarah's eyes.

A new sound caught her ear. A voice from the house above? Through the thin boards she heard a woman call, "Robert, come here. Now, boy."

She started. The tone of voice sounded familiar. As she had many times in the woods, she willed herself to become stone.

Silence. A pat of feet on squeaky floorboards. Another set of heavier footsteps. And one more set, walking quickly, almost hopping.

A pungent smell filled her nostrils. She knew that smell. Pigs' feet boiling.

And then it came.

"Steal away, steal away ..." The notes hung in the air.

Tears flooded Sarah's face. The lump inside her throat dissolved, and a salty ocean burst forth. She laid her arms under her face. She couldn't stop crying.

Still sobbing, she crawled out from her hiding place and sat on the low front step, listening. She didn't mind who saw her. The voice that sang that song had to belong to a friend. Now that she'd braved so much to get here, and stayed out of sight so vigilantly, she threw caution away in the morning breeze. She would sit here and listen and cry and someone would find her. Someone who could help. Right now her whole insides felt as if they were in a tornado, spun by a churning of emotions—fear and relief, joy and sorrow—so intense she hardly cared what happened. She could go no farther.

The front door opened and a large woman with a red-striped shawl stood in the doorway. Hands on her hips, she took one look at the raggedy girl on her front steps and called out, "Child!"

Sarah looked up.

"Where did you come from, sitting there looking like the raggedyest ...?"

Sarah looked down at her torn dress. Strips of cloth, really. She could hardly speak through her tears. "Arm ... strong ... place," she sobbed out.

"Child, where in heavens is that?" The stranger took a step and leaned down to take a hard look at Sarah's face. Her eyes looked kind, and she smelled of home. A lovely blend of pig grease and sweat and coffee enveloped Sarah. But abruptly she felt her watchfulness returning, and decided not to answer any questions. The woman could turn her in and get a reward. Her description was already in the Washington newspaper, she imagined: Negro girl, tall, well spoken, may put up a fight.

"Are you here alone, child? What Armstrong place?" The woman interrupted Sarah's thought and put a hand on her arm. Sarah winced. Hardly an inch of arm or leg was free of a cut or scrape or bruise.

"Hanover County," she mumbled automatically, from a long habit of answering questions put by her elders.

"Where in the world is that, and how in the Lord's name did you get here?"

"I walked. For ... many days ..." she blurted out. Sarah couldn't believe it herself. And was she safe even now? Should she be sitting here like this, talking, when a slaver was after her? Or could be summoned.

The big woman leaned down, pulled Sarah up, and dragged her into the house. "Robert, Benjamin, Mary, Sister, look who's here. Another one come across, by the grace of God. Hallelujah!"

Children poured into the tiny front room of the house and stared. They reached over and touched her filthy clothes and sore arms, while she stood, stiffly, every nerve tense, ready to bolt.

"Where did you come from?" they asked all at once, questions tumbling over each other. "Who brought you?" "Why you here with us?"

Sarah remained speechless. Finally, after they'd fingered her clothing and gingerly touched her bruises, they lightly stroked her arms. The smallest child, a girl, tried to pry open Sarah's curled fingers so she could take Sarah's hand in her own.

Still, Sarah did not respond. She looked around, shaking, and stared through the doorway. There, in front of her, she saw a staircase. Were the white people upstairs? Wouldn't they wake up, with all this noise? She tried to make herself smaller, shrinking into herself.

"I'm Miz Louise," the woman said, throwing her red shawl over Sarah's shoulders. Following Sarah's worried gaze, she said, with a puzzled look, "No one's up there." Understanding flashed across the woman's face, and her brown eyes lit up. She chuckled. "This is our house. We pay rent."

Sarah gaped.

"You're safe." Miss Louise smiled, then pulled Sarah into the kitchen and motioned to the table. "Poor child."

Dizzy, Sarah sat down for her first meal in freedom. Miss Louise carried steaming dishes to the table: collards, eggs, corn mush, and flour biscuits. All the food of home. Still speechless, Sarah ate as much as she could, until her shrunken stomach could hold no more. Her head nodded down on her chest and she peered out of lidded eyes.

"Sister Elsie." Miss Louise gestured toward the short, stocky woman who came into the kitchen from the back door while they ate. "My sister." The woman was followed by an older man who dragged one foot. "And Mister Frank Thomas."

Sarah nodded groggily; she tried to stand up to greet the pair, but had to steady herself by holding on to the back of the chair.

"Lord," Miss Louise said, shaking her head, "That child needs rest for a week. Take her up to my bed." Sister Elsie carried Sarah upstairs, laid her down, and gently pulled up a quilt. Before Sarah drifted off she thought, *I did it! I came all that way, by myself, and now I'm home.* Even through the drowsiness that fogged her mind she vowed, *I will never, ever go back to slavery. And I will find Esther and little Albert.*

Of those two things, and little else, Sarah was absolutely sure.

CHAPTER 14

I close the folder and remain motionless, holding on to the magical ending. Sarah made it all the way to Washington—and had a glorious sort-of homecoming. I hope she found Albert and Esther. If Dad ever talks to me again, I'll find out.

For half an hour I sit stock-still, savoring the pleasure of Sarah finding a safe haven. But I don't feel safe. I scan each person who comes into Café Suzette, and the later it gets, the more people arrive. I want to head home under my own steam, not have someone who sees me call the cops to report "the missing girl." By now Fran's probably wondering what happened to me too, since my cell went dead. I hope she didn't call my house. I don't think she'd bust me.

When I come outside at last and stand in front of the cafe, ready to charge toward home, Mom's words flash into my mind: "If you wear a Kick Me sign, people will oblige." Could I have really created my own storm system, as she tells me whenever I complain? It seemed so real though. I couldn't imagine feeling safe and trusting, with that warm feeling of "knowing" that somehow things will work out, even if I can't see how. Why does that seem so obvious today? Is that what Dad's been trying to tell me, through Sarah?

While I walk I start to rap out loud, lyrics that simply emerge from my mouth like words did on those days when I basically cursed out Dad and then Mom, but this time it's something wonderful: "I'm big and bad and bold. Comin' in from the cold." I get into the groove and snap my fingers. "I be black and I be white. If you my friend, you all right." I chant it, softly, nodding, "I be black and I be white, hey, if you my friend, you all right." Wouldn't the kids in Music be surprised to hear me now, laying down such a cool rap?

I feel myself smile for the first time since I can remember, really grin in a deep, good way that reaches into every part of my body. "I be black and I be white, if you my friend— " I'm in the groove. I snap my head and stand tall, thinking home might be all right, that somehow I'll deal, when I hear my name screamed.

"Nina!" Saundra's Lexus screeches to a stop. "Nina!" She skids over and leaps out. "Child, where've you been?" Soon she's grabbing and hanging on to me the way Miss Sarah did in my dream. "Are you all right? Where were you? Silas and Maggie— " She puts one hand to her head while the other keeps an eagle grip on my arm. "I have to call them. They've been frantic all night. The police ..." She's talking so fast I only get part of it. "What happened?" She rushes on. "Kidnapped? Why do you have your suitcase? Everybody's hysterical. Did you run away? Oh my Lord, I have to tell Maggie and Silas." She pulls out her phone, then looks up to scream, "Look at you, filthy—girl, you gave everybody a scare!" Her entire hand wraps tight around my arm, and I can tell she's not going to let go. She yanks me hard, until the snot dripping from the end of my nose flies off.

And we both start to laugh.

Yeah, this must be home. The flickering inside me flares up, like when you blow on a fire and the flames leap. It's as if I can *see* it, inside my chest. It's awesome.

"Nina!" Saundra has me by one arm and she's pulling me into her car, while she's also punching a number into her phone with her thumb. In a minute I hear her yell, "Tell Maggie I've got Nina!" To me she mutters, as an aside, "Honey, your house was headquarters central all night." Then back in the phone, "She's inside my car. We're on our way. Right now. I'll be there in two minutes." She starts to sob, and when I hear her, so do I. We're driving, weeping, and the rap floats into me again while she's bawling: "I be black, I be white, hey, if you my friend, you all right." I can imagine how I'll hold myself straight and tall, keeping that flame of *knowing* bright inside, while I stride around the school radiating the spirit of my rap. Even through my sniffles I'm shaking my head to the beat.

When we get home it's one huge commotion. Two police cruisers slash the lawn, another's pulling up, its lights flashing behind us, and five or six blue uniforms with guns are milling about on the porch. Mom and Dad and Jimi huddle on the steps with Lavonn and Tirza, whose baby is screaming, and a bunch of other neighbors are scattered around the lawn. When they see us, everyone shrieks and runs to the car, lots of them wailing—even Dad—and laughing.

"Oh, sweetie." Mom leaps when I step out of the car and locks her arms around me, burying her head into my neck and pressing herself against me so I can feel her chest heaving with sobs. Dad's right behind her, looking like I'm the best dessert he ever saw.

"Baby, where were you?" Dad's squeezing me, reaching around Mom, and I see a dark, glistening line down his cheeks. He looks at my damp green suitcase and at me. "You're the raggedyest ..." With one hand he wipes his eyes. "Don't you ever do us this way again. Ever! Please."

"I won't," I say, before I let my whole weight fall into them.

Jimi grabs my hand, holding it tight like he'll never let it loose. "Don't go away," he whispers, and when I peek out I see his eyes are shiny. "I'll give you my allowance, every week. All of it." He hands me two balled-up dollars. I don't even pretend to not care about him, the way I usually do. Instead I pull him close. "I'm a by-your-side sister. Keep your money." Later I'll rip his butt for stealing.

Mom and Dad are leaning over us both now, making a tower like old times. Mom's clinging, repeating, "Nina, thank goodness you're home. Don't *ever* run away again. Whatever's going on, you can tell us. Oh, honey, you have no idea how dangerous—don't ever ..."

Soon—after they tell the police I'm okay and promise that the cops can "debrief" me in a few minutes—we all stuff into our kitchen. Everybody's hugging me or hanging on to some part of my body, as if I might evaporate. Even Rolling Stone is sitting on my foot. At last, we unjumble ourselves, while Mom pours coffee and hot chocolate. She carries two steaming coffee cakes in her heavy cast-iron frying pans, and sets them down on the round dining table. I can tell the cakes are fresh from the oven, they smell so good—full of apples, vanilla, and cinnamon. "We've been up all night," she says, starting to cry. Yet she's still able to stay in Mom mode, telling Lavonn, "Pass the plates, please," pointing with her knife.

Lavonn gave me a squeeze when I first got here, along with everybody else, but she hasn't said anything. She's staring with those big eyes, mascara running down one cheek.

"Baby," Dad starts out, when we're finally jammed around the table. "What happened? I rushed back— " But he can't talk. He's crammed in next to me, with one arm around my shoulder, and Mom is by him, reaching over to touch me. On my other side, Jimi's holding on to my leg. It seems like everybody wants to keep their hands on me this morning. He breathes and gets his voice back, even though it's choked with tears. "Where were you?" His voice is kind, but he sounds like he's bleeding internally, that's how wretched he feels. I've never seen Dad cry before. It's scary.

"I don't know," I mumble.

"Yes, you do, sugar. Tell us."

Silence.

"Where were you going?"

I don't want to tell, but I mutter, "To Fran's."

"All the way to San Luis Obispo?" His eyes widen and he looks scared. "We love you," he says softly, when I don't answer. "What is it, baby?"

"Everything ..." Now I can't talk. My eyes are leaking again and everybody's looking at me. Then some of my trouble bursts out, after all these weeks of holding it in. "There's a boy chasing— " I can't implicate Jimi, so I rush on, hoping they won't notice that part. "I don't have any friends. You don't know what it's like in ninth grade, how the kids separate black and white and make you choose. And at home we're not a family anymore. Everything changed, and no one wants to actually do anything about it!"

"We're all family," Saundra says right away. She's passing slices of warm coffee cake topped with cut-up pears, and everybody's chomping while they watch me. "You and Lavonn and Maggie and Silas and Jimi. And Paul." Her husband. "And me. You have lots of friends," she says. "Lavonn— " She looks at Lavonn, hard, her eyes glinting.

"I'm sorry," Lavonn says. She stares down at her plate. "I wish you'd come to *Black Nativity.*"

"Cool," I say, surprising myself.

"I'll hook you up." Her round face looks up, smiling, as if she never said all those mean things. That's today—a special amnesty day, I guess, like the library has for overdue books. Today it's overdue-friends-and-family day.

Then Mom tries. "Running away doesn't solve—" She stops and pours a steaming cup of hot chocolate, hands it over, and we all sit quietly while I blow on the scalding liquid, until Dad breaks the silence. "We need to talk." His face is kind of tight, like his old, stern self, even though he still has one arm draped on my shoulder. He reaches behind the table and jabs at my suitcase, as if he can't believe it's real. I can tell he's about to cry again, but then a car pulls into the driveway, revving the motor. It's Helane, in her yellow sports car. Why is *she* here?

She hops out and charges inside, and when she gets to the dining table, she acts the same as everybody else today: hugs me and says, "Welcome home, sister." I freeze. Maybe this *is* a giant forgiveness day, but this is one person I'm not ready to welcome into my life. No way. Not yet. I look at Dad.

"Helane, honey," he says, and that word rips along my skin. He shakes his head at her. "Not now." I watch them exchange a long, complicated look, full of both tenderness and anger. Their gaze, even though it's quick, is so intimate I look away. "This is not the time or place," Dad says quietly. She shrugs, then waves good-bye in everybody's direction, and I'm relieved to see her walk toward the door. When I hear her car start I know Dad's right: today is not her day. It's mine.

Pretty soon the neighbors leave, and then the cops, who sounded annoyed that I draggled home on my own instead of letting them find me heroically. Mom and Dad head for the couch. Rolling Stone stretches out on the floor next to Mom's feet, waving his tail like Number Nine did on Market Street. It's amazing how long our cat can stretch. Jimi and I are sprawled-crunched in the big chair, with him practically squashed on top of me, but instead of punching him I actually hang on. For a minute.

Dad breaks the momentary silence. "Listen, kids." He sighs. "You've got to let us in on what's happening with you. You know, we're not your enemies."

I catch Jimi's eye. No way.

"You can't surprise us like this. We can't take it; we're too old." He tries to laugh but it comes out closer to the choked voice he had before. "I know this was a tough fall and your mom and I had a lot to do with that. I'm sorry."

Wow. I never heard Dad say that word before. Jimi and I the ones who have to say it.

"Okay," I say. I remember the feeling of confidence I had in Saundra's car and decide to ask for something. "What about Thanksgiving this year? Can we have it like we always did, with Grandpa James and Grandma Bettye here, and G'a Milt and Granny Leigh?"

Mom and Dad glance at each other. They still have their silent way of speaking, because they both say yes at the same time.

I know how Thanksgiving will be. Before we eat, Grandma Bettye will read a long, sad poem about Native Americans, possibly about their Trail of Tears, and tell us how Thanksgiving is a day of mourning for them, like we don't know by now. She'll say a prayer for healing that goes on forever; it's embarrassing. Then G'a Milt and Granny Leigh will lead us in some old Stick-to-the-Union solidarity song, which somehow at this moment doesn't seem so bad. Kind of cozy, actually, like people caring about each other. This year Dad will probably announce his newfound African roots too and conduct a weird African ritual. Ugh. But my heart perks up anyway. It wouldn't be Thanksgiving without all of that.

"And, young lady— " Dad looks at me. "You are grounded until ..." He turns to look at Mom again before he finishes. This time their eyes meet for more than a second. "Until you apologize to everyone in this family." He adds, "For theft, for rudeness to me. And to your mother for giving her the fright of her life. Don't you *ever* pull this kind of stunt again! And don't you ever break in and steal—I can't imagine—" He's sputtering. "And where *is* the manuscript?"

Before I recover, or answer, he goes on. "You are grounded indefinitely, young lady, with the loss of every privilege in the book, until you demonstrate that you can show us all the respect we deserve. And can keep your hands on your own possessions."

"Yes," I say.

He raises his eyebrows.

"Yes, sir." I squeeze Jimi's hand. These are the words I'm going to use—*Keep your hands on your own possessions*—when I get him alone. I might make him write a letter of apology to Tyrone too.

"And until you demonstrate integrity. Which theft is not—"

"We're trying our best," Mom breaks in, "and we don't deserve that snippy attitude you've got, either. We expect better from you—"

"I'm sorry, Dad. I'm sorry, Mom," I hear myself say. "I felt like Sarah was the only friend I had for a while. Dad, what happened? Did she ever find Esther and Albert?"

"We'll talk about that later," he says, looking grim. "We will be watching you very, very carefully. We'll assess your attitude as the days and weeks go by, to determine when your privileges will be restored. You had best be on exemplary behavior, young lady."

"Yes, sir," I say, thinking, out of habit, *yeah, yeah, yeah, you can't make me do anything*. But deep inside, I don't know why, a happiness stirs around, the way it hasn't since last summer. It's a lightness that makes me want to do things again. I'm looking at my dad differently too, though I'd never admit it. If he could write about Miss Sarah that way—basing her on me, he said; wow—he must understand *something*.

There's a long silence. "Can I go out and play now?" Jimi asks.

Dad laughs. "Yes, son," he says, "you're dismissed," which I know he's pretending to say all formal, but that's the way Dad really is. Old school, like he tells us.

CHAPTER 15

On Sunday I stay home at Mom's all day with Jimi, hanging out, fooling around. Late in the afternoon, when the sun's fallen behind the trees, I grab the shovel and head to the backyard, to the farthest corner. Leaves and moss cover the ground, so I have to dig awhile to find it. The earth smells damp, with a strong musty smell. I dig up so much hard dirt it looks like I'm excavating a mine. And it's slow in this clay soil. Finally, when I'm shivering like my bones are gonna break and I'm about to give up, I see the smudged corner of an envelope. My heart jumps. After I shove the spade around it to loosen a clump, I reach in, yank the dirty bundle, rip open the paper, and wipe the ring. Hey, if I'm big and bad and bold, who knows what could happen? Anyway, I'm trying to forgive and forget, the way Mom and Dad did with me. I slip the ring into my pocket; once inside I wash it, wrap a tissue around it, and stuff it into the secret compartment of my jewelry box under the crumpled money I put back.

That night when Lavonn calls I don't tell her anything about Jessica's ring, how I buried it and dug it up and who knows what will happen, but I do ask, "When's the next rehearsal?"

"Saturday. I'll text Michelle tomorrow. She's the director. Michelle is bad. Wait 'til you hear her. You'll like her."

"Thanks. Singing, that's gotta be awesome. My parents probably won't let me go since I'm grounded forever, but I'll ask."

On Monday morning, Mom lets me stay home for a couple of hours while she "supervises" and "helps" with my schoolwork. Really, she's afraid I'm going to run away again; I can tell by the eagle eye she's keeping on me, hardly letting me out of the room without watching. Finally I make my way to school and arrive right after 12:30, the beginning of lunch. The bell is ringing and kids are pouring into the halls. After I take my late note to the office, I run to Jessica's locker and catch her by herself, without Claudette or anyone else. Just the way I imagined it. Other kids are milling around, pushing and talking and, as usual, the din is deafening. I tap on her back when she's bent down in front of her locker.

She jumps up and screams, like she's happy to see me, "Nina! You're at school!"

I nod, acting cool.

"The police were at my house and everything! Where were you?" She's shouting, with an ear-splitting, high-pitched voice, and other kids stare. "Your mom called a hundred times. Your dad too. What happened?" She leans over to hug me, and for a moment it feels like old times, until I notice my friendship ring's still not on her finger.

"I'm okay," I say, looking her in the eye. "Jessica, you were my best friend." Tears start to come into my eyes, but I am not going to cry in school. I bite the inside of my cheek.

"You're hanging around with Lavonn now," she says and pulls away, fiddling with her backpack. "She's your new best friend."

"I have lots of friends," I say evenly. "But you were the best I've ever had. You and Fran."

She stops and stares at me just like the old Jessica, not some hijacked fraud, but then she ruins it. "How can we be best friends anymore? I'm not going near those kids."

"What?"

"They're rough." She laughs like she's nervous. "Scary."

"Scary?" I can't believe this.

"Yeah. Susanna, she shoved me into my locker the other day and called me a slut."

She looks frightened and for an instant my heart softens. I remember how afraid I was the first time I took the bus to Dad's, when those guys were hanging out by their car and all I noticed everywhere were black people—the assumptions I'd had. Now I've gotten to know the guys, who look out for me, and I know the neighborhood. It's all so normal. "Jessica, just 'cause one girl pushed you—" I stop. "What did you do to make her mad?"

"Nothing." Her face starts to fill with red blotches so I know she's lying. But I decide to skip it.

"That was only one person, Jessica."

"I'm staying away from—" She's got her books pressed to her chest, as if they'll protect her, and I understand how afraid she is. That's part of what's good about being friends for a long time: how well we know each other.

Right when I'm trying to keep open that place in my heart that's warm, remembering how close Jessica and I were—no matter what she's saying now—Claudette shows up and screams, "Nina!" like everybody else. I guess all the kids know.

I ignore her and keep my eyes on Jessica. I've never seen her like this, with her face so tight.

"You're staying away from who?" I ask Jessica, but she turns away from me and toward Claudette, who's tugging on her arm, saying, "Come on, Tommie's waiting."

I still ignore Claudette and say directly to Jessica, "You said I've changed." I don't care who's listening. "I have. Now I know I can be friends with anybody. Even you, except not if you're gonna act like this. But if you change too, who knows?"

She doesn't answer so I walk away, leaving the two of them standing in the hall. When I turn the corner of the hall, my confidence deflates. I feel myself flush. Dwight is standing by his locker fiddling with his backpack. "Hey, Nina!" he says, surprised. "You're back." He looks pleased.

What am I supposed to say to that? "Yeah" is the best I can manage. Even though I've been wanting him to notice me all fall, I'd like to be invisible right now, with some of that black-cat mojo Dad told us about that supposedly makes people disappear.

"Hey, I saw Tyrone's bike at our house." I must be staring at him in an odd way, because he stops tugging on his jammed backpack zipper. After a minute he continues, "Sorry he hassled you. And your brother." He's moving toward me as he talks. "You put the bike back, didn't you? Thanks. That took guts. I've got a brother who gets me in trouble too. Big time. But I guess you know that." He laughs lightly, so his dimples cut into his cheeks.

I must look awfully serious, not smiling back, because in an instant he stretches his neck, lifts one leg, and transforms himself into a stork—how does he do that?—flapping his arms, which suddenly seem like wings. He succeeds in making me laugh, but by the time I do, he's sprinting down the corridor, calling back over his shoulder, "I'm gonna text you, and maybe we can get together."

Now this is a sentence I never thought I'd hear from Dwight Jackson. He does know who I am. And he's acting as if maybe he kinda likes me.

In the cafeteria I find Lavonn and Demetre at a table by the windows. After they wave and see me head their way, Lavonn shoves over her cardboard tray to make a place. I drop into the vacant seat and open the avocado sandwich that Mom packed. Inside there's a note—*I love you*—like she used to put in my lunches years ago. "What's up?" Demetre asks. "Where were you?"

"Jessica's nuts" is all I say.

"We heard you ran away. What happened?"

I shrug, but Demetre keeps asking, so I tell them about Dad getting mad and me stealing his manuscript, then me and Mom having a fight that last morning, and me taking BART all the way into San Francisco. I only leave out three-quarters of the story: the bike, Jimi, Tyrone, Jessica, them, or anything about white and black kids. In the middle the bell rings, interrupting me anyway, and there's pandemonium. Everybody's jumping up, yelling to friends, and rushing to dump their trash.

That night, Amy calls. "Hi," she starts out, and I remember again how shy she is. She talks, all in a rush, "My mom and her boyfriend are taking me to Hawaii after Christmas, and my mom said I could invite you if you want to come. For five days."

Wow. Not only is Amy tight with Jessica and Claudette, that's expensive.

"My uncle works for the airlines and he can get us special tickets for two hundred dollars," she adds, reading my mind.

"Yeah," I stumble. I could use my own money for that—not the trip I thought I'd go on, but hey, life had a better plan for me, I guess. Or maybe it was Miss Sarah, working her magic up in the sky. "I'll ask my mom." Maybe by then I'll be ungrounded and she'll let me go. And the same as on Saturday morning, a good feeling rises out of my middle and bubbles around my body, even into my arms. It'll work out.

"Bueno," she says.

"How come you speak so much Spanish?" I ask. "Did you live in another country?"

"My mom's boyfriend is Cuban. Roberto. I'm used to his friends hanging around and he's got a big family." She adds, out of the blue, "His sister Mercedes practically lives here. So we're a mixed family too." Then she blurts, "And Mercedes' baby is black."

After that, something pops out of me—I don't know where these outbursts come from—that shocks me all over again. Only this time, like the rap, it's good. "We're gheppies," I say.

"Gheppies?"

"Yeah, G-H-E-P-P-I-E-S. Ghetto and preppy. That's what we are."

There's a silence, until she giggles. "Ha, I'm a gheppie."

Is this what Saundra meant? I still don't get how I "signed up for a big life," but everything looks a little better. I don't know why, nothing's changed—except now I'm grounded. Even the idea of going to school every day doesn't seem so bad. And who knows, next year in tenth grade, things might get "more fluid," like Mom said. Someday I might even be friends with Jessica again. If I want to. If she grows up and gets some sense. I can't believe all the crazy things she said, but the weirdest part is that I'm okay. That black cat that crossed my path might have been lucky. Or maybe it was my great-great-grandma, her and God speaking to me through the manuscript. I'm a lot like Sarah, I guess, the way Dad said when he first told me about her.

After school on Tuesday I ride the bus to Dad's house; I don't have to lug my green suitcase, 'cause this time my clothes are already there. And I'm actually looking forward to staying there for a change. Dad's gonna take Jimi and me shopping to buy bunk beds so I won't have to sleep on the Deathbed anymore. Plus, he asked me if I wanted to write a story about Miss Sarah with him, about her time in Washington, D.C. Well, we'd write it after he and Helane do the research. It's sad; they think she never found her sister and brother, though they're not sure—that's one of the things they want to research.

Dad also told me there's a girl on his block who looks like she's my age, which shows how clueless he still is; just because she's around my age doesn't mean we'll be instant friends. Adults are so weird. But I guess since I'm stuck with two homes, I might as well have friends both places, so I'll see what that girl is like.

I don't have to choose friends, the way Jessica threatened, or Lavonn told me that day she was so mad. Amy and I might start a Gheppie Club. Our anthem could be my rap: "I be black and I be white ..." or whatever you are, and the club would be open to everybody. We'd have hecka fun. I bet there are lots of kids who'd want to join. Who knows? Someday even Jessica Raymond might want to be a member. But still, even if she doesn't, as my great-great-grandmother said, *I came all that way by myself, and now I'm home.*

Author's Note

Though Sarah Armstrong is a fictional character (like Nina Armstrong), all the events described in the novel-within-a-novel are factual and actually happened to somebody enslaved in Virginia before the Civil War. Details of plantation life — and escapes — come from slave narratives: interviews with people who had been enslaved or, in a few cases, who were able to publish their own stories.

The story of the white abolitionist who appeared to Sarah in the field is based on the true story of Dr. Alexander Ross. He was a scientist from Belleville, Ontario, who made regular trips to the southern U.S. states for "bird watching." His exploits and adventures (including one dramatic arrest and release) are frequently described in Underground Railroad literature.

And Henry "Box" Brown, who escaped from Richmond, Virginia in a large wooden box, was another historical figure whose wife and children really were suddenly sold into slavery, and who in 1849 — in actuality several years before the fictional Sarah meets him — did have friends mail him to an Underground Railroad station in Philadelphia. He became a noted abolitionist speaker in later years.

Many of the fugitives who made it to Washington, D.C., did elude recapture until, following the Civil War, they were permanently freed. It is quite reasonable to imagine that a strong, literate, and clever young woman would have been able to successfully make her way in the alley culture of Washington, D.C., where lots of former slaves and free people helped new runaways.

If Sarah Armstrong were real, I think she would have made it.

And a true story inspired this novel-within-a-novel. It was a tale of flight from slavery I heard from the family of Washington, D.C.'s, congresswoman Eleanor Holmes Norton. Her great-grandfather was enslaved on a Laroline, Virginia plantation until he fled in the 1850s. Though no one knows the details of the flight he took while still a teen, he did succeed in reaching Washington and founded the Holmes family, which resides there to this day. I've told more of this family story in my biography of Congresswoman Norton, *Fire in My Soul.*

Many longtime Washington African American families have similar histories. So Sarah Armstrong, while a composite, is a could-have-been-true figure. In any case, I salute her determination, and though she is fictional, she inspires me to persevere in my own life goals.

Acknowledgments

I am indebted to colleagues and friends Muriel Albert, Betsy Blakesly, Suzzette Celeste, Lan Samanatha Chang, Ronnie Gilbert, Jewelle Gomez, Rosemary Graham, Nellie Hill, Pat Holt, Zee Lewis, Ruth King, Wendy Lichtman, Emily Polsby, Patricia Ramsey, Lesley Quinn, Lynn Wenzell, and Maxine Wolfe, each of whom offered invaluable encouragement and advice during the writing. They are truly godmothers of this book. And to Marissa Moss, who read many, many versions in their entirety and came up with this terrific title: a special thank-you.

Some of my best editors were the teens who read the manuscript and made excellent suggestions: thanks to Page Dennis, Jenna Anne Rempel, Asa Stahl, Elias Stahl, and Danielle Wilson. Thanks also to teacher Deborah Godner at Berkeley High, who offered me unlimited access to her fascinating ninth-grade classroom.

I am fortunate to have an outstanding agent in Caryn Wiseman, who is also a superb editor. Her suggestions enriched the text, and her passion for the project sustained me.

Jacque Alberta, my enthusiastic Zondervan editor, had numerous wise ideas for deepening Nina's character and the plot; it is a better book for her insights. I also deeply appreciate Sara Maher, who oversaw the fabulous *Black, White, Other* trailer, plus created an outstanding marketing campaign, and Candace Frederick, publicist extraordinaire.

I am grateful to my family for their constant support of my writing endeavors, and especially to Carole, who, as always, scrutinized every single draft with her keen and supportive eye, as well as to Malcolm, Karen, Mardi, and Mama Barb, who each read early versions, and to my father, Morton Steinau, to whom I had the great privilege of reading the first four chapters while he lay dying, at age eighty-seven, in a Cape Cod hospital. Receiving his blessing on this work was a great gift.

Above all, I am appreciative of those who made the dangerous journey to the North, helping, with their determined feet, to end the practice of human slavery in the United States.

Discussion Questions

1. How does Nina see herself at the beginning of the book? At the end? What changed?
2. Why do you think Nina ran away from home?
3. Are there other things she might have done to help resolve her "Who am I?" question?
4. How has Nina's understanding of race changed by the end of the book? What does it mean to her to be "black"? To be "white"? To be "other"?
5. How do the people around Nina define *race*? Compare her mother's attitude to her father's. What did Nina's mother mean when she said, "Race is not real"?
6. Nina's journey is physical, spiritual, and emotional. What does she learn about herself on each level?
7. What echoes did you notice between Nina's contemporary story and her great-great-grandmother Sarah's tale?
8. How did Sarah "know" it was time for her to flee the Armstrong plantation? Have you ever had that flash of knowing, which gave you a calm surety about acting?
9. What trigger event(s) made the difference for Nina, leading her to return home instead of continuing on to her friend Fran's house?
10. What do you think about the idea that Nina might have been wearing a metaphorical Kick Me sign?

11. Did Nina's parents or friends change, or was her lifting heart primarily a result of her own internal process? What was that process?
12. Who were Nina's allies, and how important were they to her understanding about her ability to create her own social space?
13. Have you ever felt "other," really different from your peers? Explain.

Follow-up Actions

Allies

1. When you've felt "other," did you have an ally—a friend, teacher, parent, or other person who had a clue about what you were going through, and cared? What did your ally do, and did it help?
2. What makes it easier to talk about feelings when you wonder how you fit in? Are there certain people who let you know they don't judge you, no matter what you say?
3. Have you ever been an ally for someone who was perceived as "other" in any way?
4. Can you think of a person who might need an ally? What could you do to reach out?

Oral Histories

1. Do you have any ancestors—far back in history or in more contemporary times—who inspire you the way Sarah Armstrong inspired her great-great granddaughter Nina? Does your family tell stories about ancestors, or even about their own lives?
2. If you've never done so before, record an oral history from either or both parents about *their* parents, grandparents, or older ancestors. All you have to do is ask, and either take notes or record their stories. It definitely will give you fresh information about your own history; you may be stunned.

Glossary

Abolitionists African Americans and white people who were determined to end slavery as a legal system of labor in the United States. Particularly in the thirty years before the Civil War, they agitated constantly for the compulsory emancipation of enslaved people. Abolitionists had newspapers, gave speeches, and led rallies, trying to convince lawmakers in Washington to abolish slavery. Their determination and fervor made the slavery question the prime concern of national politics for an entire generation. Some of the most famous abolitionists were Frederick Douglass, Harriet Beecher Stowe, Sojourner Truth, Wendell Phillips, Harriet Tubman, William Lloyd Garrison, and Susan B. Anthony.

Ash cake Made of either cornmeal or wheat flour, the dough was wrapped in damp cloth and put in hot ashes on the hearth to bake.

Bounty hunters These were people who caught escaped slaves and received a "bounty," or fee, for their services. Before 1850, people who reached free states — the Northern states, where slavery was not legal — were permanently free. But the Fugitive Slave Act of 1850, passed by Congress as a "compromise" when California was admitted as a free state, thus tipping the balance between slave and free states, said bounty hunters or owners could lawfully go into free states and capture runaways. The act even made it against the law for anyone to help escaped slaves elude recapture.

At the beginning of 1850, before the Fugitive Slave Act, there were fifteen slave states and fifteen free states.

Cat-o'-nine-tails A whip with many "tails" — that is, separate strips of leather bound together near the handle. When ol' miss flicked this whip in the story, each strip of leather could catch one of the children, or hit different parts of a child.

Contraband Literally, illegal goods. When enslaved people ran away they were known as "contraband," because they were stolen property—stolen by themselves!

Drinking gourd The constellation of stars we know as the Big Dipper. It pointed the way north.

Driver Usually enslaved himself, this person was put in charge of groups of other slaves. His job was to keep them working and "well behaved." Some drivers empathized with people in a similar position and tried to use whatever privilege they had to help, without endangering themselves. Others used their power brutally, trying to win favors.

Driver's horn This was often a conch shell. As Mary Reynolds, an ex-slave interviewed in the 1930s, recalls, "The conch shell blowed afore daylight and all hands better get out for roll call or Solomon bust the door down and git them out." (*Bullwhip Days: The Slaves Remember*, 18.)

High-yellow Very light-skinned black people. This was usually, though not always, a derogatory term, for people with clearly mixed ethnic ancestry.

Hoe-cakes A cake made from cornmeal and water, and cooked on a hoe over the fire. People also cooked them in frying pans, but still called the flat cakes "hoe-cakes."

Hogshead Large barrel for tobacco leaves to be packed in and shipped to market.

Langston Hughes One of America's most important twentieth-century poets. He was prominent in the Harlem Renaissance of the 1920s, when he was called the Poet Laureate of Harlem, and wrote, among other famous works, the poem that inspired the title for the play *Raisin in the Sun*.

Jump the Broom Enslaved people, without legal status as persons, could not legally marry. But they created their own ceremonies to signify the joining of a couple. This one is thought to be a mix of rituals from different African regions. Friends laid a broom on the floor, or held it a foot above the ground. The lovers "jumped over the broom" together. Sometimes they faced east to signify new beginnings, like the rising of the sun. Then they were considered married.

Sometimes slave owners sanctioned this ceremony, which signified the couple's step into married life, and held it on their porches. But without legal standing as a couple, the bond could be broken at any moment by an owner, as happened in the fictional case of Sarah's parents—and happened often in real life during the time of slavery.

Middlin' meat Meat cut from the middle of the hog.

Mister Charlie or **Mister Charley** Derogatory name used by African Americans for the prototypical oppressive white man; the male version of **Miss Ann**. An article by John Cowley, "Shack Bullies and Levee Contractors: Bluesmen as Ethnographers," in *The Journal of Folklore Research* 28, nos. 2–3, pp. 135–62, recounts the story of the Lowrence family, a set of seven brothers. The oldest was named Charley. These brothers were infamous contractors of cheap labor, using mostly African Americans to build the levees alongside the Mississippi River in the 1920s. A number of songs quoted in the article refer to "Mr. Charley" specifically in this context, giving rise to speculation that the repeated reference to a "Mr. Charley" by Southern bluesmen was undoubtedly a reference to Charley Lowrence.

Overseer A foreman who ran operations on a whole plantation, or sometimes part of it. Almost always a white man, though occasionally free African Americans were hired to do the job.

Pattyrollers White men who patrolled the roads as a kind of extra police force. Since they were patrollers, the name developed into "pattyrollers."

Pallet A bed. Usually it was a thin mattress, stuffed with old rags, corn shucks, or pine straw.

Peck (of meal) A measurement, like a cup.

Pot likker Water that vegetables have been cooked in, making a tasty vegetable broth.

Quarters The area of the plantation reserved for slave cabins, which were usually one-room, shingled rectangles, though sometimes they were made of brick.

Remit A handwritten pass, required for travel. All people who appeared to be of African ancestry had to carry either a pass—supposedly from a white person—giving permission to be away from the place they lived, or they had to carry official Free Papers, stating they were free blacks. Pattyrollers checked for passes or papers. If none could be showed, a person could be—and typically was—arrested.

Underground Railroad An organized group of people who helped fugitives find their way north to freedom, either in the northern United States or Canada, where bounty hunters could not get them. One of the most famous conductors—a person who led others along the way—was Harriet Tubman. A runaway herself, she made nineteen trips back into the South, rounding up groups of enslaved people and leading them north. She was so successful that owners finally offered a reward of $40,000 for her capture.

The phrase *Underground Railroad* was born, so historian William Evitts believes, "when one slave owner chasing a runaway lost track of him near the Ohio River. He complained that it was as if the slave had disappeared on 'an underground road.'"

Whip Sometimes made out of raw cowhide two or three feet long; sometimes a horse whip; other times a hickory branch taken from a nearby tree, or a leather belt, or stick.

Sources

Ira Berlin, "The Slaves' Changing World," *A History of the African American People*, eds., James Oliver Horton and Lois E. Horton, New York: Smithmark Books, 1995. This essay by a renowned scholar gives details about life in Southern states from 1800 until the Civil War sixty years later. This excellent article is accompanied by reproductions of paintings, photographs of artifacts used on plantations, and drawings. They are as helpful as the text in showing what daily life was like then.

Ira Berlin and Leslie S. Rowland, eds., *Families and Freedom: A Documentary History of African-American Kinship in the Civil War Era*. New York: The New Press, 1997. Gives details about family life in the years just before the Civil War, during the time when Sarah Armstrong was a girl.

Raymond Bial, *The Strength of These Arms: Life in the Slave Quarters*, Boston: Houghton Mifflin, 1997. Gives good examples, with pictures, of exactly how some of the cabins looked, what kind of eating utensils enslaved people used, and other details of daily life.

Paul D. Escott, *Slavery Remembered: A Record of Twentieth-Century Slave Narratives*, Chapel Hill: University of North Carolina Press, 1979. Actual stories by ex-slaves.

J. William Evitts, *Captive Bodies, Free Spirits: The Story of Southern Slavery*, New York: Julian Messner, 1985. Young adult nonfiction by a historian, who details various ways the enslaved people in the South resisted captivity.

Julius Lester, *To Be a Slave*, New York: Dial Books, 1968. This wonderful little book, a young adult classic now, relied on slave narratives to tell stories about what it might have been like to be a slave.

Gerald McDermott, *Anansi the Spider: A Tale from the Ashanti*, New York, Holt, 1988. A children's book about Anansi, the West African trickster spider, who journeys into misadventures, is rescued by his six spider sons, and finding a globe of light in the forest, puts it up into the sky to become the moon. It's a wonderful tale from Ghana, the West African country used as a port of departure by slave traders. It is likely Sarah's people were from Ghana, or at least passed through, coming from another West African country on their way to the United States.

James Mellon, *Bullwhip Days: The Slaves Remember, An Oral History,* New York: Avon Books, 1988. This treasure trove has direct excerpts of interviews made in the 1930s with survivors. "A typical interview occurred on the rickety porch of a former slave's shack ..." the book begins. Their remarkable life stories show a great variety of experiences under slavery and give insight into surprising details of daily life. One sentence on a "pit school," for instance, remembered by Ms. Mandy Jones, provided inspiration for Sarah Armstrong's own pit school.

Charles Perdue Jr., Thomas E. Barden, and Robert K. Phillips, eds., *Weevils in the Wheat: Interviews with Virginia Ex-Slaves.* Bloomington: Indiana University Press, 1980. This is another collection of interviews with ex-slaves, but this one focuses exclusively on Virginia. "In November 1936, an all-Negro unit of the Virginia Writers' Project under the direction of Roscoe E. Lewis began interviewing ex-slaves in Virginia and during the next year interviewed more than three hundred elderly Negroes as part of this project," says the introduction. It gives more fascinating stories about people who were themselves, or whose parents were enslaved. From this book I also got details about the food, work, and stories of escape.

Kwaku Person-Lynn, "Why Do We Jump the Broom?" *AfrocentricNews.com*, 2003, www.afrocentricnews.com/html/Person_lynn_jump_the_broom.html (accessed May 18, 2011).

Doreen Rappaport, *No More! Stories and Songs of Slave Resistance*, illustrated by Shane W. Evans, Cambridge, Mass: Candlewick Press, 2002. Big picture book full of examples of people who resisted slavery, many by running away.

William Troy, *Hair-breadth Escapes from Slavery to Freedom*, Manchester, England: W. Bremner, 1861. This book, as the title indicates, focuses on fugitives; people left in so many ways, from Henry "Box" Brown's audacious mailing of himself to daring flights on horseback. But most people walked the way Sarah Armstrong did, alone or in small groups. They simply kept heading north. Many were captured, but many escaped.